MW00584405

PRAISE FOR ANDREA RANDALL

November Blue

The women in this series are bold, strong and independent. Yet they aren't intimidating or stone cold. Their hearts are vulnerable, they are loyal with a passion, and they love deeply and intensely. ~ **Flirty and Dirty Book Blog**

The heated scenes between Bo and Ember were magic. ~ **Tough Critic Book Reviews**

Andrea Randall has a way with words and I can't wait to see what emotion she stirs up next ~ **Candy Coated Book Blog**

Who ever said that the sequel never lives up to the original never read an Andrea Randall book! ~ **The Book Avenue**

I love that this is no cookie cutter romance and it felt more like poetry...or a song than a book at times. ~ **Michelle Pace, co-author of The Sound Wave Series**

It's hard not to get sucked into the world of Ember and Bo ~ **SMI Book Club**

...an excellent writer with a superb talent at crafting words ... that grab ahold of your heart ... An eloquent, master wordsmith - **All the Raeje Book Blog**

I could gush about this book for days...If you read one book of Andrea Randall's this should be it. There's something in here for EVERYONE to love. ~ **Word Blog**

In the Stillness

They had the kind of love that just makes you shake. Cry. Laugh. Ache right down to your soul. It was an irreplaceable love. The kind that, once taken away leaves a hole that no other person can ever fill. ~**Aestas Book Blog**

Gorgeous writing. Eloquent, but in a raw, realistic way. A delicate subject matter, distressing thoughts, and yet, a wondrous growth that the reader experiences every step of the way, with the characters. ~**Maryse's Book Blog**

This is easily the best book I've read all year, and I will be hard-pressed to find a book that will bring out of me such a strong reaction as this book. In the Stillness is a stimulant of the best and worst kind; it is truly captivating and commensurate with the suffering of so many in society. ~ **Romantic Reading Escapes Book Blog**

Author Andrea Randall has written a gut-wrenching, 5++ star piece of dark perfection. This is a journey of redemption, healing, loving, acceptance, and moving forward. ~ **K and T Book Reviews**

ANDREA RANDALL

Books by Andrea Randall

November Blue

Ten Days of Perfect

Reckless Abandon

Sweet Forty-Two

Marrying Ember (February 2014)

Bo & Ember (March 2014)

In The Stillness

Nocturne (with Charles Sheehan-Miles)

Something's Come Up (with Michelle Pace)

SWEET
Forty Two

If you enjoyed this book, please share it with a friend, write a review online, or send feedback to the authors!

www.andrearandall.com

Edited by Lori Sabin
Cover Design by Sarah Hansen at Okay Creations
Cover Photo by Erica Ritchie

DEDICATION

For Melissa Brown:

The most romantic person in the universe.

ACKNOWLEDGEMENTS

I'D LIKE TO start, a little unconventionally, by thanking Georgia. Yes, the main character. She made me work for her. She didn't reveal herself easily, which is no surprise to any of you who just finished the book. I started working on this book in April and Georgia and I played a very long and frustrating game of hide-and-seek. I even put this story on the shelf and wrote "Nocturne" with Charles Sheehan-Miles in the meantime. When I got back to it, though, we were finally on the same page. Thank you, Georgia, for making me really find you.

Sarah Hansen: This cover is exactly what I wanted. Thank you!

Erica Ritchie: Thank you for working with me to create a fabulous picture story for the November Blue series. I'm looking forward to the Ten Days of Perfect cover makeover, and the rest of the series.

Lori Sabin: You're a beautiful soul, and I love you dearly as a friend. Thank you for your sharp and critical eye as you tackle my raw manuscripts. I learn more with each project we work on together.

Ashley Wilcox, ACS Tours and Michelle Preast, Indie Bookcovers: Ashley, thank you for organizing all of the blog involvement for this book, and for keeping me organized as well. Michelle, thank you for the wonderful art that accompanied the blog tour.

My November Blue Series beta readers: Lisa Rutledge, Lindsay Sparkes, Erin Roth, Sally Bouley, Laura Wilson, Pamela Carrion. You ladies rock!

Charles Sheehan-Miles: Thank you for your support every single day. Every. Day. It was, and always will be, the words.

DREAMS...

"THIS LAND IS incredible. Who owns it?" I look around on the most perfect summer day that's ever existed.

Rae slows down so her horse is walking in step with mine. "The Greysons. Lauren and Warner were friends with my parents forever. We'd come up here all the time as kids and get lost on purpose." Her smile makes me feel like I'm right there with her. Back in her memories.

"Did they have kids?"

Rae nods. "Older, though. Well, the girl was around Bo's age, but she was never interested in him, and I don't think he was in her. They were good friends. Zoë is her name. The boy, Kevin, was in college before I was in high school. I don't really remember him."

The breeze picks up, and loose strands of Rae's black hair whip from under her helmet. Summer breezes are the best; you hear them coming before you feel them, and they're always warm. She closes her eyes and takes a deep breath through her nose.

I love you.

I can't say it. I want to so badly, but I can't. The way she lets her lips part as she's lost in her smile begs me to say it. It's too soon, though. Too soon. We've only been together for two months, even though it seems longer. Everything is so effortless with her.

Rae is optimistic, bright in ways her older brother, Bo, can't be, especially with all of that brooding he's doing over his ex-girlfriend, Ember. I still don't really understand what happened there, but Rae assures me it will all work out for them in the end. Apparently Bo and Ember are meant to be. If the level of snark and brood one shows during a breakup is directly proportional to the "meant to be" factor of a couple, those two are goddamn soul mates. That's what Rae says, too. She uses the term soul mate as if it doesn't come with centuries of baggage attached to it.

See? Effortless. Love is love. Soul mates are soul mates. And she is perfect. My term, not hers.

We come to the head of several trails that all disappear instantly into thick woods. My heart races a little in anticipation. Reality knocks, but I know I can stay here a while longer. In this dream. Before it's shredded into a nightmare.

Normally I wake myself up when we get here, to the trail. Sometimes I push it, though. I just want to be with her a little bit longer.

"Which trail are we taking?" I ask, holding my horse back. He's as anxious here as he was when it happened. Like he knew what was coming.

Rae points with her chin to a trail on the left of the tree line. "That one. It's shaded and this sun is brutal today."

I nod and back my horse up a few steps so she can take the lead.

I really should wake up now, but she still has more to say. And one more smile to give.

Not yet. Just a few more minutes.

"Oh," she sighs in relief, "thank *God* for shade."

My horse leads me just behind her and I'm grateful to find out she's right. I didn't realize how hot the sun was until I was in the coolness under the branches. Huge trees. Evergreens, pines, maples, and probably a few others my two years in Boy Scouts didn't teach me, create a narrow tunnel of nature that we travel down in single file fashion.

Rae turns around and smiles.

Wake up. Now.

I don't, though. I'm greedy tonight and want to hear her voice one more time.

"You with me, Regan? You got really quiet."

"This trail...it's...wow." I gesture with one hand to the grandness of the earth around us.

She giggles.

I forgot she'd done that.

"Right? Come on, let's get going. This trail is long." She commands her horse to pick up its step, and it follows loyally.

I do the same with mine, but make it slow slightly as a low hum filters into my ears. It sounds like a far away tractor, or lawnmower, but I didn't see anyone else in the large pasture we just crossed. And, she just said the trail was long.

Leave. Now. Open your eyes, Regan.

My throat closes and I try to swallow. Nothing. My horse pulls back as I try to push it forward. He shakes his head and lifts his front legs slightly. Warning. I'm not trained enough on horses to know that, though. I think he's just not submitting to me.

You've seen this enough, man. Open your eyes. Wake up. Wake up!

The humming is louder now and I don't say anything because I'm trying to find the source. Rae is several yards ahead and seems to hear it, too. Her head moves slowly side to side as she continues her stride forward.

Then, I look up. It's there. Huge. Grey like brains and dangling from a branch just above her.

It's too late.

The bees come.

CHAPTER *One*

BEGIN AT THE BEGINNING...

Regan

"THANK YOU GUYS for letting me stay with you while I look for a place." I yawned and poured milk into my coffee, looking at the boxes surrounding Bo and Ember's new kitchen.

Through the window over the sink, the calm waters of Mission Bay greeted me. North Cove, to be exact. And I was...envious. Soft, crystal blue waves lapped up onto the almost-white sand that was a couple of dozen yards from the sliding doors off of the kitchen. The house was tucked neatly into the cove, and I could see the tiny bungalows and cottages that lined the cul-de-sac of water on all sides. None were over a story high, allowing for a full view of the small mountains just beyond the bay.

Inhabited by mainly year-round residents, it was a far cry from the ocean side of Mission Blvd. Or "wild side", as the neighbors called it.

I knew I'd never be able to afford to find a place like this on my own, so I was taking in what was sure to be one of my last waterside morning vistas.

Ember's parents had maintained a condo here since the late eighties, even after they moved to Connecticut to send Ember to high school. They'd offered to have Bo and Ember move in with them, but Ember had gone on and on during late night drinking sessions about boundaries. Before she wavered, though, they were able to find a bungalow to sublet for six months a few houses down from her parents.

Relaxed boundaries, then.

Bo entered the kitchen and set his coffee mug in the sink before he put his hand on my shoulder for a second. "Any time, man. You know that." He gave it a slight squeeze before picking up a box labeled *Sandals.*

"A whole box?" I raised my eyebrows, eyeing him over my steaming mug of motivation.

He shrugged. "I…guess…" He chuckled, so did I.

Little things like that were starting to come more naturally again. Laughing.

"You boys find something funny?" Ember sauntered into the kitchen looking more ready for the day than I'd ever looked any day of my life.

Her long auburn hair was tied back, and she wore short denim shorts and a green tank top. She was gorgeous by any standard but didn't flaunt it. I'd met her when she was in the middle of an emotional mess after her breakup with Bo. I still wasn't clear on all the details from when they met to when they broke up, but I didn't think I needed them.

I wasn't the one sleeping with her, so I figured it was safe for me to push the teasing a little. "You can only wear one pair at a time, Ember. Why do you need so many?"

"San Diego." She arched her eyebrow and fished through another box, producing a pair of kitchen shears.

"Huh?"

"We're in San Diego, Regan. It's sunny three hundred days a year." That was the only answer she felt she needed to offer. She gave Bo a quick kiss before running the scissors along the seam of the box as he held it.

She was right. It was San Diego, and I hoped that this place held more answers than why Ember needed twenty-five pairs of sandals. Just after I'd come back from Ireland, Ember sent her mother some audio and video recordings of me playing, without telling me. I would have resisted had she suggested it, but I'm glad she did. Her parents wanted me immediately and called me themselves to ask that I consider coming out with Bo and Ember to record in January. I was still jobless, but with a nice cushion in my bank account from when I'd taught in Ireland the year before, so I had nothing to lose.

"Here they are." Ember exhaled in near-relief as she lifted a pair of gold sandals out of the box and slid them onto her feet.

Bo cleared his throat, seeming to stifle a laugh. "Ember, I told your dad I'd meet him at the studio this morning to help him set up that new equipment. You two all right here?"

"Of course, tell Dad I'll be by around lunchtime." Ember rose up on her toes as Bo slid his arms around her waist and rested his hands on the small of her back. "I love you."

"I love you," Bo whispered as he kissed her.

I turned quietly on my heels and snuck out the back door onto the cool sand. No matter what room I left, or what country or state I entered, she was there.

Rae Cavanaugh.

Bo's younger sister, and my girlfriend, who had died tragically the summer before. We were together for less time than she'd been gone, but her death overrode all internal sense of time. Seeing that horse buck her from its body and watching her lay lifeless on the ground changed my internal makeup.

Her death stuck to me like thick, cold mud, dried under the hottest sun I'd ever felt. It tugged at my skin, ripping the hair from my arms one at a time before I could brush the dust free. Dust. One day, seemingly just like that, I was able to stand up and brush it all off like dust.

Still, when I looked across the room into Ember's eyes, or watched Bo bow his head slightly before each time he played his guitar, she was there. She was there when I bailed after the funeral and escaped to Ireland for three months, ditching the closest friends I'd had in years. Rae was there, snuggled amongst the ruins of centuries old castles on the edges of family farms, and she was there in the quiet moments before I drifted to sleep. She was in my dreams.

Dust lingers, and I was desperate to wash it clean, but I didn't know how. I didn't even know if I could, but I had to try.

"Hey, you okay out here?" Ember quietly slid the screen door open and met me in the adjoining Adirondack chair.

I nodded. "Of course."

"You know, Bo found a great therapist here. If you want to set—"

I bit the inside of my cheek. "It's okay, Ember. Really."

"Ireland isn't therapy, Regan." I could tell she rolled her eyes without even looking at her.

"Says the girl who's never been there. Anyway, I'll be fine. CJ's plane lands in a couple of hours, and he and I will be exploring some while I apartment hunt. That way I can get out of your hair and let you and Bo play house." I tried to smirk but couldn't when I looked at her.

Ember's eyes softened in a way only hers could. Just barely. Just enough. "No rush, you know. You're welcome here any time. All the time."

My sister was several years older than me, and I didn't spend a lot of time with her growing up. While Ember and I never directly talked about it, it was like we'd adopted each other as brother and sister. I knew she was worried about me because I didn't talk much about Rae, but there wasn't much I felt I needed to say. I just needed to get settled in my own apartment, get playing with the band, and the rest would take care of itself. I needed to push through this.

Just a little longer and I'd be okay.

"How long is CJ planning on staying, anyway?" Ember's nose scrunched a little as she formed her question.

"Ha, don't worry, Em, I won't let him touch your things."

"Mmm." Ember arched her eyebrow as she took a sip of her coffee. "Thank you. Okay, love, I'm out to run some errands, then I'll be at the studio the rest of the day."

"You have fun, and I'll try to make sure CJ is in bed with a dose of penicillin by the time you guys get home."

Ember choked on her coffee as she laughed. "This. This is why I love you. Later."

"Later."

A couple of hours later I was waiting in San Diego International Airport. CJ had, in true CJ fashion, invited himself out for a visit. I'd only been in San Diego for about a week, and was still looking for my own place to live, but he said it was too cold in the Cape to wait for me to get my act together.

"Hey, asshole!"

And, there he was.

CJ's movements didn't match his looks as he brightly bounced toward me. He was clearly hung over, his usually-gelled hair sticking straight out on all sides, making him look like Animal from The Muppets.

Okay, maybe his movements perfectly matched his personality.

"What up, cuz?" I high-fived him, pulling him into a half-hug.

Even though he was a couple of years younger than me, my mother had always demanded that I play with him, given he was an only child and my sister was out of the house most of the time. I looked after him for as long as I needed to, but once high school came, and we went to different schools, he no longer needed me. While I was always taller, he doubled in size across his shoulders and in every muscle of his body. CJ could take plenty good care of himself and was able to find many girls who could take care of what he couldn't.

"Let's get this party started, bro. It's cold as balls back home, man. God, it's gorgeous here! You lucky fuckin' bastard. What's up first?" With his ADHD in full effect, CJ bounced beside me as we walked to my car.

"How's the band been going?" I asked a few minutes into our drive.

"Slow right now, our next big show will be St. Patrick's Day." CJ's hands rapped lightly against the dashboard as he looked out the window. "So, where are we going?"

"We're going to head down to South Park, I think. I've heard great things about the neighborhood, and it seems affordable."

"Oh no shit! E's Tavern is in South Park. We *have* to go there." His drumming got louder as he smiled.

I looked at him out of the corner of my eye. "What's so special about E's?"

"Well, for one, they've got live music. Stage, open mic nights, everything. You could play there when you're not recording. But, most importantly," he stopped his drumming and arched an eyebrow, "Georgia's there."

Of course.

I couldn't help but laugh when he flicked his tongue ring against his teeth as he wiggled his eyebrows. "Do I even want to know?"

Probably not.

"Oh," he returned his attention to the road, and his fingers to the beat, "you'll know."

"What'd you run out of women on the East Coast who bought your shit, so you had to outsource?" I'd always wondered how he avoided sleeping with the same girl twice.

CJ's face crinkled a bit. "Fuck no, dude. I've never slept with her. It's...*Georgia.*"

"Surprisingly, CJ, I don't follow your logic. Georgia is female, yes?" I watched him grin as I sipped from my water bottle.

"Yeah, but it's not like that. We went to high school together until senior year when her dad pulled her out of school and moved her here. He used to own that bar in Provincetown we played at in high school. *Dunes,* remember?"

I nodded. *Dunes* was kind of a dive bar, but it was the only one that let us play on weekends when we were teenagers. I had no recollection of Georgia, though I *did* have a clear memory of the owner of the place, and it wasn't a pretty one. He was kind of straggly with your standard town-drunk demeanor. The fact that he had children at all was concerning on a number of levels.

"Anyway," CJ continued, "we stayed friends after she moved, and..."

I cut him off as I spit out my water. "I'm sorry," I coughed, "what the hell did you just say? Friends? And a girl? In the same sentence?"

"Fuck off," he mumbled, sitting back and crossing his arms.

"Okay, okay, no need to get your panties in a bunch. We'll go to E's to meet your *friend*." My air-quotes around the last word was a little too much and earned me a punch in the arm.

E's Tavern was on Ash Street, and from the outside looked as much like a grocery store as a bar. The bright-blue painted wood exterior had me fearing I'd end up in the middle of a happy hour for senior citizens. Reminding myself that I was in the middle of South Park quelled my fears. I'd heard from a lot of friends around the country that this hip area of San Diego was where I'd want to make a home for myself. Checking out the wildly painted bungalows all around me, and hearing the saxophonist playing on the corner, I'd say they were right.

"We can't stay here for too long, Ceej. I still need to find a place to live." I slammed my door shut and shoved my hands into my jeans' pockets.

"Relax, dude. We'll have a drink or two, I'll catch up with Georgia, and we'll go." He held the door open as if he'd been there a thousand times before.

Stepping in, I was indeed relieved. E's was a spacious tavern with lots of dark wood. Tables and mismatched chairs painted different colors scattered the floor and a sizable bar wrapped around two sides of the interior. It was a Saturday, but it was only late afternoon, and the place was pretty busy. That was a good sign, and once I spotted the large square stage in the far corner, I took that as a *really* good sign. South Park just might be my neighborhood after all.

Halfway on our walk up to the bar, I stopped dead in my tracks. CJ was right. I knew her when I saw her. *Georgia.* Not because I recognized her from somewhere, but because all the energy from the bar orbited around her. CJ's face lit up a second before the short girl with bleach blonde hair tied up in a red bandana looked up from pouring a drink, and shrieked.

"CJ!"

"G!" The smile on CJ's face was more honest than I'd ever seen him look. It went all the way to his eyes, and he didn't even stick out his tongue ring.

Ignoring social convention, this girl gripped the edge of the bar and leapt over it as if it were a pommel horse. The closer she got to us, the shorter she looked. She was a good foot shorter than me, putting her around 5'3", but her smile and fierce indigo eyes made up for the difference in an instant. She wore a short-sleeved red plaid shirt tied at the waist, which was perfectly positioned to show off a silver belly button ring, and *short* jean shorts with frayed threads hanging from the hem.

As she jumped into CJ's arms and wrapped her arms around his neck, I noticed the boots. Black combat boots with an inch or so of red and black striped socks peeking out from the top. I don't know what struck me as most odd — that she was wearing all of that, or that she pulled it off like she could never wear anything else. CJ swung her around once before setting her down.

"How the hell have you been?" she asked as he patted her head like she was his little sister. A diamond stud in her nose caught the light as her face pulled back into a bigger smile.

"Better, now. Georgia, this is my cousin, Regan. Regan, this is Georgia Hall." I swear to you he was blushing.

Georgia

The name CJ scoffed at when I'd asked if he'd slept with her. Given that reaction, I'd assumed she was...something other than this intriguing girl with amazing curves standing in front of me.

I stuck out my hand. "Nice to meet you, Georgia."

Looking me head-to-toe once with an intense look in her eyes, she finally stuck out her hand. "Nice to meet you, too, Regan. I gotta get back to the bar." Turning on her heels we were left to follow her to the deep mahogany bar. It was then that I caught a black keyhole tattoo behind her right ear.

Interesting.

Just as we gave Georgia our drink orders, the phone rang at the far end of the bar, and she had to answer it.

"So...Georgia..." I turned to CJ as he continuously drummed his hands on the bar. He never stopped.

"Yep. Pretty hot, huh? How about that ass?" Blushing CJ left, and vile CJ returned with a mock ass-slapping gesture.

I rolled my eyes. "Classy. So, what gives?"

CJ looked genuinely confused. "What do you mean?"

"You've known her a long time, she's pretty good looking...and you've never?"

"Nah, it's...complicated. Her mom got sick and left her dad, and then Georgia moved out here...it's not important. We're just friends." He nodded toward the middle of the bar, signaling Georgia's return.

"Here you go, boys." She leaned forward and set our pints of Guinness in front of us.

As she pulled her hand away I noticed a tattoo on the thumb side of her left index finger, running the length of it. I'd assumed the first tattoo I'd noticed was a one-off. A dare. A flight of fancy.

More than one tattoo, though, takes guts. Judging by the type and location of the two on Georgia, though, I was betting she had more.

I wanted to know where they were.

I didn't look long enough to read what it said, because I got distracted. I can't be sure, but it looked like she'd unbuttoned an extra button on her shirt. Either way, there was a lot of cleavage staring CJ and me in the face. He wasn't even looking, which made me uncomfortable since he was the pervert, and *I* was the one who couldn't look away. I shouldn't have been looking. Though, I suppose the fact that I wanted to was a good sign of some sort of moving forward.

Or, it was just cleavage.

"Thanks, G. What's the matter? You look pissed." CJ took a large gulp of his dark beer, never taking his gaze from her eyes.

"Fuckers," she muttered. "We had Celtic Cross lined up to play tonight and they bailed. Their drummer can't hold his liquor, apparently, and is too hung over."

"Lightweight." CJ chuckled, drinking more of his beer.

"Anyway — hey," Georgia stopped her train of thought as her beautiful eyes widened, "you still play, don't you?"

"Won't ever stop." He smirked.

"Come. Tonight. I'll try to get some other people in here. You can pull something off, can't you? It's going to be packed in here tonight and they *need* music. Please?" She batted her short, dark eyelashes and he caved.

CJ nodded in my direction. "Regan plays the fiddle. Not just plays...owns. I bet we could get Bo and Ember to come along too. They play guitar, sing..."

Georgia smiled brightly and looked right at me. "Oh, so those gorgeous eyes of yours can read more than just my breasts?"

CJ spit some of his beer back into his glass. "Burn, dude."

"I…uh…" I looked down immediately, vowing to never look back up.

Georgia leaned in so close I could feel her breath on my neck. "It's okay," was all she said before she turned away and took care of some patrons at the other end of the bar.

"Let's get out of here before you embarrass yourself some more." CJ slapped my back and hopped off his stool.

"I don't even think that's possible," I grumbled as I followed him toward the exit.

CJ shouted across the bar as we reached the door. "See you tonight, G. Is nine o'clock okay?"

"You got it, Ceej. Nice meeting you, Regan." Her voice brightened at the end of her sentence as if she were mocking me.

Kill me now.

"Bye." I waved without turning around.

There was no way I'd be playing at E's now.

CHAPTER *Two*

I'm not like other girls

Georgia

"YOU SURE THAT tall drink of water is coming back tonight, G?" Lissa snatched my vampire-red lipstick from my fingers, as we got ready for the night's shift.

It didn't look right on her, but it made her feel right. In the end, that's everything.

I snatched the lipstick back. It looked *and* felt right. Tonight would be a gold mine. I felt it.

"Did you say *tall drink of water*?" I chuckled without smiling, my mouth formed in an *O* as I finished my second coat of a sure thing. "Yeah, he'll be back. CJ's never turned down a gig as long as I've known him."

"No, I mean that guy he was with."

I grinned, recalling those hazel eyes on me. "That's his cousin, Regan. I don't know anything about him."

Lissa finished spiking her jet-black pixie cut and closed the cap of her hair wax. "What about CJ? Is he fair game?" She pulled down the neckline of her spaghetti-strap tank top.

"Knock your socks off, Liss." CJ was a sure thing. He'd always been.

Not with me, though. With us it was...different. He was safe, and so was I. I gazed in the mirror, remembering our joint conquests in high school. Teaming up to find the hottest people in the bar my dad owned became a game. A game we both got damn good at in no time.

Lissa whistled to get my attention. "What's that look? You want CJ? You can have him. That Regan guy looks like he'd be a good time."

"Have them both, for all I care. I've got tips to make and I'm not counting on my old high school friend." After applying eggplant-colored eyeliner on my top and bottom lids, I hiked the hem of my dress as far up as it would go and still be considered a dress. The unwritten rule with nighttime attire was to take more risks than daytime.

So were we.

"Jesus, Georgia," Lissa laughed as she headed for the bathroom door, "anyone listening in on this conversation might think we were getting ready for a night of street walking, not bartending."

"Some nights there's no difference, really." I arched an eyebrow and she smiled in response as we headed back behind the busy bar.

Even with my heels, I was still a couple of inches shorter than Lissa. She was waif-ish, with a dash of untreated Anorexia. Our differences in appearance worked to our advantage. It was easy to spot within a few seconds which patrons were eyeing whom, and we used that, to the delight of our wallets.

I'd been counting on Celtic Cross to draw a huge crowd, which would translate into great tips. Their last minute cancellation had me panicking until CJ walked in this afternoon. It was almost like it was a few years ago; the last time we saw each other in person. Almost.

I hadn't done a very good job of keeping in touch over the last few years, but he'd done his part and kept quiet about my reasons for leaving Massachusetts.

"I love when you wear your hair down, you should do it more often." Lissa was counting her drawer and I was counting mine.

"I guess." My reverse bob was an easy choice for looking good tied up or left down. Mostly, I favored it up in a bandana. I looked to the clock and to the crowd. *CJ better show.*

Lissa pulled out the cutting board and a bin of limes. I grabbed a small knife and stood next to her, carving out perfect wedges the customers would barely notice. She elbowed me playfully. "When are you going to stop slumming it with us and finally open that bakery?"

I let my head hang as I sighed. "I'm not opening—"

Lissa cut me off as she rolled her eyes. "I don't want your excuses, sister."

"My hours are too irregular to successfully operate it. I'm here till three, at least, then I'm tired, Liss. I just want to go to bed." I tied my apron around my waist and smoothed out the front as my lie prepared to wrinkle up the truth.

Just before I got sucked into another "get the hell out of here" conversation with Lissa, CJ burst ceremoniously through the door and walked straight toward me. To onlookers, he might be intimidating. He was probably 6'3" but his shoulders were so wide it made him look like a brick wall. His dark hair was shaggier than it used to be, but it looked good on him.

"Hey, gorgeous, do you...wanna wear some clothes behind that bar?" He lifted his pierced eyebrow as he tossed his drumsticks on the bar.

"Are you suggesting I put on *more* clothes?" I leaned back and grabbed the Jack Daniels, mixing CJ's drink before he ordered. It was always the same, and, sometimes, same was nice.

He looked up and pensively ran the barbell in his tongue across his lips. "No. What was I thinking?" He stuck out his tongue and I smacked his shoulder. *Sex addict.*

"Do *not* stick your tongue out at me, Ceej. Lord knows where that thing's been since we last saw each other." I slid his drink to him. "So...where the hell are your friends?"

CJ looked over his shoulder, and as if choreographed for film, Regan strolled through the door with a violin case slung over his shoulder with a red strap. His loose jeans were tattered at the knees and pockets. I couldn't tell if that was from a lot of wear, or if he'd spent too much money and purchased them that way. He was wearing a white long-sleeved button-down shirt with the sleeves rolled up to the elbows. Black converse sneakers and his hair tied back away from his neck in a messy ponytail completed his homage to carelessness.

Regan nodded to me and CJ as his long legs carried him to the bar. Before I could say *hi*, he was followed in by a god and goddess.

I shit you not.

The guy was a couple of inches over six-feet with thick hair as black as Lissa's. It was styled to look messy but he didn't look like he tried very hard. I was annoyed already. He held hands with what was easily the most beautiful girl I'd ever seen. Her long auburn hair had beach waves I just knew she was born with, and I felt my shoulders stretching back and my spine lengthening, as I stood straighter. I hated her. The effortless perfection of others got under my skin. Like God was mocking me.

"Thanks for waiting for us, Ceej." The girl rolled her eyes and she and the guy set down heavy-looking guitar cases I'd totally missed them carrying in, what with all the good-looking air hovering around them.

"I'll always wait for you, sweets." CJ stuck out that goddamn tongue ring, and she flipped him off as Regan and the other guy laughed.

It seemed she was well acquainted with CJ, and thankfully for her, hadn't slept with him. I cleared my throat and shot a snooty look to CJ, encouraging his social skills to make an appearance.

CJ whipped his head around. "Sorry, G. You met Regan earlier today..."

Regan nodded but would barely meet my eyes. He must have still been uncomfortable from staring at my breasts earlier. Given I had a hell of a lot more than cleavage showing tonight, I doubted he'd be able to look at me at all.

"Hi Regan," I teased. Sometimes it was *so* easy to make a man blush. He murmured his hello and then grumbled something about heading backstage or outside to tune. As if E's had a backstage.

CJ ignored the awkward exchange and gestured to the dynamic duo of attraction. "And, these are my friends who live up in Mission Bay. Bo and November."

Naturally, they smiled in unison. Bo took my hand, and I was instantly filled with the need to make his mouth mine. Given he seemed pretty tight with CJ, though, I decided against it.

"Nice to meet you, Georgia. CJ told us a lot about you on the way over here." The way his voice wrapped itself around my guts told me he was a singer.

I forced a smile. "Good to meet you."

On habit I snapped my gum, then immediately cursed myself for the classless noise. The urge to fit in with them was overwhelming. I snapped my gum one more time to remind myself that those feelings could fuck right off in the direction from where they came.

I held my hand out to the girl. "November?"

She smiled all the way to her Cheshire cat green eyes. "You can call me Ember."

Of course I can...

"Nice to meet you, November."

But I won't.

"Oh for fuck's sake, Regan, don't get your panties in a wad," CJ groaned as I forced myself to break my gaze from Ember. She looked familiar, but I couldn't place from where.

"Problem, boys?" I took a deep breath and leaned my elbows onto the bar.

"Prince Prodigy here needs to know where we can *put our stuff.*" CJ threw some air-quotes around the end to accent his juvenile state.

I stared at Regan until he looked me straight in the eyes. The hazel eyes I remembered from earlier in the afternoon had taken on more of a yellow edge. Fierce. Humming with agitation of some sort. I decided not to play any more games with him for the time being.

"We don't really have a separate backstage area, but you guys can head over there and set up whatever you need to. You're on in ten, okay?"

"Thanks, G." CJ swallowed the rest of his Jack and Coke in one gulp and picked up his sticks as he slid from the stool.

Bo, Ember, and Regan had already made their way to the stage.

"Hey," I stopped CJ just before he left the bar, "what's wrong with your cousin? Did he sit on one of your drumsticks or something?

"I'll tell you if you tell me where the fuck your accent went." He scrunched up his forehead as he nodded his chin in my direction.

"I didn't—" As my face heated, CJ smiled.

"I'm just giving you shit, kid. I teased Regan about losing his, too, when he went away to that preppy fuckin' high school with all of those band geeks."

Despite being the same age as me, CJ sometimes called me *kid.* He didn't seem to have rhyme or reason to when he did it, but hearing it was like going home. To the good stuff.

Grateful that I wouldn't have to enter into a discussion of the parts of me I'd given up during my move to San Diego, I breathed a sigh of relief. "I miss hearing it sometimes, though, so don't go losing yours, too."

CJ waved his hand. "Don't worry about Regan. He's just bent out of shape because he can't find a place to live and is itchin' like hell to get out of Bo and Ember's palace of love." CJ thrust his hips a few times for effect.

"Nice, Ceej. Just get the hell up there and keep people happy... and drinking."

A few minutes later, I headed toward the stage to announce the group. "Hey, guys. You've got about three minutes. When I announce you...what do I call you?"

"The Fucking Lunatics!" CJ sounded serious as he fist-pumped the air.

"Okaaay...any other suggestions?" I scanned the group. Thankfully, Regan let out a laugh.

"Just say we're a sub-set of the San Diego Six. We're recording with them this winter. Well, minus CJ." Regan nodded to Bo and Ember.

Then, it clicked. I darted my eyes to Ember. "*That's* where I've seen your picture. You're Raven and Ashby's daughter, right?"

Ember nodded and smiled. I don't think she'd stopped smiling since she walked in the bar, actually. "I am. You listen?"

I'd been a fan of the Six since I moved to San Diego a few years ago, but demanded of myself that I keep that fangirl shit under wraps.

"I do. They're good. Good for you guys for getting to record with them."

Regan smiled as I talked with Ember. The way one eye squinted a little more than the other when he smiled made me uncomfortable, as if he was studying me under an invisible microscope. I was determined to keep him at arm's length since he couldn't keep his eyes off of me. He seemed nice and I wanted to leave him that way. So, just before I turned on the mic, I leaned in and perched my lips about half an inch from his ear.

"The Six is good, Regan. Real good. Can you keep up with them?" I challenged.

He shrugged, an unreadable look taking over his face. "They seem to think so."

I hadn't heard a single note come from his fiddle, despite his earlier insistence that he get to the stage. For all I knew, he could be a complete fraud dressed up in David Garrett clothing.

"Well," I whispered with a smile on my lips, "prove it."

"Prove it?" He tilted his head almost incredulously, a cocky grin forming at the corner of his mouth.

"You heard me. Make a believer out of me with that thing." I touched the edge of his fiddle, and he pulled it back slightly. My eyes shot to his and I found him looking at his instrument possessively.

Ok, then.

With a quick lick of my lips, I looked at the microphone. "E's is happy to present...Last Call."

I headed back to the bar without looking back, but heard CJ's excited "Fuck yeah! Last Call!" as I situated myself for the night.

Lissa shouldered up next to me as I went back to my end of the bar. "What was that?" she shouted in my ear as the musicians did one final round of tuning.

"What was what?"

"That look you gave Regan. Your *go* look. I thought you weren't into him." Lissa stepped back and looked down her long eyelashes at me.

Before she could respond, CJ struck the snare drum, as Bo started a familiar tune on an electric guitar. "Smooth Criminal".

"What the..." I looked past Lissa just as Regan raised his bow and struck it across the strings.

Holy shit...

Regan

She didn't look back when she returned to her station at the bar. I don't know how I missed it earlier in the day, but she had a third tattoo on the back of her neck. It looked like a rocking horse of some sort. I'd already spent far too much time staring at Georgia's body for one day, so I looked away. Though, the way she attempted to pass off that scant piece of fabric for a dress, it didn't seem that she wanted me to look away.

Or anyone else for that matter.

I didn't know what Georgia's game was, but when she challenged me about my ability with the violin, it lit something inside me. I don't even know why I cared what she thought. I'd met her only hours earlier and had made kind of an ass out of myself.

Still, when she asked me to make a believer out of her, I asked Ember to sit the first song out while Bo played the electric guitar, and we started "Smooth Criminal". It's my go-to "wow" piece for people who have an attitude about classical instruments.

Then, her jaw dropped.

Yeah, that's what I thought.

Just as I pulled the corners of my lips up into an *I told you so* grin, Georgia's seemed to curl into a sneer and she abruptly turned around and got to work behind the bar. Mission accomplished. I'd regained my social footing from my breast-staring fumble earlier and was on even keel with her again.

As the song went on, I looked around the bar. It was an eclectic mix of customers. Hippies, hipsters, and hip-replacements all mingled together, drinking and enjoying the music. I planned to spend some time after the set mingling with the crowd to see if anyone had any leads on apartments or sublets. Anything.

"Smooth Criminal" ended, and as the cheers rose to a roar through the bar, Georgia's eyes found mine. I watched as her tongue ran across the front of her top teeth with her mouth closed. The look on her face was unreadable, but the guy's hand riding up her arm as he ordered another drink was loud and clear.

She looked down as if she'd caught two people having sex, turning her attention and smile to the guy with a buzz cut and black-rimmed glasses at the bar.

"Dude." Bo interrupted the jealousy that had no business brewing in my stomach.

"Sorry. Uh..." I cleared my throat and looked back at CJ who was shaking his head and grinning. He never missed a thing.

"Ha," Bo continued, "she *is* intriguing...but we've got a set to finish. You and Ember do "Foolish Games" next, okay?"

"Sure. Ember, you ready?"

Ember's eyes drifted between the bar and me. Curiosity mixed with concern. "Yep...are you?"

It made me uncomfortable when they made comments about me and other girls in the same sentence. It had been several months since Rae died, but I couldn't tell if my moving on would give them permission to, or if it was the other way around.

Either way, I wasn't ready for anything, and as I heard Georgia giggle purposefully from behind me, I knew I certainly wasn't ready for anything with a girl who had a boyfriend.

I had to get her out of my system. Fast.

"Just give me a second." I set my violin on the stool and weaved through a group of girls making out with each other before reaching Georgia at the bar.

She walked toward me, and despite the noise around us, I could hear each dedicated click of her heels on the sticky wood floor.

"Takin' a break already?" She folded her arms on the bar in front of her and leaned toward me like she'd done earlier in the day. This time, though, I remained fixed on her eyes.

I chuckled. "I figured before I continued I should check in to see if I made you a believer."

Any look of surprise that showed on her face dissolved into a grin. "Regan...I've believed as many as six impossible things before breakfast."

That's it. That was her only response before slowly lifting her chest off of her folded arms, turning, and strutting over to a guy with spiked hair and a black t-shirt with "Pink Floyd" across the front vying for her attention.

With my eyebrows pulled in, I returned to the stage in a daze.

"You okay?" Ember settled onto her stool and adjusted the guitar over her shoulder. "What'd she say?"

"I..." I looked back at the bar and watched Georgia thread her fingers through the spikes of the Pink Floyd guy's hair. "I have no idea."

"What were the words she said, Regan?" Ember chuckled as she tuned.

"They made no sense." I tuned with her as she looked over my shoulder, undoubtedly at Georgia.

"Well," she shrugged, "it's probably for the best, anyway. Her eyes and hands have been all over everyone in this bar."

Defensiveness overrode common sense. "Isn't that just...her job?"

Ember's eyebrow hooked incredulously. "*That's* not her job." She nodded, and I followed with my eyes to see Georgia leaning *all the way* forward as a different guy whispered something into her ear.

He tucked a piece of paper in between her breasts and she set herself back on her heels and kept working.

I wanted to kick his ass, and it made no sense.

I shook my head. "God, whatever. Let's play. Ready?"

Ember's look relaxed. "Mmmhmm."

As we settled into the song, I reminded myself that girls like Georgia were good at making guys want them. Crave them. With skin-baring clothing, wicked eyes, and a bottom lip pinched between their teeth, they owned us. All of us.

Through each piece, Georgia's hips swayed to the beat, but she never pulled her attention away from her customers. Her tips. Once every other song, or so, her eyes would flash to mine, and I'd look away. She was scrambling my sense of reality with one stone-blue gaze. One smile. One laugh.

It was clear why she and CJ were such good friends as I watched her move with seductive determination through the bar with a tray of drinks in hand. Each time she set down a glass she'd bend a little further forward, inviting eyes to places they had no business being.

Her game bothered me just as much as CJ's did, maybe even more since I knew how men perceived women who behaved like that. I hadn't seen her take a drink all night, and I was pretty sure drinking on the job as a bartender was barely tolerated, so she couldn't even use intoxication as an excuse.

She was intentional, this girl with a rocking horse tattooed on the back of her neck.

She was intentional and made absolutely no sense.

We finished our set and packed up our gear with an hour left before the bar closed. I just wanted to get out of there and go home. It was the first set of that length that I'd played in some time, and I was exhausted. The finger pads on my left hand screamed for a break.

"Great set, Ceej." Georgia met us on the stage, kissing CJ on the cheek.

"Thanks, kid." He smiled as he held her waist for a second.

It was then that I got a better look at the tattoo on the back of her neck. It wasn't just a rocking horse. It was one with wings. More confused than I'd been before, I shook my head and slung my violin case over my shoulder.

She and CJ were engaged in quiet conversation about something CJ appeared to take seriously, given he was paying attention at all. I wandered to the bar and sat next to Ember.

Ember bumped her upper arm into mine. "That was good, Kane. Real good. You're back on top of things, I'd say."

I grabbed her beer and took a sip. "It felt good. Two weeks and we start recording, right?"

Bo laughed from the other side of Ember. "I knew the bug would bite you in due time."

Even though I'd agreed to come record, I wasn't sure if my heart was in it. But, Bo and Ember could see the desires of my heart written across my face. I was all in.

Ember tilted her chin to where CJ and Georgia were still talking. "What's with her? How does CJ know her?"

I filled them in on what little details I knew.

"Dunes?" Ember crinkled her nose at the mention of the bar Georgia's dad used to run. "That place is such a hole."

"Yeah, she's been out here for a few years. I don't know anything about her, really."

Ember raised her eyebrows. "She really does leave little to the imagination, though, doesn't she?"

I leaned to the side and saw Georgia and CJ walking toward us. Georgia's breasts bouncing as she moved.

"Be nice," Bo mumbled.

"I intend to," she shot back.

Georgia cocked her head to the side as she wiggled her way between Ember and me. "What's the matter, Regan? You look...lost." She bit her lip. Her eyelashes swooped down for a fraction of a second before she looked back up, red in her cheeks.

She was flirting with me.

No.

"Just tired."

A tiny groan of a noise fled from her throat as she smiled. "Well, rest up. Janice wants you back here tomorrow."

"Janice?" I asked.

"The owner. Customers told her they want more." Then she looked at me in a way that was so intimate, I felt like we should be alone. "I want more, too."

"I don't know..." I looked between my friends, who all seemed eager to accept.

Bo shrugged. "It would be great practice before we hit the studio."

Ember eyed me cautiously before nodding in agreement with Bo.

CJ slapped me on the shoulder. "Come on, dude! I'm only in town for a week. Then how much will we get to play together?"

"What the hell..." I sighed as CJ cheered. He was easy to please.

"See you tomorrow, then." Georgia smiled, and for the first time since I met her a few hours before, it reached her eyes.

I nodded. "Tomorrow."

I ordered a drink from the 6-foot, too-skinny bartender with spiky black hair. She set the Guinness in front of me while looking me over, suspicion lazily forming her lips into a half-grin.

"What?" I asked, the noise of Bo and Ember asking Georgia for details about tomorrow lost in the background.

She just shook her head, looking behind me for a split second before looking back at me with a full smile.

"Enjoy the ride."

"What are you talking about?" I shook my head.

"You'll see." Her eyes flickered behind me once more. I knew Georgia was still standing there. I could smell the brown sugar perfume I remembered from earlier in the afternoon.

"I doubt it," I challenged.

She chuckled, and as she walked away she said in a sing-song voice, "We'll see."

Turning around, I found Georgia linking arms with what had to have been the fourth or fifth customer I saw her get that cozy with over the course of the night.

No, I thought.

We won't see.

CHAPTER *Three*

WHO ARE YOU?

Regan

THE GANG AND I had some sound-check issues we wanted to correct before Sunday night's gig, so we showed up at E's around six o'clock. CJ had insisted on staying until closing to catch up more with Georgia, and I didn't see him until he rolled in around five in the morning. Needless to say, he was moving slower than I would have liked for someone that needed to move a multi-piece drum set across the stage to accommodate our set-up.

"Come on, Ceej, you slept till we woke you up to drive over here. Get your ass in gear or get off the stage." I set a coil for sound cable on the stool and went over to his set, pushing the bass drum with my foot.

"Pull the bow out of your ass, Regan. And, don't touch my fuckin' drums."

Bo shook his head with a smile, moving stools to the side. But, Ember wasn't about to let me get away with my attitude.

"You've been kind of bitchy all day."

I loved when she used the word *bitchy* to describe Bo's attitude, sometimes. But not mine.

She was right, though.

"Sorry," I sighed, "I guess the stress of trying to find a place to live is grating on me."

"No luck last night, huh?"

"No. I talked around the bar for like an hour, but no one knew of anything available right now."

"Craigslist?"

"You mean *Crazylist*? I'm good."

Ember snickered and picked up the cord I'd been winding and deposited it in its appropriate place. "You know there's no hurry, Regan. Don't stress it, okay?"

I nodded. I was stressing it. I loved both Bo and Ember, but soon we'd be spending 12-18 hours a day together in the studio, and living with them on top of all of that would become a challenge. Especially with Bo suggesting to me each week that I go to his therapist with him one time. To, *you know,* he'd say, *talk about Rae and stuff.* There was no stuff. Why couldn't they just let me move on in peace?

Once we were all set up, Bo and Ember left to go grab some dinner before we went on around eight.

"You want to go get some food?" I asked CJ.

He crossed his arms around his broad chest. "Are you off your period, now?"

I had to laugh. "You're a dick."

He nodded. "I accept your apology. No, though, to dinner. I'm going to go sleep in your car for another hour."

"You really are a useless pile of shit, CJ, you know that?"

"You won't say that when all the girls are cheering," he called over his shoulder as he snatched my keys off the bar and exited for the parking lot.

With a frustrated sigh, I turned to the bar and sat on the middle stool. The place was just starting to get busy, and I was hoping for some food before our set.

"What can I get you?" The skinny tall girl with the spiky hair from last night asked. Though, her hair wasn't spiky tonight. Or black. Well, most of it was black, but she had bright blue highlights across the top of her head.

"Do you have food?"

She looked behind her to a set of double doors, turning back around with a smirk. "We have a kitchen."

"Great, food's that good, huh?" I rolled my eyes.

"Settle down, I'll get you the boneless wings. *Those* are good. You like 'em hot?"

"As hot as they make them."

She arched her eyebrow. "We'll see."

"You keep saying that." I challenged her assertion from last night that *we'd see* about Georgia.

"I keep meaning it. It's Lissa, by the way."

"Huh?"

"Lissa is my name." She stuck her hand across the bar.

"Oh...Regan. Nice to meet you." I shook her hand.

"You were amazing last night."

As she pulled hers away, she let her fingertip drag across my palm. Her inflection suggested way more than my playing ability. One look into her nearly black eyes told me she was trouble. The kind CJ wouldn't mind getting into more than once.

"Thanks. It wasn't my first time." I couldn't help it.

Lissa threw her head back in a light laugh that didn't match the sharp edges of her frame. A second later she disappeared around the corner, and I rested my forehead on my fists for a minute before a provocative voice lured my eyes back up.

"What's the matter with you? Last night's show rocked." Georgia dried the insides of pint glasses as she talked. She was in dark, ripped jeans and a fitted purple tank. Her hair was tied back with a black bandana.

As she set the glass down, I noticed a bruise around her wrist that nearly matched the color of her shirt.

"What happened to your wrist?"

She picked up her arm as if she were viewing the mark for the first time. "Huh, who knows? Anyway, what's up your ass?" She and CJ seemed to share an idea of where all of the attitude in the body was held.

"I still can't find an apartment." Reluctantly, I continued, "You know of any?"

She looked up in thought for a moment. "No. I live in La Jolla, so I don't know much about what's open around here."

"La Jolla?" I sat up.

"Don't contain your surprise..." She rolled her eyes and picked up another rack of glasses.

"That area is...really nice."

"What, I can't have nice things?" She blew a giant pink bubble, her tongue collecting the sticky gum from her lips after it popped. I studied the way her lipstick didn't budge, even when her tongue slipped back into her mouth.

"That's not what I meant, Georgia."

About ten-seconds too late, Lissa came back with my order of wings.

"Here you go, good-lookin'." She set the plate on the bar with some napkins and silverware.

"Thanks." I looked around her to try to continue my conversation with Georgia, but she was nowhere to be seen.

"So," Lissa filled a plastic compartment with cherries, and lemon, lime, and orange slices, "is your cousin as big of a pig as he acts?"

I snorted, which was a bad idea given how hot the wings were. "Probably worse."

She nodded, and with a twisted grin on her face, went about her work. Thankfully I didn't appear to be on her radar for whatever it was she did with those eyes.

Several minutes later, Georgia returned from a room in the back. Her relaxed wardrobe had been discarded, and she was wearing tight red shorts—very short—with a black tank top covered in cherries. Her right wrist, the one with the bruise, was decorated with a thick black cuff that had silver squares set through the middle. She looked like a 1940's pinup girl with her hair tied back with the same red bandana I'd seen her wear the day before.

She stood at the tap for a minute, filling three pint glasses. She gracefully navigated through the crowd in several-inch high black high heels to a table in the back.

"See something you like over there?" Lissa took my empty plate from my hands.

"Why does she do that?"

"Who do what?" Lissa looked around behind me.

"Georgia. Dress like that." I looked away as Georgia bent over to give a beer to someone across their table.

Lissa frowned slightly, almost sardonically. "Surely you've been in a bar or two in your day." She stepped back, holding her arms out and turning once.

I could see she wasn't dressed much differently than Georgia. Lissa was wearing an electric blue skirt that matched the highlights in her hair, and a black tank top without straps. I think my sister had called that a tube top. She was right. At nearly every bar I'd been in, the female bartenders played up their assets. That's just part of the culture. But as I chewed my lip and stared into my empty pint glass, I wished it wasn't.

The familiar clip-clop of Georgia's dangerously high heels signaled her return. Peeking up slightly, I caught Lissa staring at me for a few seconds before she returned to the other end of the bar.

"Regan," Georgia set the empty tray down in front of me, "I wanted to run something by you."

"Shoot." I wished she were still wearing those old jeans and that purple tank top. Purple did killer things for her eyes.

"Well," she said as she leaned forward the way I'd seen her do all last night. I didn't want her thinking I expected that from her. "The apartment across from mine is open. It's *right* on the water. Like, leave door, cross street, fall off small cliff into the ocean. I know it seems far from here, but it's only about a twenty-five minu—"

"Yes!" My tongue and my lips produced the answer before my brain caught up. "But, why the hell didn't you mention this earlier?"

She shrugged, her cheeks seeming to blush a little. "I didn't know if you'd be interested. From what CJ told me last night, you were intent on live down here in South Park."

"It seems like an awesome neighborhood, but I just can't find a place..." I ran a hand through my hair, then tied it back.

"You could always stay with me," Lissa piped in. "Where'd you tell him there was an opening, G?"

Georgia shooed Lissa away with a wave of her hand. "Mind your own damn business for once."

"Fine," Lissa exaggerated a sigh, "guess I'll just have to go flirt with CJ."

I looked behind me and found him reentering the bar, stretching his arms overhead.

"Don't worry." I laughed a little. "You won't have to do that much work. He's kind of a sure thing."

"Funny," Lissa looked between Georgia and me, "that's what she said last night. You two share a brain or something?"

Georgia shook her head. "No, we just know CJ. So," she turned back to me, "want to come look at the place tomorrow? I'll get the key and show you around."

"That'd be great." Relieved and overwhelmed at the turn my housing search had taken, I smiled and slapped the edge of the bar.

"Georgia! Order up!" A stern male voice hollered from the back.

She curled her lip, flaring the nostril that held that tiny stud. A look that would have told the guy to shut the hell up, had he been able to see it. "All right, off again. Good luck tonight."

Georgia darted back to the kitchen, returning with a full tray of food and hurried off to three different tables.

"What was that about?" CJ asked as he sat down.

"I think I just found a place to live."

"With Georgia? Lucky..."

"No, hormone central, the place across from hers."

CJ ordered a beer from a very attentive Lissa. "That's going to be one hell of an adventure."

I looked over to the corner of the bar at those tiny red shorts, wondering what I'd done in my moment of housing desperation.

"I'm sure it will, Ceej."

Georgia

"Here ya go, Jake."

Jake winked at me as I set his beer down, leaning back in his chair just far enough to study the length of my shorts from behind.

"Thanks, sugar." He licked his lips.

I smacked the back of his head. "You know I hate that nickname."

"Aw, come on. It's sweet, just like we were."

His friends whistled in mock-reverence at his apparent accomplishment of getting me in bed.

"Sweet? We?" I tapped the pad of my index finger on my bottom lip as I looked up at the lights. "Ah, yes, as sweet as five minutes can be." I strode away from the table as the whistles turned into jeers and teasing.

That boy didn't have a goddamn clue. It was a shame, too, given what a Ken Doll he was. I'd left the bar with Jake six weeks ago, and, bless his heart, he returned every single Saturday and Sunday since, asking for "another chance."

"Last night that good?" Lissa bumped her bony hip into mine once I got back behind the bar.

"What?"

"That smile?"

"Oh, ha, no..." Out of the corner of my eye I caught CJ and Regan turn their heads in our direction. "Six weeks ago was *that good* for Jake."

Lissa looked over my shoulder. "Oh for the love of...is he still following you around like a puppy? Can't he take a hint?"

Without asking, I slid two beers in front of Regan and CJ. Looking at them, still talking to Lissa, I continued. "Hints don't matter if you know what you want. You just go until you get it."

CJ grinned and nodded. Always on my wavelength. Regan, though, looked down and shifted in his seat. He didn't particularly strike me as a prude, and I'm certain CJ would have warned me if anyone in his gene pool behaved in such a manner, but he always looked uncomfortable when I was around.

"When'd you dye your hair?" CJ cocked his head and looked at me like he was working through an algebra equation.

"Wow, it's only taken you twenty-four hours to realize my hair is a different color than the last time you saw me?"

"What color is it supposed to be?" Regan piped up.

I lifted an eyebrow as my eyes slowly shifted to him. "It's *supposed* to be any color I want it to be."

He rolled his eyes. I didn't much care for his "I'm too good for this scene" attitude.

"Black." CJ blurted out, sounding annoyed if my ears interpreted things correctly.

"What the hell's your problem?" I felt like I'd been asking people that all night.

CJ shrugged, staring at me rather incredulously. "That guy, G? Really? He looks like a massive douchebag."

Regan and I laughed at the same time. "CJ," I caught my breath, "I've been picking up guys like that for as long as you've taught me how they operate."

"Did you just call me a douchebag?" His eyes lit up like a kid at Christmas.

"I did." I set my hands on my hips.

"Well, none of us deserve you." He winked. I'd never seen him wink to any girl he was taking home, so I'm not sure exactly what the hell he ever meant by it.

"As long as you know that, I'd say we're all set here." Just then, the door opened, escorting in those annoyingly beautiful people. I nodded to the door. "Your band is here."

Holding hands as they walked, they made my stomach churn.

"What's that look on your face?" Regan's rich voice sent chills down my back. Where he couldn't see.

"Do they ever stop smiling? Are they always that happy?" I nodded to the prom king and queen.

Regan's eyes seemed to dull for a minute. "Which do you want me to answer first?" He tried to chuckle, but it wasn't sincere.

"Neither, my food order is up." Before the syrup that was Bo and Ember could ooze over the bar and onto me, I made a break for the kitchen.

Standing next to the stainless steel counter, waiting for the rest of my order, I ran through as many busy thoughts as I could to keep my mind away from last night.

Lissa saddled up next to me, snapping her fingers at the line cook before speaking to me. "You okay?"

"Yeah."

No.

"I saw you leave with Dex last night."

"You did." I nodded, bile rising through my body.

"Aw, shit," she groaned, "is he bad? He looks like he'd be amazing in bed."

My shoulders twitched a little. "He was...okay."

"That blows. Will he be in tonight, you think? You know, part of the puppy brigade with Jake."

"God, who knows." As I reached for an oversized bowl of soup, my hand slipped, dumping steaming hot liquid down my right arm and the front of my shirt. "*Shit!*"

Lissa tossed me a rag as I silently cursed the asshole who would order soup in a place that rarely dipped below seventy degrees.

"Shit, are you okay?" Lissa shrieked.

"Ugh, I need to change my shirt, and take this fucking cuff off, now that it's probably ruined. Can you take the food to my table?"

"You got it." Her voice faded as I pushed through the double doors and walked to the back room.

I cursed again when I crossed the threshold and tore off my cuff, casting it onto the tattered couch.

"G?" CJ rapped on the doorframe, causing me to jump. "I heard you yell from the stage. Thought I'd come check..." He trailed off, his words plunging somewhere into our past. One we never talked about.

"I'm fine. Fuckin' soup." I peeled off my soaked tank top and pulled on an *E's Tavern* T-shirt, rolling up the sleeves and tying the back into a tight knot with a hair elastic, right above my lower back.

CJ didn't even flinch when I was just in my bra a few feet from him. We'd spent so much time together smoking pot in the back room of *Dunes* back in Provincetown, I'm sure he'd caught more than a glimpse of me in my bra a time or two.

"Well, as long as you're okay..."

"I'm fine, CJ," I snapped.

"Christ, all right. What is it with everyone today? Anyway, Regan says the apartment across from you is open"

"It's in La Jolla, right on the water." I took off my leather cuff and wrapped it in some paper towel, hoping to salvage it from the cream of mushroom.

"The fuck is that?" CJ paced toward me, pulling his hands from his pockets.

I lifted the bracelet. "Just a cuff I picked up at this second hand store down the str—"

"*No,*" he tenderly wrapped his fingers around my forearm and grazed his thumb across my purple wrist, "*this.*"

"A bruise." I tried to keep my voice even, but knew CJ would tear down the facade in a second. He could see through any half-truth of mine as if I'd left the shades open and was walking around the inside of my conscience naked. I pulled my arm back and he released it without a fight.

CJ's eyes darkened and narrowed at once, as if he were morphing into someone else. Someone only I knew. "That doesn't look like just a bruise."

"Whatever it is you think it looks like, it's not."

"That guy you left with last night. Him?" He crossed his arms over his chest, taking up a majority of the doorway with his massive shoulders. I sighed as I rolled my eyes. "Don't give me that look, G. I'm not overreacting."

"Actually, you are a little. This isn't senior year. I'm not that girl anymore." I squared my shoulders to his, my hands on my hips.

"Yeah?" he challenged. "Then, who are you?"

I smiled, trying to break the angry red cloud between us. "Come on, Ceej, you know who I am. We built us. Remember? We learned from each other. How to pick 'em, how to bed 'em."

CJ would give me pointers on how to look attractive, rather than desperate. How to play hard to get. I taught him the same thing. Despite how piggish he might seem to some, he actually uses those techniques every goddamn night. It's not that he's a pig, really. It's that the girls get mad they ever fell for it.

"It's different for us, Georgia. I'm a guy."

"Uh-uh, don't you dare start that shit with me. It's not different, that's the whole goddamn point. Don't go all gender roles on me now, Kane." I waved my finger in his face and he took both of my arms in his giant hands, just like they were his sticks.

He sighed. "You're right. Sorry." The top of his left cheek twitched a little. He didn't believe the words he was saying, but he wanted to. I needed him to, too. He cleared his throat. "You gonna tell me what happened to your wrist?"

I shrugged. "Guess Dex thought my bedroom walls were red." I laughed at his confused look, trying to cover up the nausea I felt at constructing yet another lie. And, throwing Dex under the bus with it. "God, read a book once in a while."

Just then, Lissa appeared in the doorway. "Knock, knock. You cleaned up, girl? You've got thirsty customers. Including Dex."

I froze. Just for a second, but CJ's grip tightened before he let go. He caught my reaction and seemed to file it away as he slid his hands into his pockets. I needed to keep CJ far away from Dex. Far away from asking about the reality of last night at all.

"Great." I scraped some sarcasm from the back of my tightening throat and slathered it across my words.

I slid past CJ without meeting his eyes. I needed a shot, and for CJ to get on stage, and for Dex to eat and leave. All at once.

That way no one would get hurt.

No one.

CHAPTER *Four*

OFF WITH THEIR HEADS!

Regan

EMBER BOUNCED HER knee as her high heel dangled off the dowel in the stool. "God," she groaned, "where the hell is CJ?" She'd been tense all afternoon. I didn't know what was sticking to her, but Bo seemed to be checking her for live wires, as well.

Thankfully, CJ strode out of the back hallway a second later, just behind Georgia.

"Couldn't wait until later tonight, CJ?" Ember did little to control the volume of her voice. Bo's eyes widened as they darted between Ember and CJ.

Georgia stopped in her tracks and walked with baleful control toward Ember, who paid her no attention. Until Georgia was standing an inch away from her, angry eyes narrowed until I could nearly only see her pupils.

"Wait until later tonight for what?" Georgia's chest heaved between her narrow shoulders. She'd changed out of her tank top and was wearing a black bar t-shirt that she'd manipulated to still show her belly button. I loved that her stomach wasn't overly tanned or tight.

"Let it go, Georgia," CJ grumbled as he pushed past me and settled behind his set. Georgia shot him a killer look. Turning around, I found him mirroring it back to her as he stretched his head from side to side, rolling his shoulders back. He shifted his eyes to me. "Let's warm up."

I turned back around and found Ember tying back her hair as Georgia continued to stare at her, taking one, two, three steps backward before she turned toward the bar.

"What the hell?" I whispered.

"What?" Ember shrugged. "She's a bitch."

"I swear to God, Ember, shut up." CJ was speaking through clenched teeth.

"Oh fuck off, CJ. She is. She's given me nasty looks since she first laid eyes on me. She hangs all over everyone at this bar like she's the damn ocean breeze, and she gets *offended* when I suggest she was fooling around with you in the back room? Please." She turned and adjusted her mic stand.

CJ stood up so fast his stool crashed into the wall behind him. "I *said* shut up!"

"CJ." Bo stepped between the drum set and where Ember was sitting. CJ hadn't moved more than just to stand up, but I found myself inching toward him, as well.

I gotta hand it to Ember. Despite the first row of people in front of the stage going silent at the sight of my bear of a cousin a millisecond away from losing his temper, she calmly turned around. The way she maneuvered on her stool made her look like she was on a rotating display in a jewelry case.

Ember didn't have a chance to reply. Out of the corner of my eye, I saw a flash of blonde hair dart past me. Georgia snaked her way around me and behind the drum set. I couldn't see the look on her face, but it seemed to calm CJ. She placed one small hand on his shoulder and I watched them relax before my eyes. Just as quickly as she came, she left without ever addressing the rest of us.

I scanned the faces of my bandmates, each looking more confused than the other. "Are we...set?"

CJ readjusted his seat and raised his sticks. "Let's start with "Window"."

I threw my head back in hard laughter, and Bo and Ember followed. *Guster* was the least CJ-like band on the *planet.* He often sat out last summer when we'd fool around with some of their songs. Why he'd choose that song, especially when Ember had just royally pissed him off, was confusing at best.

"Fuck you guys. Are you in or not? You start vocals, Ember, and Bo, can you back off and I'll take over second vocals? It will sound better that way." He cleared his throat and held his sticks out. "*What?*"

"Nothing," we all answered at once. *Nothing* as in Ember and CJ had never sung together, not to mention I hadn't heard CJ sing in years. He could, and well, but he never did.

Bo and I tuned quickly and Ember set her stool aside and let her hair down. She shifted some mics around and moved one back to CJ, who just nodded at her.

Georgia hopped back up on stage, taking hold of the mic in front of me in order to announce us. As the applause rose, I leaned over and whispered in her ear, "How'd you do that?"

"Do what?" she whispered back playfully. She smelled like basil, or mint, or something. I liked that she didn't always smell the same.

"Calm the beast." I tilted my head to the back of the stage. CJ's quick temper was rarely easily quelled.

She shrugged. "He's not that complicated." Georgia turned on her heels and with a skip-step was off the stage and back into the crowd, a fourth tattoo peeking from the bottom of her shirt. Rather than head down to the lowest part of her back, like tattoos on the other girls in the bar, hers seemed to go up further. It looked like there were little feet, or leaves, dancing up her spine.

Bo spoke his thanks to the crowd and counted us off. He strummed the up-tempo intro, and as soon as I joined in, my eyes fell on Georgia. She'd just set drinks in front of a table of girls, and she turned toward the stage, her empty tray hanging loosely by her side. Ember entered the song beautifully, and Georgia's eyes moved to her, a faraway smile brushing her lips.

As CJ's entrance neared, I felt myself holding my breath. Ember tensed, too. My eyes, though, stayed on the way Georgia held on to stillness in the middle of the bustling crowd. My fiddle hung by my side during those measures, but I'd have given anything to be able to hide behind it as I watched Georgia take in CJ's voice. He was good. His tone was as solid as I remembered, just a hint of rasp creeping in behind his cigarette addiction.

Ember sang with her eyes closed a lot, so I couldn't even get her visual reaction to the emotions Georgia shot through her eyes. I almost missed my entrance with CJ. Just as I pulled the bow across the strings, someone from behind the bar shouted to Georiga, causing her to jump. She turned quickly, but I didn't miss the sight of her tattooed finger sliding underneath her heavily made-up eye as she bobbed and weaved through the crowd.

What the hell?

I followed her trail to where a guy had called out her name. I'd assumed he was someone working there, with the authority he'd put into his voice, but he was sitting on the patron side of the bar. I recognized him from the night before. He seemed to be a regular here, but she certainly wasn't happy about his presence. She stood with the empty tray hugged to her body, her head tilted to the side.

Before I could judge their relationship further, CJ picked up the tempo of the song. I followed, but not without turning around to see if he was aware of what he was doing.

He was. Looking around me toward the bar, CJ's forehead scrunched and his nostrils flared. Something was definitely weird. A few seconds sooner than it should have been, the song was over and CJ was on his feet.

Ember stepped in front of him. "CJ, that was great. I'm sorry about—"

"Yeah, yeah," he cut her off, "it's fine, just...do the next song without me, okay? "Foolish Games" again or some other folksy bullshit that doesn't need me, K?"

"Uh, y-yeah, sure..." Ember trailed off in an almost-daze, looking back at Bo. "Does that keyboard work?"

As they worked on the mechanics of the next song, I grabbed CJ's arm. Now, even though he's my height, and I'm older, CJ still had about twice the distance between his shoulders as I did. He wasn't heavy, per se, but I wouldn't stand in his way if he were running down the sidewalk. I had our childhood on my side, though, when I stopped him. I'd been like an older brother to him, and more times than not, he would at least listen to me for a few seconds before doing whatever the hell it was he wanted to anyway. Given the fury framing his eyes, I had to give it a shot.

"What the hell, man..." I made sure he was looking directly in my eyes as I spoke. If he wasn't, he likely wasn't hearing me.

"Nothing, I just...gotta sit this one out, okay?" His glare rose back over my shoulder. I looked to find him eyeing the guy who was still talking to Georgia, even as she served customers around him.

His accent was thicker than usual, which meant one of two things. Either he was drunk, though I knew he wasn't. Or, unfortunately, he was looking for a fight.

"Want me to go over with you?" Bo and Ember were ready to play "Foolish Games" so I could play or sit out, as well.

He shook his head, setting a firm, hot hand on my shoulder. "No, it's cool."

"CJ..."

"Regan, I'm not seventeen, okay? You don't need to hold my hand. I just need to...just let it go." He gave my shoulder a squeeze that I'm sure he meant as reassuring, but it wasn't.

I watched him edge his way to the bar, but he went nowhere near Georgia, or her end of the bar. He sat on the far side, but never took his eyes off the guy I'd only seen once before, and was fairly certain CJ didn't know.

"Hey," Bo stepped between me and Ember, who I didn't realize had taken her seat next to me, "what's his deal?"

"God, who the fuck knows? He insists he's fine."

"Well, whatever," Ember sounded irritated still, "we've only played one song and we've officially been on stage for like eight minutes. This shit's unacceptable. Let's goooo."

I arched an eyebrow in her direction as I looked at Bo, who just shrugged with a slight grey expression pulling over his face.

What the hell was up with everyone tonight?

"Okay," I sighed, "'Foolish Games'?"

"Yep." Ember nodded, settling onto her stool. She usually stood while she sang, but she always, *always* sat for this song. It was like it was too much emotion, or something.

"Let's go." I winked at Ember as I mocked her tone from earlier. She allowed a small smile, gave Bo a thumbs up, and he began the piano intro.

There's no official violin part written for that song, so I kind improvise as needed, usually in the chorus. Ember's voice was mournful and I eyed her with concern. With her eyes squeezed shut, she may as well have been a closed book—she held everything in her eyes. Something was wrong with her. Big time.

Not only was she uncharacteristically bitchy to Georgia— someone she barely knew—but she was fidgety and unfocused between songs. Concern rose as I tilted my head to view Bo. I caught him look up at Ember once before taking a visibly deep breath, and looking back at his hands, his eyes closed for long blinks every few seconds.

Everything started turning in counter-clockwise motion around me. Out of nowhere, I was brought back to last summer when I'd rehearsed this song with Ember. Suddenly, Rae's laughter looped through the spaces between my strings as my hand shook. She was beautiful. She was kind.

She was fucking gone.

For six goddamn months I'd been able to keep it at bay, the feeling that my chest was being unzipped, one bloody layer at a time. The feeling that once it was finally open, everything that mattered would spill out, and I'd be swallowed into it. I trusted my fingers and hands to finish the song as my chest and stomach volleyed between churning and free-falling. Beads of sweat sprung across the back of my neck as my head began a slow ascent over the rest of my body.

Panic attack.

I'd heard Bo talk about them with Ember sometimes at night when they were sitting outside and I was making tea before bed. Something about his hands going numb. Not being able to breathe...

I needed to finish the song and get the hell outside before I lost my shit in the middle of a group of strangers.

My eyes darted to CJ, but fell first on Georgia who was standing right next to the guy CJ had been eyeing as he swallowed a pint of Jack and Coke. This guy had a tight buzz cut. He was tall and lanky, roughly my build, but he had big hands. Really big.

The only reason I noticed how big they were, I realized a second after we played our last note, was because one of them was pulled back in the air, seeming to hover for a second over Georgia.

Before I could register what was happening, CJ blasted through the people between him and Georgia like he was a snowplow in a blizzard. I can't be sure it was real, given I was in the throes of a massive panic situation, but it looked like people were cast aside like rag dolls.

"Shit!" Bo growled as he brushed past Ember. "Stay here," he commanded her.

With world still working in slow motion around CJ, who looked like a wild animal, I was moving just as slowly, turning back around to see him reaching for the guy's neck.

Fuck.

I clumsily handed my violin to Ember, who grabbed hold of it before it hit the floor. Bo made it to CJ before I did, breaking the force of CJ's hands with his forearm. Just enough time for me to get there and pull CJ's arms behind his back. All of a sudden my ears worked again. Two too-short bouncers busied themselves with the drunk guy I heard Georgia call *Dex* as he spit in her direction.

CJ's voice attacked my senses loud and fast.

"What the fuck did you do to her, you bastard?" he yelled over and over as if repetition would give him the answer he needed.

"Do to her? She's a fucking cock-tease. And crazy." Dex pulled against the bouncers, but CJ pulled tighter against us, and freed enough arm to punch Dex square in the nose.

CJ growled through frighteningly ragged breaths. "Don't you *ever* talk about her that way, you dickless pig."

There wasn't any blood right away, and the bouncers dragged Dex to a far corner of the bar.

Bo and I regained control of CJ, and Georgia stood on her tiptoes in front of him. "CJ, calm the *fuck* down!" An edge of panic leaked from her authority.

Bo and I repeated CJ's name, trying to get him to come to his senses before everyone ended up in jail, but he couldn't hear us. I could tell by the rigid set of his muscles from his wrist up to his neck. When he was that angry, nothing worked except his sense of touch. Sense of punch, really.

"I'm not going to calm down, Georgia. Not after Brandon gave you that concussion."

He started to say more, but Georgia's hand cut across his face so sharply, I could almost feel it. With a single slap from one small waitress, the overfull bar fell silent as Georgia's facade melted into tears.

"You fucking bastard," she whispered, "you said you'd never tell."

CJ's shoulders sank, strained muscles dissolving their strength underneath my hands. "Go," I mouthed to Bo, eyeing the door. I'd watched the bouncers move *Dex* to the far corner of the bar, meaning the main door was clear for us to escape through.

Looking over my shoulder as Bo pushed CJ through the door, my chest ached as I watched Georgia wave off a hand from Lissa, disappearing down the hall in a hurry. Just before the door closed, I saw Ember chase after her, nodding to Lissa to follow her.

CJ shook free from us the second the door closed. He'd clearly let us lead him from the bar, almost like a security blanket. Truth is, he could have flicked us off of him like bugs if he'd tried hard enough.

"CJ," Bo started breathlessly, "what...the fuck?"

"Let it go." CJ dug his hands into his pockets and started for the parking lot.

Feeling was just returning to my brain as I teased out what was real from the nightmare that was my internal trip through a fun house on stage. I let Bo search for motive in CJ.

"I won't let it go, man. You were a dick to Ember earlier, then you—"

"Oh shut the fuck up, Cavanaugh, your bitch of a girlfriend was nasty to G—"

"Dude..." Bo's voice dropped a dark octave as his hand wrapped into a fist at his side.

That was my cue.

"Shit. Guys." I ran a hand over my head. "Neither of you need a broken hand. Fair?" CJ hadn't turned around but shook his head and mumbled *whatever.* I continued, taking shallow breaths as I wiped my hands on my jeans. "What was that about, Ceej? Who's Brandon?"

CJ's voice was impassioned with a dash of defeat. "Forget it. Just fucking forget about it, okay? He was some bastard boyfriend of hers in high school who got drunk and beat the shit out of her one night. That's it." With slumped shoulders, CJ reached my car, pulled my keys from his pocket, and got in, slamming the door and reclining the seat, his hands covering his face.

Bo and I stared at the darkened car for a minute before either of us spoke.

"Do you think anyone called the police?" I grimaced at the thought of CJ's less than stellar record.

Bo shrugged. "Doubt it. They'd have been here by now."

As the melody of Rae's laughter once again bubbled through my senses, I had to speak to override it.

"Ember followed Georgia down the hall as we were leaving." It felt like tattling.

"Jesus," he grumbled, running a hand over his face, leaving it over his mouth for a beat.

"What's really going on with you two?"

Bo closed his eyes and lowered his head, shaking it a few times. When he opened them, he turned for the door, holding it open for me without looking my way. "You all right, Regan? You seemed a little off at the end of that song."

"I'm fine. I just saw CJ, and, you know..." I lied. There was enough going on tonight without getting into a therapy session with Bo in a bar parking lot.

I looked around for a second before stepping back into the bar, wondering how in the hell I even ended up here.

Georgia

Shit shit shit.

I kicked the door to the back room open, thankful for the faulty latch. I needed to kick something. I took comfort in slamming the door behind me, but someone stopped it. I kind of wanted it to be CJ, so I could kick his ass.

But, almost worse, it was Hippie Barbie and her merry band of judgmental facial expressions.

"Get the hell out of here," I snapped as I retreated to the far corner of the room.

Ember looked over her shoulder, letting Lissa in before she closed and locked the door behind her with the chain. "Um, no, I won't get the hell out of here. Are you okay?"

Her voice was as sing-song-y as it was on stage, but I could barely hear it as I remembered the way she'd looked at me when I came out of the back room with CJ before their set.

"Yeah," Lissa interrupted, "holy fuck, Georgia, what the hell was all of that about?" Her words shook like the muscles in my legs.

"It's fine. It's over. Seriously, leave me the hell alone. Lissa, you have tables. Take mine or send them home. I need a few minutes." I turned toward the window and rested my forehead against the lukewarm glass.

Ten seconds later, amidst unintelligible whispers, I heard the chain swing free, and the door open and close. I jumped when I heard it latch again.

"It's just me," Ember whispered.

"I told you to leave." I crossed my arms in front of me as she leaned her back against the door.

"I will…as soon as I know Dex has left the bar and parking lot. I don't think anyone called the cops, which is good news for CJ, but bad news for you." She studied her cuticles as she spoke, looking like she was fighting something inside with the steep downward angle of her eyebrows.

"Where is CJ? I'm going to kick his ass." Wherever it was, I'd hoped it was far from Dex.

Ember shrugged, finally looking me in the eyes. "Bo and Regan took him outside. I think there's been enough ass-kicking for the night."

She took a deep breath, pried her back away from the door and walked toward me in the annoyingly casual way that was meant to make it look like she wasn't really approaching me. Kind of like she was at a tag sale, her fingertips skimming the surface of the desk and the back of the couch as she got closer.

"How often does that happen?" she asked when she was about five feet from me.

"Excuse me?"

"How often does he get in your face like that?"

"It wasn't—"

"It wasn't what?"

"My personal life is none of your damn business. I don't need you looking at me like some battered wife."

"Okay, then who's Brandon?"

Fuck CJ.

"Also none of your business." I wasn't going to discuss my bastard of an ex-boyfriend with *her.* I hadn't intended on discussing it with anyone, let alone all of E's.

I knew CJ knew the weight behind every word Dex had spoken. But his interpretation of the bruise on my wrist, mixed with Dex's attitude, led him to spill the Brandon secret everywhere. *It's the lesser of two evil secrets, G.* I had to chant that in my head on repeat.

Ember cleared her throat. "I've known CJ a long time—"

"Not as long as I have."

Ember rolled her eyes. "Whatever. I've known him long enough to know that he basically doesn't give a shit about anyone. Except you."

I cleared my throat to keep the vice at bay. "Yeah, so?"

My eyes burned like hell, but I wasn't about to give in to tears. CJ betrayed my trust.

Before she could respond, a loud knock rattled the door.

"Ember, you in there? It's Bo...and Regan."

"Can they come in?" Ember tucked some hair behind her ear.

I shrugged. "I guess. I've got to get back to work anyway." I started for the door, but Ember held up her arm.

"Just wait until we can be sure he's gone, okay?"

I conceded, leaning back against the door. This was the wrong kind of attention. All wrong. It could have been worse, though. I had to repeat that in my head. Some secrets were so deep I could hardly feel their roots in my veins when I was in mixed company.

That's a lie. They were always there. The secrets. Snacking on my soul.

Ember slowly slid the chain out of place and let her arm fall loosely at her side as she stepped back. "Is he gone?" She looked between Bo and Regan as she re-latched the door behind them.

"He is," Regan answered. "I double checked with Lissa. His friends dragged him out. He was pretty drunk."

"That doesn't matter, Regan," Ember snapped.

Bo hesitantly placed his hands on her shoulders, lifting a finger to her chin when she wouldn't look at him right away. "He knows, Ember. He was just saying..."

"Sorry." She sighed. "Where's CJ?"

Regan stuffed his hands in his pockets. "My car. The sooner I get him home, the better."

I stared at Regan's tattered Converses. Old, not purchased that way. "No one called the cops, right?"

His weight shifted to his left foot. "Right. If you don't want to be alone tonight, you can come stay—"

"No."

"Georgia," Bo spoke in the same nursery rhyme volume Ember had pestered me with since she followed me back here, "Lissa said for us to tell you that you can go home for the night. Use the back door..."

"What?" I looked around at three apparently concerned faces. "Like I'm a refugee? Christ, nothing *happened*."

Ember opened her mouth to speak.

"No," I stopped her. "Nothing happened. Dex is gone. And, I intend to finish out the rest of my shift so I can earn my money. *Some* of us don't have rich parents who put us up in North Cove." I brushed past her for the door.

"No," she scoffed in the most irritatingly sarcastic exhale, "some of us are *forced* to live in *La Jolla* instead."

I stopped in my tracks, my hand resting on the doorknob as I exhaled slowly through my nose. I scanned three sets of eyes before resting on Ember's perfectly green irises.

"It must get tiring, huh? Strutting around like you know everything?" With the tension in the room dialed all the way to *Exit*, I did just that, finally getting to slam the door behind me.

As I wiped down the tables at the end of my shift, anger seeped into every muscle of my body. Thankfully, Lissa and the rest of the staff left me the hell alone so I could finish out my shift without hassle. But I was still pissed at CJ and intended to track him down to tell him just that.

"Night, Liss," I called over my shoulder as I adjusted the straps on my backpack.

"Night, girl. You good?" She tried to sound casual, but CJ's outburst clearly had her shaken.

"Yep." My tone was clipped as I pulled the thick wooden door open and walked into the starlit night.

My heart pole-vaulted into my throat at the sight of a broad shadow leaning against my car.

"It's just me, G." CJ's voice rumbled through the parking lot.

"You mother fucker!" I yelled as I sped toward him, reaching for his face with my hand, but only making it as far as his shoulder.

He grabbed my shoulders and held me at arm's length. Just far enough that I couldn't hit him.

"Georgia, calm down." He sounded bored.

"Do you have *any* idea what the hell you did in there tonight?

He ducked his head to meet my eye line. "Yeah, kept you from getting hit."

"Yeah?" I stepped back and crossed my arms. CJ let go, but didn't put his hands in his pockets. "And what do you think you're keeping me from now that you've pissed him off and embarrassed him in front of a bar full of his friends?"

CJ ran a hand over his over-gelled hair. "He doesn't know where you live, though, right?"

I shrugged.

"For fuck's sake, G, you take them back to your place, still? I thought we talked about that."

"I..." My shoulders sank under my tears. "I did flirt with Dex last night and left the bar with him. But, only to walk him to a cab. You know, make sure his drunk ass didn't try to drive home. The bruise wasn't from him, CJ."

CJ held me at arms length. "Who is it from?"

I shook my head, looking to the stars in an effort to stop the stream down my cheeks.

"G..."

Looking back at CJ, I found the only person left in my life who knew everything. I swallowed hard and tucked some hair behind my ear.

Immediately he knew. I know he knew because he whipped me back into his body and tried to wring the pain from me with a tight hug. It was deep in my bones, though.

"I didn't realize it had gotten bad again, G. You should have told me."

As I sniffled into his shoulder, I tried to come up with something defensive to say. There was nothing. I should have called him. Told him in the back room, instead of letting him construct an outlandish story in his head about Dex and me that was cemented far from reality.

"Stay with me tonight," he whispered into my hair.

"I can't. I have to go to the—"

"Not tonight, G. You know how she is after a rough night. It's still the same, isn't it? She'll be too medicated to know you're there."

I wanted to say yes. That I'd spend the night with my old best friend. "I can't, CJ."

"Georgia."

I was too tired to deny him a third time. So, I just sighed.

CJ growled. "God. Whatever. You're not going back to your place tonight."

"You're not the boss of me."

The second it spilled out of my mouth I knew he'd laugh. And he did. So did I.

"You're insufferable." He grabbed me into a hug.

"Insufferable? Word of the day calendar?" I smiled into his chest.

He laughed, bumping my head against his chest. "Screw off."

"Where are you staying?" I pressed my chin into his pecs as I looked up, smiling as he looked back down.

"With some friends in North Cove."

"Mission Bay? Classy."

"Not as classy as *La Jolla*."

"Hey now," I teased, "that was all my dad's choice. Not mine."

CJ opened his driver's side door. "Ride with me. We'll come back for your car tomorrow. How is your dad, by the way?"

"Dead." I yawned and plunked into his car.

"What the hell? When?" He eyed me like I was insane.

Not yet, I wanted to tell him.

"What?" I shrugged. "Last year. Don't act so surprised. He was an alcoholic, CJ. His liver ran out of motivation. The house in La Jolla was his, though."

"Scumbag..." CJ mumbled and shook his head.

I shrugged. I knew he didn't totally mean it. CJ knew the full story, but that meant he also knew every dirty detail. My dad had been a schemer his whole life: shaking your hand with one hand, and tying your shoelaces together with the other. But there was something about him that women loved—a charisma woven through his gap-toothed smile. It'd done my mother in, which is why I'm here.

When she left, though, he did the best he could for me. Even if it wasn't enough, it was his best. When I'd tossed a fistful of loose earth over his final bed, I'd taken comfort in that.

CJ merged onto the highway and reached over the center console, silently grabbing my hand. I held it all the way back to his friends' place, shoving my guilt down for one night. Relieved not to be in the driver's seat for once.

CHAPTER 

It is far better to be feared than loved

Georgia

CJ and I didn't get to bed until well past four in the morning. Once we got to his friends' place, we sat on the beach and talked until our words got lost in yawns. He took the floor and gave me the pull-out couch in the office where he was staying. I'd assumed that Regan was in the house as well, but I didn't know whose house it was, and everyone was asleep, anyway.

While it was Monday, and I technically had the day off, I wanted to get some coffee in me and get back to the bar to pick up my car before I had to show Regan the apartment in La Jolla. The house was quiet and the sound of waves, like crinkling paper, swept through the windows.

I tiptoed to the kitchen and found the coffee pot already on and full. Looking around for a moment, I didn't see or hear anyone. Gazing out the window over the sink, I spotted someone's feet in the air. Like, straight in the air. As they appeared to stand on their head.

"G? You all right? It's fuckin' early." CJ's morning voice always sounded like a polar bear on valium. I don't know why he even bothered with the AM half of the day.

As he clomped into the kitchen behind me, I leaned my head forward, squinting to make out why that person in the sand looked familiar. Dawn didn't provide excellent contrast, though. Just as CJ shouldered up next to me, I figured it out.

Then smacked him.

"You bastard, you brought me back to *her* house?" I pressed my finger against the glass.

"What?" His eyebrows drew together, eyes barely open as he followed my finger. "Oh...yeah..."

"She's a bitch, CJ!" I whispered as loudly as I could.

"You're still mad about her thinking you and I hooked up? Christ, Georgia, half the Cape thought that for years." He cracked his neck and pulled down two coffee mugs.

"No, it's not that. It's that she took pride in judging the hell out of me last night. And the night before, though it didn't bother me as much then because I didn't think I'd ever see her again. Plus, you got pissed at her too, remember?"

"Yeah." He yawned. "And since when do you give a flying fuck what people think?"

"Besides, she's not a bitch." Regan stepped down into the kitchen, rubbing his eyes, interrupting my poor attempt at answering CJ.

"You coulda fooled me."

I didn't care what people thought.

I thought.

Regan was wearing black board shorts and...that was it. All except for the elastic that held his deep copper hair away from his face. I stepped aside so he could reach the coffee, and as he did, I caught the muscles in his back move as he poured the coffee and put the pot away. Eyeing his back from his neck to the tops of his hips, I didn't see any tattoos. No references to his beloved violin or his renegade appearance. Nothing on his freckled back to display who he was. Or who he wanted people to think he was.

Interesting.

"All right, maybe Ember isn't a bitch," CJ raised his eyebrow to Regan, "but even you have to admit she was being kind of snatchy last night."

Regan slurped his first slip of coffee, hazel eyes settling on me for a moment before he responded to CJ. "Snatchy?"

"Where's your accent?" I blurted out. CJ told me he'd teased Regan about it. I don't know why I even asked him.

CJ laughed. "Boarding school boy here doesn't have an accent. His must be hiding the same place yours is." He playfully smacked my ass, and I squealed.

I felt myself blush as Regan caught me eyeing the v-shaped crevices barely holding up his shorts.

With a grin, he leaned in and whispered, "It's okay."

I'm sure I had the same mortified look on my face as he'd had when I said the same thing to him just two days before, but he didn't laugh. He winked and poured more coffee into his mug.

He fucking winked.

"Anyway," I cleared my throat and gestured to the window with my hand, "what the hell is she doing?"

"Sirsasana." We all turned slowly toward Bo who was walking into the kitchen, rubbing his eyes.

"What?" CJ sounded drunk on confusion.

"Sirsasana," Bo repeated. "A headstand."

"I'm going back to bed." CJ set his mug on the counter and disappeared down the hallway.

Momentarily ignoring that I had to leave soon, and my ride just went back to bed, I looked back out the window. "How...long does she stay like that?"

Bo reached above me, in all his shirtless glory, and took down a coffee mug. "Usually five or ten minutes, I guess. Probably a little longer today. She's thinking."

"What's going on with you two?" I sipped steaming coffee and watched Regan's eyes widen. I pursed my lips at him. "Like you're not wondering, too? They were a disaster last night."

Regan looked like he wanted out of there, fast.

Bo stared out the window for a second, lightness coming into his face. "It's okay, Regan. She's right. We were off balance. Ember thought she was pregnant."

Regan and I formed a duet of choking on our coffee.

"Precisely." Bo chuckled. "Don't say anything, though."

"Your secret's safe with me, man."

Looking at Regan as he spoke, I was filled with the sensation that his words held exactly their weight.

I shook my head. "You said *thought*, right? So what's with the broody headstand?"

Bo sighed. "It just freaked her out, is all. Not being ready for kids. We haven't been back together that long, we're not married..." He shrugged, but didn't seem to buy his own spiel. *Good Dad* glittered in his eyes. That man wanted children, *and* I had a hunch he'd rock it. I hoped that Ember chick wouldn't screw it up.

"*Back* together?" I hadn't intended on being so nosey.

Regan chuckled. "That's not a story you want to hear at six in the morning. Trust me. I haven't even pieced it all together."

"Funny." Bo playfully punched Regan's lean shoulder. "I'm heading out there to check how long she's been like that. She loses track of time, sometimes."

"Godspeed, bro." Regan mocked a military salute as Bo headed onto the sand to his Nature Valley girlfriend.

As the door slid shut, I became hyperaware of my proximity to Regan, which was no longer necessary given we were the only two left in the kitchen. All I had to do was step to the right, just to get to the other side of the island. And, I couldn't do it. Next defense? Sarcasm.

"Going surfing?" I pointedly stared at his shorts, which, if I'm not mistaken, had slid down an extra inch when he'd retrieved his coffee mug from the cabinet. Though the coast was loaded with surfers, it was more densely populated with those who dressed as if they were.

"Yep." He rinsed out his mug and placed it in the dishwasher.

"Seriously?" I let out a suspicious laugh.

"Seriously." Regan turned around and leaned against the counter, curling his hands around the edges. He was a little more tense and quiet than I'd have expected for someone who could do what he did with that violin on stage. Suddenly the lack of tattoos wasn't a surprise.

"Well…be safe. I'm gonna go wake up CJ to take me to get my car."

"Yeah," Regan drew out, "you know as well as I do that that's not gonna happen. When he's out. He's out."

I knew he was right, but there was no way I was going to hang out in Barbie and Ken's Bayside Bungalow all day.

"I'll take you. Let me get my shirt." His triceps flexed as he pushed himself away from the counter.

"No, that's okay, you've got plans. Hanging ten and all of that."

Regan let out a hearty laugh. "More like choke-on-saltwater. I suck. Brilliantly. Plus, you've got to show me that apartment today."

"Oh, right. Yeah…" I stammered.

"That's today, right? You said Monday."

"No. Yes. I did. Um...can we jet now, though? I know it's early, but that's fine." I shook the tingling sensation from my fingers, hoping he wouldn't notice.

"We can go now." Regan's eyebrows drew inward as his voice softened. In a blink, his long, slender fingers were on my cheekbone. "Are you okay? You look pale all of a sudden."

"I'm okay." It came out as a whisper. It was getting harder for me to tell the difference between panic attacks and something more serious. But in the kitchen with a stranger was no place to start that conversation.

There *was* no place to start that conversation. It just kind of happened. Mid-sentence and I'd be floating fast and slowly all at once with Alice down that hole.

"Okay. Let's go." Looking up, I found Regan with a grey tank and his black Converses, and no recollection of the amount of time that had passed.

Looking out the window in an attempt to reorient myself, I found Bo and Ember sitting in the sand, staring at the water. They were never leaving each other. That was the message scrawled across the scene of her head on his shoulder while his fingers glided up and down her arm. I hated that it was so obvious.

I hated that I'd never have that.

I cleared my throat. "Yeah. Let's go."

Regan

"Do you want to just swing up to La Jolla right now and then I can take you back to get your car?" I glanced at Georgia out of the corner of my eye, who seemed to have glued herself to the door of my car. Her arm was pressed against the door, and if she had moved her head a fraction of an inch, it would have rested on the glass.

"No, I have to go a little further north later today, so bring me to my car at E's and you can follow me back." She looked out the window as she spoke. Not at the cars passing by, though. Further out. Like into another time, or something.

I took a deep breath and struggled to form the next words. "Sorry things got so crazy last night. How are you?" Georgia didn't seem to be the kind of girl who liked to be asked if she was okay.

I was right.

She arched her eyebrow as she whipped her head around. "I'm *fine.*"

"Is Dex your boyfriend?"

"Are you deaf to social cues, or something? What about my tone makes you think I want to talk about Dex at *all*?" She leaned her head against the window.

Ok, then.

I twisted my lips and focused on the road, grateful that the drive back to E's would be twenty minutes, tops. On second thought, that seemed like a really long time.

At a red light I turned toward her. She was in faded jean shorts, but they weren't as short as the ones I'd seen her in behind the bar. They were rolled up to her mid-thigh, the part where the inner thigh curves in just slightly. She was wearing one of those tank tops with the way oversized armholes. The kind *designed* to let lookers-on view the side of the bra.

Hers was red. Bright red. That wasn't the most interesting part. Okay, it was, but what caught my eye after three seconds was a tattoo just below the lacy red fabric.

"What does your tattoo say?" The driver in the car behind me laid on her horn, kindly letting me know I'd been sitting at a green light for who knows how long. I moved forward as Georgia gestured kindly back to the driver with her hand out the window.

"You lookin'?" She smirked as she looked back at me, her eyes simmering.

"Seems you made sure I would with that shirt." I bit my lip to keep from smiling too big.

"It is far better to be feared than loved."

"Excuse me?"

"My tattoo. It says *it is far better to be feared than loved.*"

"Ah," I nodded, swallowing once to keep the heaviness away. "Not true, though..."

Georgia snorted. "Clearly you've never been in love."

My head started to float a little, just like it had last night. I shifted in my seat, stretching my head side to side in hopes of stopping it.

"Am I wrong?" she pressed, teasingly.

"You're wrong." I felt cold sweat sprout along my hairline. Two deep breaths later and I felt regulated again.

"Then," Georgia sighed, "you've never been feared." All jest drained from her voice as she rooted her elbow on the armrest and shook her hand through her hair.

With a quick glance, I could see that CJ was right when he teased her about dying her hair. Deep, black roots shown between her fingers. *She'd look excellent with black hair.* I was relieved to see our exit coming up.

It was barely seven in the morning as I turned into the parking lot of E's tavern. Georgia and I had ridden the rest of the way in strained silence. Just when I'd thought I'd learned a great deal about women from spending so much time with Ember, I felt like Georgia was speaking a different language. The attitude she displayed with her mouth was at odds with the vulnerability in her eyes. CJ mentioned that her dad was kind of a loser, so I chalked it up to daddy issues.

"Here we are. That blue car yours?" I headed toward a Chevy Cavalier.

"That's me. He's not my boyfriend, by the way."

I put the car in park. "What?"

"Dex. He's not my boyfriend." She reached behind my seat and pulled her small canvas backpack into her lap. The smell of mint still lingered on her pale skin.

"Oh. Well...what the hell was that all about last night, then?"

She rolled her eyes. "He's just a jacked up ex-jock with Narcissistic Personality Disorder."

"Aren't they all?"

"That friend of yours, Bo, isn't, right?"

"How'd you know Bo was a jock?"

She shrugged. "It would have been a damn waste of those shoulders if he wasn't."

"Well," I laughed, "I think he was the quarterback."

"Of course he was." She rolled her eyes, not mockingly, but seemingly to cue me into her thoughts on high school caste systems.

"But didn't you leave the bar with him?"

"Who?"

"Dex."

"Sure," she smiled as she opened the door, "I leave the bar with a lot of people, Regan. Dex, though...I didn't go home with Dex. I walked him to a cab. Follow me back up the highway. K?"

"Will do." I barely got out the end of my sentence as her door slammed to a close.

Craving spearmint gum the whole way, I followed Georgia's ten-year-old car up I-5.

Once we navigated into La Jolla, her car took left turn after left turn, it seemed, until we were dangerously close to the water. Turning left down one more road, there were buildings to my left, and nothing to my right. Air. And, apparently, a cliff.

Georgia pulled up in front of a white building with a garage on street level. Next to the garage, in the same building, was what appeared to be a small bakery. There was no name on it, and the lights were off. I pulled up behind her, checking my surroundings once more, before succumbing to the glaring reality that I'd never be able to afford this place.

"Yo," Georgia rapped on my window, "we're here, rock star."

I got out and looked up at the top floor, which held large picture windows. "You...this...this is the place?"

"Yeah, follow me." She pulled a key from her pocket and headed up the stone stairs that wrapped around the building, making the entrance in the back.

Once inside the narrow entryway, I saw an "A" on the door to the right and a "B" on the door to the left.

"This is the one that's open." Georgia stuck the key into the "B" apartment lock and opened the door, letting me in first.

Light.

God, the light. Windows from the front and side were like broken dams, flooding the room with bright Pacific sun. The large rectangular space looked more Cape Cod than La Jolla. The floors were bamboo and the walls were distressed wood planks, painted white.

Blue.

The back wall looked blue, but that was a window that canvassed the perfect sky and ocean. Their meeting point was the furthest point in my new living room. There was a small galley kitchen to the left, and I assumed a bedroom and bathroom on the right, but I just stood at the window, breathing in the enormity of it all.

"I can't afford this." I shook my head and turned my back to the view, not wanting to torture myself.

Georgia met me at the window, wrapped her tiny hand around my bicep and turned me around again. "You haven't even asked how much it is."

I wondered if she could feel my pulse pick up as she stood silently gazing out the window with me. Her hand still wrapped around me.

"The ocean might be blue, G, but it bleeds green. You lived on the other coast, you know that."

"Did you just call me G?" She looked up, but wasn't blushing like she did when I'd caught her checking me out in my shorts earlier.

"I did." It slipped out, but felt natural. Maybe it was because that's typically how CJ referred to her.

The skin around her eyes creased a little, as if she were smiling, but her mouth didn't turn up. "Please take it."

"How much is it?" I winced, bracing for the huge price tag. I had a shitload of money in savings, but wasn't interested in blowing through it inside of a year on rent alone.

Her head tilted to the side as her eyes narrowed in thought. After half a second she spoke. "How much can you afford?"

"That's hardly an answer."

"It most certainly is an answer." She started bouncing on her toes like she was a child waiting in line for a balloon animal.

I sighed. "It's not an answer to that kind of question."

"And why not?"

Our conversation was making me dizzy.

"Don't get all flustered. Let's go ask the owner of the building."

"Oh, they're here? I figured since you had the keys they wouldn't be here."

"We're early, remember? Sunrise headstands and whatnot?"

I laughed. "Yeah."

Georgia slid her hand down my arm and locked it around my wrist as she led me through the apartment. This was the brightest I'd ever seen her. Excitement looked good on her.

She dropped my arm as she knocked on the door to apartment A, bouncing from foot to foot. Knocking one more time with a huge smile on her face, she animatedly rolled her eyes, and fished another key from her shallow pockets.

"Did you say you lived across the hall?"

She turned the key. "I don't have keys to anyone else's apartment..."

I felt more confused with each second I spent with her. She was like this Rubik's Cube that changed patterns around each turn. Impossible. I wanted to try to solve her, though. I hadn't sorted out if that was a good thing or a bad thing before the door flew open.

Her eyebrow arched, teeth biting back a huge smile.

What?

I stood with my mouth open, eyes searching the apartment behind her, and she laughed. "This is my building, Regan."

What?

"You live here, yeah..."

She stepped back, holding the door open and waving me in. "My building as in, yes, I live here, and I own it."

While the layout of this apartment was the same as the one across the hall, it was fully decorated. A cream colored couch was up against a bright aqua wall. Fishing line ran the length of the apartment, suspended five or so inches from the ceiling. There were four rows of it, and woven between them were bright sheer scarves. Yellows, blues, greens...I felt like I was in some sort of fairytale.

My words were coming out a few seconds apart. "The whole building? How in the hell? What?"

She giggled. For the first time in the few short days that I'd known her, she let out what could only be described as a giggle. I didn't call her on it, though. She'd have kicked my ass.

"Yes, the whole building. It was my dad's. He bought it like twenty years ago. When he died, I got it."

This was the first I'd heard her talk about either of her parents.

"Oh, I'm sorry, I didn't realize he'd passed away. CJ didn't tell me."

My pockets were all bunched up inside, fumbling my attempt to nonchalantly do something with my hands. I always had to be productive with my hands, especially in awkward situations. Music was the perfect outlet for that, but this was hardly the time for a violin solo.

"No worries, I just told CJ last night, anyway. Not his fault." Georgia walked deeper into her apartment and held her arms out. "So, you see, this place is nearly identical to yours. My dad had it all as one space, but six months ago I had it renovated into two units. I didn't need all the space. And, the rent will help with...life."

"What about your mom?"

Her shoulders stiffened for a split second before her exhale. "Gone."

"I'm so sorry." I met her at her picture window. My hand hovered over the small of her back, but I hesitated, instead brushing it across her shoulder blades.

"Don't be. It is what it is. This view is perfect, though, isn't it?"

I breathed in reverence at the identical view to the apartment across the hall, allowing for her change in subject. "Yeah, about the rent..."

"Five hundred."

"Ha!" She jumped at my loud response. "No fucking way. That's insane."

"No," she snapped, "that's not insane."

Her face was all screwed up, happiness swirled with something distant.

"Sorry." I exaggerated my response as if I were on the playground.

The lines around her mouth relaxed. "No, I'm sorry. I'm not kidding. Five hundred. The apartment has sat empty since I renovated. I haven't trusted anyone else to take it."

"Trust? You met me like two days ago."

Georgia turned for her bedroom, talking to me over her shoulder as she shuffled through her closet. "Yeah, well you're CJ's cousin. I trust him with everything."

"I have to tell you," I called back, "I half expected black walls with neon spray paint everywhere or something."

"That's awfully assumptive of you." Georgia came out wearing a long black skirt and a blue t-shirt that had a faded design I wasn't going to be caught dead staring at for too long. She was wearing flip-flops that highlighted the stark vertical difference between the two of us.

"You've left me no choice." I grinned. "I met you when you were wearing short shorts and combat boots, then I've seen you for two nights at the bar wear basically nothing at all. Now, this..." I gestured to the most conservative outfit I'd seen her in yet. "Can you blame me for expecting *anything* but this?"

"Well, you see," Georgia got toe-to-toe with me and lifted up on hers so she could whisper in my ear, "I'm never sure what I'm going to be from one minute to another."

I placed my hands on her shoulders, holding her at arm's length. "You speak in riddles."

"Do I? Maybe you hear in riddles." She stepped back, shoving some things into her backpack.

"That bakery downstairs...is it ever open? Who owns it?"

"Which do you want me to answer first?" She seemed annoyed.

"The second."

"I do."

"*You* own it?" My eyes may well have bugged right out of my head.

She shrugged. "Yep, I'm full of all kinds of surprises." She seemed to be trying to wink with her voice, if one could do that, but it fell a little short and my stomach dropped a little.

"When is it open?"

"It's not, really. I don't have a ton of time to run it properly. Just mainly for catering and stuff." She was growing flustered by the second. Who knew a bakery could be such a sore spot? "Do you want the place or not, Regan?"

I wasn't sure if living across from Georgia was what I wanted to do. Well, it was what I *wanted* to do, but I didn't know if it was right. I didn't have a clear read on her, and she caused all kinds of feelings to stir up inside me that I definitely wasn't ready to feel. I was curious. With each second that passed I wanted to get closer to her than my brain was comfortable with.

"Why do you trust me so much?" was the first sentence out of my mouth.

"You haven't tried to get in my pants." She slid her backpack over her shoulders and looked at me as if she'd said the most normal thing on the planet.

"I've known you for, like, a minute."

"Precisely. You're good, Regan. I need some good around here." It was as if a grey scarf had slipped from the ceiling and surrounded her eyes as she spoke.

"I'll take it." That was the only thing to say.

Georgia walked toward me and slowly wrapped her arms around my neck as she squeezed me close. "Thank you," she whispered.

"I...you're welcome." I went to set my hands on her lower back, but her backpack stopped me, so I settled for the curve of her hip.

Not a bad compromise.

Georgia's muscles froze, and for a moment her eyes locked on mine. I didn't want to pull my hands off of her hips in reaction, so I left them there. And took a deep breath because I felt the overwhelming urge to kiss her. It could have been the relief and excitement of finding the perfect apartment, but more than likely it was the lavish garnet color painted across her smile. She was smiling. Slightly, but it was there. The color in her lips seemed to make its way up to her cheeks.

She'd been looking at me with her eyes only, not moving her face from the level of my chest, but when she tilted her chin upward, her expression fully exposed and vulnerable, everything got too real.

I had to kiss her.

In the span of my emotional volley, she cleared her throat and took a step back. My hands felt cold as she shimmied her hips away from my hold.

"Okay, so you remember how to get back to Mission Bay? I've got to go north, so I can't drive you back." She moved to the door.

"I remember. When can I move in?" I asked this in the hopes that my line-crossing moment hadn't just lost me the best apartment I'd ever seen.

Georgia handed me a key. "Any time. Get me the first month's rent whenever. See ya." She stretched way up on her toes, gave me a quick kiss on the cheek, smiled, and bounded down the stone stairs.

As I closed her door and unlocked what was now mine, it hit me. While I'd seen Georgia bounce across the line between excessively seductive and perfectly badass, the only time I'd seen anything soft and bright from her was in her interactions with her coworkers and with CJ. The girl that leaped over the bar and gripped CJ into a squealing hug was the same girl that offered me the apartment in her building.

She trusted me. Seemed relieved I hadn't tried to "get in her pants."

"Crap," I whispered to myself as I gazed out what was now *my* picture window.

Pressing my forehead into the single-pane of glass I let out a low groan.

I'd just been friend-zoned by Georgia.

Living in her building certainly *was* going to be a ride. Maybe Lissa was right, after all.

We'll see...

CHAPTER *Six*

QUEEN OF HEARTS

Georgia

MY BREATHING DIDN'T get ahold of itself until I was a good two miles away from the apartment. He'd wanted to kiss me, and under normal circumstances I would have allowed him to. But, by design, he was going to be living across the hall from me. I needed friends, according to my therapist. I wondered, though, if she'd meant that I should rent an apartment to someone I was incredibly attracted to.

Probably not.

But, given the resignation that I'd be alone for the rest of my life, I thought it would be okay to have someone nice and good looking living across the hall. Just to remind me what being human feels like. Even if I could never act on those feelings, it would be nice to *feel* them. While I still could feel, that is.

Merging onto the highway, heading North, I had to take a cleansing breath to erase the cool scent of the hazel-eyed, brassy-haired hottie from my senses. It was time to focus. To prepare.

A half an hour later I was pulling into the parking lot of Breezy Pointe. Sounds pleasant, right? A small town on the coast, maybe? A picnic spot where one might spend careless Sundays in the sand?

It was designed that way. To make you think a million happy thoughts before you walked through the doors and were confronted by every awful thing you wanted to fix.

"Hi Wendy." I smiled to the sixty-five-year-old nurse at the desk. I didn't see her too often, as I usually came right after my shifts at E's, and she worked the day shift.

"Georgia Rose, how are you?" Her voice held a hint of the southern sweet tea she carried with her from Texas when she moved here last year. She always said my name like *Jo-ja*. I loved it. "You didn't come last night?"

I shook my head. "Bad night the night before. I..."

"Needing a break is okay, Sugar. We all need them. Given the last few months you've had...well, I'm glad you got some rest." *She* was allowed to call me *Sugar* all she wanted. She had a heart big enough for the both of us.

"Thanks. Can you check to see if she's...available?"

Wendy nodded as she handed me the sign-in binder. She picked up the black phone, pressing a few buttons as I stared at the cheap art posters on the wall behind her. For a place that costs so much money, you'd think they might want to buy something other than a screen print of a shitty sunflower field. I vowed to call my photog friend, Kate, in Illinois this week to ask her to send me some canvas shots.

"Georgia." Wendy's tone indicated this was not the first time she'd called my name. I was busy making plans to pretty up the place I'd been spending more and more time as the days wore on.

"Sorry, what?"

"You can head on back."

I took my visitor badge and smiled through the sad gaze she gave me as I wandered to the locked door for the unit.

After being buzzed in and giving a silent greeting to the nurses at the desk, I made my way down the hall.

1826.

I paused at the familiar door, tracing the curves of the numbers with my eyes as I caught my breath. Typically, I'd be able to visit her in her room. Still with a nurse present, but at least in her own space. Not today, though. Not after Saturday night left me shaken and with a bruise on my wrist. It'd been over a year since she'd had an episode like that.

Just one more locked door separated me from the visiting area. Another nurse greeted me at the door and escorted me in.

"How is she today?" I checked my backpack and jewelry at the nurses' station before going further.

Daniel, the nurse who seemed to always be here, gave a stern nod. "Not excitable. We're not sure yet if the sedatives haven't fully worn off or if she's back on the immobility end."

I swallowed hard as we entered the large, bright space, gilded with damaged dreams, disappointment, and fear. The sign out front scribbled something about *hope*, but I'd only ever been in here when hope failed.

Daniel started discussing some of the protocols they'd put in place over the last twenty-four hours, but as soon as I saw her slender figure in the wheelchair by the window, all other attention fled my body as I walked toward her. She was facing me, and I mumbled a small prayer under my breath that she'd recognize me.

"Mama," I whispered, kneeling in front of her, trying to find the focus of her eyes.

Her head didn't move, but her eyes did. The empty brown holes fluttered over my face before settling on my eyes. They opened a little wider, just as her lips parted.

Please, please let her say something.

She tilted her head to the side, her greying brown hair laying over one shoulder, and with a slight smile she quietly spoke. "Baby."

Tears clouded my view of the faraway woman I still called *Mama*. Taking her hand, I smiled and nodded.

"I'm here."

Catatonic Schizophrenia.

The name doesn't look pretty, doesn't sound pretty, and the effects on the person and their family are a self-contained Antichrist to pretty. At that point there were several other diagnoses on the brink of landing on her chart, but the original catalyst was catatonic schizophrenia.

"Georgia?" A delicate male voice called from above.

At the sound of my actual name, my mother's eyebrows drew in, and she mouthed *Georgia*, looking between me and the floor for a few moments before turning her wheelchair to face the polka-dot caps of the ocean.

I cleared my throat, sniffing once as I stood. "Hello, Dr. Carver."

Dr. Carver was well seasoned. Easily in his early sixties, with a head of thick salt and pepper hair. The only wrinkles he had were around his eyes and mouth, and only appeared when he smiled. I admired that despite the work he'd chosen to dedicate his life to, he spent most of it smiling.

"Take a little walk with me?" He held what I presumed to be my mother's chart as he tilted his head to the hallway that hosted his tiny office.

I looked back at my mother with a sinkhole slowly caving in my stomach. Moving slowly, I put my hand on her shoulder. "I'll be right back, Mom, okay?"

A thin, cool hand reaching up and resting on mine for a second was the only response I got. It was good enough for now, and far better than Saturday's responses.

I walked to Dr. Carver's office with my head down, feeling somewhat like I was on my way to the principal's office. He was quiet, too. There were very few good reasons to have to sit in a doctor's actual office, and I wasn't betting this was one of them.

"Please sit."

I did. Then, waited.

"Georgia," Dr. Carver started with great hesitation, "we've known for some time that your mother hasn't been seeing the progress we'd like. What happened Saturday was a setback—"

"She has catatonic schizophrenia, Doctor. By definition she swings between excessive mobility and immobility." I cut him off by reciting basic medical information to a man who'd been practicing medicine since long before I existed.

He patiently cleared his throat and clasped his hands on the desk in front of him. "I'm aware of her admitting diagnosis, Georgia. That's what concerns me. Typically, this type of schizophrenia can respond well to benzodiazepines, which she's on, and psychotherapy, which she's involved with." He took a deep breath. "As you're aware, the length of time between her hospital visits have been shortening..."

"Yes, I'm aware."

"Is she still living with her sister?"

I shook my head, looking down. "No. My aunt Susan had a baby a few months ago. It wasn't really...you know..." *Safe.* I couldn't say the word, but it made itself known inside my hesitation.

"So she's been living on her own?"

I nodded. "She's refused for six months to move into the vacant apartment in my building. I finally had to rent it out today." My throat closed around the words. I'd known she'd put up a fight, but I hadn't counted on it being a forever fight.

She didn't want to live with me.

He sighed. A long, heavy, preemptively apologetic sigh. "It's time we actively consider adding ECT to her treatment plan."

"*No.*" I stood with such force that my chair slid several feet behind me, tapping the back wall of his small office.

Dr. Carver didn't flinch. I'm certain he's dealt with more startling situations than my brewing temper tantrum. "Georgia. ECT, in conjunction with medications, like the ones she's taking, has time and again proven the most effective for patients with catatonic schizophrenia."

Electroconvulsive Therapy. Sounds fancy, right? Shock therapy is what it is.

"Dr. Carver, when I became her healthcare proxy she made it *very* clear to me that ECT was not up for discussion. I intend to honor her wishes."

I wiped my palms against the soft cotton of my skirt. I knew she wasn't getting better. She only had to be hospitalized when she slid to either end of her catatonic spectrum. She'd been spending less and less time in the middle, making living on her own a dangerous option.

However, she still had life left in her. I could feel it as sure as I could feel the sun was out even if my eyes were closed.

"Georgia...the combination of medicine we have her on right now is the best she's responded to. Why don't we help that along with a round of—"

"No. I'm not sending her into seizures in the hopes that it rewires her brain so she can function normally again."

"It's not *just* a hope. It has a very high success rate of—"

"I'm aware of the numbers, Dr. Carver. I'm also aware of the potential negative side effects. So is my mother. Again, the answer is *no*."

Dr. Carver stood and squared his chin toward me. "Your mother is here on her own accord, isn't that correct?"

"Yes." I scrunched my forehead, wondering what this lead-in was all about.

"If her history is any indication, she'll likely be released within a few days. If she gets worse and has to eventually be involuntarily admitted, we'll be completely out of proactive options unless you okay the use of ECT."

Normally Dr. Carver would walk me back down the hallway and into the visiting room. This time, however his statuesque figure remained rooted by his desk, and I took that as my cue to leave. I knew he was her doctor and not my friend, but with one movement of his hands into his white coat pockets, he drew his line in the sand. He wasn't going to budge on his opinion of the ECT.

Neither was I.

Upon returning to the visiting room, I was thrown off balance by its emptiness. Not just the absence of other patients, but the absence of my mother.

"She got tired," Daniel said as he waved to me from across the room. "She went to bed. This is her usual time."

I ran a hand through my hair, tightening it at the back of my neck. "Of course. I'm so used to coming here when she wakes up around three in the morning...I just lost track of what time of day it was."

I remained in my lonely spot on the floor until a firm arm wrapped around my shoulders. "It's okay, Georgia. It's tiring. Go home and get some sleep. See you at three?"

I looked up at Daniel's compassionate eyes, wondering how long he'd be able to hold onto that empathy. "Do you ever go home?"

"Sometimes." He smiled and squeezed my shoulders. "I usually work doubles. No wife. No kids. Why not? I love working here."

I could have given him about twenty years worth of "why nots", but I just smiled back and made my way through the maze of secured doors and hallways until I was back in my car, resting my head on my steering wheel and begging to hit the bottom of this rabbit hole.

Regan

"That's fuckin' awesome, dude. You're going to love living with Georgia. She's a trip." CJ rummaged through Bo and Ember's refrigerator. "Get your act together in the next couple of days and I can help you move in."

"Thanks. I'm not moving in *with* her, CJ. It's across from her. And, I expect your lazy ass to help me." I shifted on the stool at the center island.

Ember set a plate topped with salad in front of me. "Wait, she stayed here last night? How did I miss that?"

"Because," CJ spoke into the cheese drawer, "you were busy in *siracha*."

I laughed as Ember scrunched her nose. "I was *what?*"

"You were in your headstand this morning." I chuckled at CJ's interpretation of Sanskrit.

"Oh." She raised her eyebrow at CJ, indicating *idiot*. "Anyway, are you sure you want to do that? I mean, it seems like you'd have to deal with a lot of...foot traffic."

"What do you mean? It's a residential spot, apart from the bakery that's downstairs." I reminded myself to ask Georgia again about that place.

Ember grumbled as CJ cluttered the island with a pound of meat and cheese, and other CJ-sandwich necessities, like mustard, mayo, and ketchup. Don't ask.

"What I mean is, she seems like she's pretty...popular with the patrons at the bar."

CJ slapped together a sandwich, took a bite, and responded with a mouth full of turkey. "What the hell is that supposed to mean?"

"Oh come on, guys," Ember looked exasperated as she played with the strings on her hoodie, "each night we were there she left with a different guy, and was all over everyone else. Don't you think it's all a bit...much?"

My stomach twisted as CJ's eyes shot to Ember defensively. "First of all, princess, she's an adult. Second of all, she doesn't do anything different than I, or half the other guys at Finnegan's do every weekend, so you don't need to judge her."

"I judge *you*," Ember mumbled between bites of organic lettuce from her parents' garden.

"And I judge *you*," CJ shot back. "Seriously, what do you care what she does with her time?"

Ember dropped her fork onto her plate. "You want to know why? I've spent nearly five years working for a domestic violence organization. It doesn't matter how much we want gender roles *not* to matter, CJ. They do. The fact is, Georgia is almost infinitely times more likely to get raped than you ever will be by behaving the same exact way you do. And, the fact that *you* encourage her makes you incredibly irresponsible. You call yourself a friend? I call you clueless."

"Regan," Ember turned to me before CJ could respond, "if you do take that apartment, promise me you'll be careful, and that you'll keep an eye out. For her."

I swallowed a forkful of seeds, nodding as my throat constricted around Ember's implications. I hadn't, honestly, thought much about Georgia's safety in her actions. I'd spent too much time thinking Ember was judging her, being a bitch because she perceived her as slutty. Maybe that was an impression I'd had, too.

It frustrated me that she behaved the way she did. She was beautiful, funny, charming, and badass. I didn't know enough about her, and I wasn't close enough to her, though, to suggest she lead her life any other way.

Looking up, I found CJ red-faced and holding his sandwich in mid-air, staring at Ember. "What makes you think she's going to get raped?"

"It's not what I think, CJ. I was just telling you statistics. When she behaves like that, it's going to invite the wrong kind of guy one of these times. It doesn't cross your mind, CJ, because you're not like that. You'd never do that. But, unfortunately, not all guys are like you. And, when alcohol and/or drugs are involved, even *more* people get into trouble."

CJ didn't respond. There was no attack, no smart-ass comment. He simply sat in silence. We all did.

After cleaning up from lunch, I tracked CJ down outside in the sand. His feet were buried as his forearms were propped up on his bent knees. I sat next to him, mimicking his position and staring out into the water until he was ready to talk.

"It's not like that with her. Georgia..." He let his head fall, staring between his knees.

"Like what?"

"She's not...just she's not like *that.*" CJ's hands bounced, as he seemed to search for words that weren't coming.

"I'm not worried, CJ. You said you two hung out a lot in high school, and whatever—"

"I'm worried. Her dad died."

"Yeah, she told me. And her mom..." I sighed. There was so much loss everywhere.

CJ's back straightened. "She told you about her mom?"

"Yeah," I nodded, "gone, too."

"Oh," CJ looked at his knuckles, "yeah. Now they're both gone."

"When did her mom die?"

CJ shook his head. "It was all just really bad..."

I wrapped my arm around his shoulder and he didn't move. He didn't pull away. Even though I'm not his brother, I suddenly felt extreme guilt for not being around for him during the time I'd gone away to boarding school and then to college. It seems a lot happened in the two years CJ had left of high school while I was at the conservatory.

"Just keep an eye on her for me, okay? She's been through a lot, and I didn't even know about her dad until last night." CJ's face broke down a little as he covered his face with his hands.

I hadn't seen him cry since the last time I kicked his ass when I was twelve and he was ten, so I wasn't absolutely sure that's what he was doing. Still, I gave his shoulder another squeeze just in case.

"I don't really have much stuff." I broke the stiff silence. "Do you want to swing by the place and check it out with me?"

CJ rubbed the back of his neck. "Sure, is she gonna be there?"

I shrugged. "Not sure. She said she had something to do north of La Jolla today. She didn't say what."

"Let's go, then. I want to have time today to play around in that recording studio where you lucky bastards get to spend the next few months."

I stood, reaching a hand down to help CJ up. "Let's go, brother."

"Now this...*this* is a view!" CJ pressed his forehead...and his palms against my once-clean picture window.

"Yes, and forevermore I'll gaze at your greasy forehead print at sunset, wishing you were here." I slapped the back of his head and handed him window cleaner and paper towels I'd picked up at the grocery store on our way over.

It only took us one trip to get all of my things from Bo and Ember's place over to my new apartment. There was a futon and a dresser left in the apartment, so I moved them to my bedroom, vowing to pick up some other furniture later in the week.

"I'm gonna miss you." CJ tossed the used paper towels into my still unlined trashcan and walked toward me with his hands in his pockets.

I raised a cautionary eyebrow. "Like miss me, miss me? Or, get ready for one of CJ's smart-ass jokes, miss me?"

He laughed. A full laugh that stripped away his punk exterior. "No, I mean really miss you. You just came back last summer, then everything with Rae..." He pulled one hand out of his pocket and rubbed it along the back of his neck.

He didn't bring Rae up often. I wasn't sure if it was because he was emotionally stunted, or because he was unsure how to handle the conversation. The way his eyes never left my face, though, suggested the latter.

"It's okay, man. It gets better everyday." I sighed, resting my back against the expansive living room wall.

CJ shouldered up next to me. "No, it doesn't."

I turned to look at him, and found him staring at me with a look on his face as dry as scotch. "I..."

"Just because you find better ways to deal with it, doesn't mean it gets *better.*"

As his words worked a perfect circle into my gut, I slid down the wall. "You're right. Nothing is *better*. Easier some days? Maybe. But nothing can possibly ever be better."

CJ followed my lead and sat next to me, knees bent, hands clasped between them.

"I'm sorry, man...I might not believe in love for myself, but you two definitely loved each other."

"We did." Tears infiltrated my eyes as the unsettling tingling returned to my hands.

"Don't be ashamed to talk to someone. Anyone."

I whipped my head in his direction and softly chuckled. "What did you just say? Did you just give me mental health advice?"

He started to answer, but I cut him off. "Nah, you're right, I think. Maybe. No, you're definitely right. I almost kissed Georgia today, for fuck's sake."

"You *what?*" CJ's eye's widened, and if his voice had eyes, they would have widened too.

Burying my face in my hands, I groaned. "Dumbest move ever, right? This girl I barely know offers me this incredible apartment on the cheap and I try to make a move?"

"Eh," CJ laughed, "maybe your excitement got a little redirected."

"You're an asshole. Seriously, though. I didn't mean to. I don't even...she's not really my type. And even though I couldn't admit it to myself at the time, when she pulled away I felt a huge sense of relief. Like I'm carrying around guilt, or something. About Rae."

CJ punched my shoulder. "*She* backed away? Burn, dude. Burn. Way to put the Kane family name to shame."

"CJ," I sighed, "somehow I doubt that our forefathers dreamed that the activities you concern yourself with would be *dignifying* to our family name."

He stood and held out his hand. "You're wrong. I'm definitely a legend."

"In the healthcare industry, maybe." I mumbled as I reached for his hand. He pulled his away, sending me back to the floor.

"I'm always safe, dude." He used his helping hand to give me the finger.

"Whatever. Ready to go see the recording studio?" I stood and fished the apartment key from my pocket, heading for the door.

"Only if I can bang on the drums," he jested.

"Only if that's the only thing you bang while we're there."

"*Damn it*," he playfully hissed. "Good one."

As we drove to the studio, I replayed the bonehead move I'd made to try to kiss Georgia, and prayed that she'd just forget about it.

There was still too much of Rae swimming in my heart to let my lips confuse someone else.

CHAPTER *Seven*

I'M NOT MYSELF, YOU SEE

Regan

"OOOOH, MAN, THIS place!" CJ slapped his hand off the roof of my car as we stood in front of the recording studio.

"You haven't seen the inside yet, you freak." I closed my door and headed for the brick building with a faded *Blue Seed Studios* sign.

"You don't always have to see things to know how awesome they are." As he stood and looked at the door in reverence, I wondered if he ever knew the depth in some of the things he said. "Do Ember's parents *own* this studio?"

I nodded. I swiped my badge in the key reader to the left of the door, and with one click we were granted access to the place where I'd be spending eighty-five percent of my time for the next few months. I'd only been in here once before, when Ember gave me my key card and the grand tour, so everything still felt new. Even though I'd been in several recording studios all over the world, walking down the halls of this one felt like my first day at the conservatory.

Fresh. New. Full of promise.

Despite the three month hide-and-seek from myself in Ireland following her funeral, I held hope that working on this album with my friends in a new place could bring me a sense of closure in Rae's death. She would have been so excited for me. Despite being a student at UNH, with a few semesters left, I'm certain that if she were still alive and Bo presented me with this opportunity, she'd have told me to take it.

She always lit everything with positivity from the inside. Even when she'd spent a few hours one night filling me in on all the Bo and Ember Saga details in the middle of their bizarre breakup, she held on to the floating dandelion seeds of hope.

"They're meant to be together. I don't know how long it will take, or what it will take to get there. But...they'll get there." She told me that one night in the sand under the stars. The Big Dipper was right over us, and I remember that because I'd looked up at the black sky and wished the constellation would scoop us up and hold us in that moment forever.

"Woo!"

I'd been wandering down the hallway mentally in the past, but CJ's cheer summoned me back. He respectfully turned the handle to the studio and let himself in.

Not surprisingly, a few members of the Six were around.

"Hey, Natalie. This is my cousin, CJ." I spoke to the ethereal blonde who was tightening the skin across the top of a large African drum.

She stood, and while I knew she was probably fifty years old, she looked like she could get away with telling people she was thirty-eight or younger.

"Nice to meet you, CJ. Please, call me Journey."

CJ shook her hand, biting his lip to surely prevent the insidious laughter I knew was brewing. "Sure thing. Nice to meet you."

I turned to the other woman in the room. "You're still Magnolia, right?"

Both women came apart in soft, amused giggles. "Yes," Magnolia answered. "Please, call me Mags. Don't worry about Journey. She was just baptized under the seventh sun last week. Not everyone is used to the new name, yet."

Mags, with short chestnut hair and wide set brown eyes, continued playing with the strings of her mandolin as *Journey* returned to her drum. CJ slowly turned his head in my direction, stupefied, and mouthed, "*Seventh sun?*" to me. I shrugged, miming to him to keep quiet.

That was all the reintroduction to Blue Seed studios that I needed. Now, all we needed was the return of Raven and Ashby, who were Ember's parents, and their friends, Michael and Solstice Shaw.

"Hey there! Nice to see you again." Sunshine seeped through the room. Not a person with that name, just to clarify, but the feeling that came when Willow Shaw spoke.

She was the daughter of Michael and Solstice, and had been childhood friends with Ember before Ember and her parents moved to Connecticut for Ember to attend high school.

"Hi, I'm just showing my cousin around the studio, if you don't mind." I held out my arm for a side hug as she casually conquered my personal space.

Something else I'd have to get used to over the next few months.

"No worries. Actually, I'm glad you're here. My dad rewired for the new microphones last night, and we need to check some pitches. Can you get your vio-fiddle-whatever-you-call-it and play for a few minutes?"

She seemed to be nervous as she tucked a strand of her sandy brown hair behind her ear. Her hair was long and wavy, like Ember's, and they had nearly identical jade coloring in their eyes. Guess growing up counterculture made you look like sisters. Her skin, though, was pure caramel. Her mother was black, from Haiti, and her father was white. I briefly wondered if, like the bartenders at E's, she ever felt the need to dress in a certain way to get attention. Likely not...

"Yeah, Reeg, go get your fiddle-dee-doo, and I'll show Willow, here, how this painfully forsaken drum set sounds. Does *no one* play this?" CJ stared at the abandoned set in horror.

Willow toyed with the ends of her hair. "They're not really using that for this album but, um...you can try it out..."

My brain tried like hell to beg her cheeks not to turn red during her exchange with CJ.

They did.

There was nothing more I could do.

"Be right back." I attempted a look of warning to CJ, but he ignored me as he drew his sticks from his back pocket and sat on the stool, ready to strike.

The set, and Willow in due time I was sure, if he wasn't scheduled to leave in a few days. Who was I kidding? That was plenty of time for him.

A few minutes later I was set up in front of the mic, with headphones on, and a mic hanging twelve inches from my strings. Journey and Mags were seated on the couch in the corner of the recording room, while CJ asked Willow questions I knew damn well he knew the answers to in the sound booth.

"Okay," I interrupted Willow's hair-tossing giggle with a clearing of my throat, "do you want me to play anything specific or..."

"Just whatever comes out. Give me some low and high notes. Anytime."

I closed my eyes, taking a deep inhale that filled me with thoughts of Rae and our last few days together. Sun, grass, kissing under the

Weeping Willow, and her smile. A heavenly smile seen, now, only by God and in the moments I let it slip into my memory.

I let my bow fall across the strings on my exhale in any manner they chose. They chose Chopin's *Nocturne.* I kept my eyes closed for a few seconds until my shoulders found their sway. Until my fingers stopped shaking. I hated my hands for making me play this. The melody alone sounded like I imagine fingernails sound when they dig into the dirt surrounding the grave of a loved one.

So painful, one would be wise to pray the notes into nothingness. So evocative of feeling altogether, you beseech their continuance.

Opening my eyes when I was certain the pain had no place else to go, I found CJ looking smug as Willow wiped tears from her eyes, adjusting slides on the soundboard. Journey and Mags held hands on the couch, Mags's head on Journey's shoulder.

I wasn't sure if they were a couple, or if the song simply made them want to cling to each other as the vulnerability of life bled through the connection of my bow and strings.

As I pulled the bow away from its lover, and the notes drifted into the nothingness in which Rae resided, I let myself feel it. Not all at once, as I was in the company of relative strangers, apart from CJ, but I had to acknowledge it was there.

The hole.

I'd heard Bo describe it on more than one occasion as a "Rachel-sized hole," and I'd brushed it off, half-joking that she was so tiny it'd be like a pinhole. I was wrong. Jagged walls of memories and touches and hope shot up around me, leaving me in a crevasse so steep on both sides I just had to sit. Sit and be in it.

I was still standing, of course, having learned to somewhat control my physical responses to emotion. That didn't keep their eyes off of me.

"Regan..." Willow's mouth pinched shut at the end of her sentence.

"Never leave us. Ever." Journey wiped under her eyes as she accosted me with a patchouli-scented hug.

I smiled, squeezing back. Squeezing away encroaching feelings of emotional nudity. I needed to feel this. More. And often, if I was going to be able to let go of it.

What I knew for sure was I was in no place to go around kissing anyone else. Or almost kissing.

"I won't leave the group, if that's what I'm in, but I do have to leave now. Just for the night. I'll be back in the morning. You coming, Ceej?" I slid off my headphones and set them back on their hook.

CJ met me in the recording room. "Where are we going? We just got here."

"I've got to track down Georgia."

"Whatever." CJ pouted as he slid a hand across the small of Willow's back. "I'll see you tomorrow. Or in a little bit, if you'd like to stop by E's in South Park," he spoke into her ear."

"I'll be there," she whispered just as I was about to roll my eyes.

I couldn't babysit CJ or his potential submissives tonight. Tonight, I had to apologize to Georgia.

Georgia

The clocks were all stuck at different times, so it seemed. The start of my shift had been hours ago, but it seemed like I'd just gotten there and had been there for days all at once. I couldn't even tell myself I wanted to go home and rest. There was no rest. Not while my mother was there.

Thankfully, it was football season, so Monday nights at the bar rivaled the crowd size of a summer Saturday night. Hungry and thirsty sports fans would prevent me from staring at the unmoving clocks.

"What was your car doing here this morning?" Lissa couldn't look me in the eyes, even as she arched her eyebrow.

"What were you doing noticing?" I knew before I finished the inquisition. Lissa's car was left in the parking lot of E's at least two nights a week, depending on where she decided to sleep.

"No need to get defensive, I just thought you always brought them back to your place. You weren't drunk last night, either, right?"

"Nosey, much?" I snapped as I slammed the tray of fruit garnish on the bar, sending several orange slices to the floor.

"Sorry." She rolled her eyes and her tone rang of an elementary schoolyard.

I sighed, discarding the victimized orange slices into the trash. "No, I'm sorry. It was a long night. I went home with CJ. Not *with* CJ, but we just caught up. Then I had to show Regan the apart—"

Shit. Lissa hadn't known I was showing the apartment to him. Or anyone.

"You. Slut." She whipped my butt with a wet bar rag.

"Ow! What?"

"I saw the way you were lookin' at him all weekend. Clever move, though, to have him pay you for...that." She wiggled her eyebrows and I realized exactly why she and CJ never made it out of the bar together. They're too much alike.

"He needed a place, I needed a renter. Stat. That's all. Besides, he's CJ's cousin, I couldn't..."

It was a last-minute decision to ask him to take that apartment. Hanging on to it meant that I was still planning on encouraging my mother to move in there. For six months she and I had the same discussion. I had to honor her wish to live alone as long as she physically could, considering other wishes of hers were becoming harder to grant.

Regardless of having to root my heels in the floor as he leaned toward me lips-first earlier in the day, I still couldn't. I needed normalcy. Consistency. Something about his eyes—no, that's cliché—something about the way he moved as he played on stage told me he was safe. Passionate and disciplined. Intense, maybe, but it was harnessed. Released only on stage and, I assumed, in practice.

"Well save your *couldn't speech* for another time. Here he comes." Lissa's lips curled up in guilty pleasure.

Walking toward me in a march-like manner was Regan, followed by an evidently irked CJ, whose shoulders were tense, like he'd just been turned down by a girl. I took a deep breath, and plastered on my "Welcome to E's" smile.

"Hey, boys, what can I—"

"Can I talk to you for a minute? In the back or outside?" Regan's hands hung at his sides, but I watched the rhythm of his thumbs rubbing against the pads of his fingers as he waited. He was nervous. If his hands hadn't given him away, his voice would have. It bordered on overconfident. Overcompensation.

I looked to CJ, preemptively furious that he'd told Regan everything, and Regan was going to back out of the theoretical lease. CJ simply shrugged and pointed to the Guinness tap.

Looking at Regan as I handed CJ his beer, I drudged up some confidence of my own. "Sure, can you give me a few? This game's almost over, then it'll die down here for another hour or so until the next one starts."

"Yeah, no problem." He dropped onto the stool next to CJ and laced his fingers together, turning every other knuckle white.

On my way to deliver food to my table, I slid him a pint of Guinness without him asking. I needed him to mellow the hell down.

Fifteen minutes later the crowd at the bar started yelling in frustration.

"What the hell happened?" I asked Lissa as I came up the stairs from changing a keg.

"Damn Patriots game is delayed an hour. Snow. Where on earth gets 6 inches of snow in a couple of hours?" She gestured to the snow globe that encircled Gillette Stadium splashed across every TV screen in the bar.

"Great," I groaned.

"What?" CJ and Regan spoke in unison in front of empty pint glasses.

"Game delay. Now the people who are staying to watch the game are either going to get disruptively drunk...or just leave." I heard my bank account plead for mercy.

Regan shrugged. "Want me to play something?"

"Thanks, Regan, but I don't know if this crowd is really the fiddlin' type." I set a hand on my hip, delighting in the offense on his face.

CJ laughed, but set his sticks on the bar. "We could come up with something. Willow's on her way, too. I think she sings, or plays something..."

Regan put a hand on CJ's shoulder. "I'm surprised you got that much information out of her, given you spent most of your time in the sound booth staring at her breasts."

"Nice one. He must have learned that from you, Regan." I laughed as CJ and Regan whipped their gazes toward me.

"Burn!" CJ hollered, drawing attention from both ends of the bar.

"Whatever, want us to play, or not?"

I'd waited half an hour to see him smile, and when he did, he did it right. His eyebrows lifted, revealing soft creases in his forehead as his slightly imperfect teeth briefly seized my sense of reason. I had to say something.

"Play." In my head it sounded louder, but it came out as a whisper.

Watching Regan walk away from me, and to the parking lot to, presumably, get his violin, I couldn't help but stare at the way his clothes regarded his body as a perfect rack. One for which they alone were designed. Nothing was too tight, or too loose. He didn't belittle those around him with flashy brand names. Though he could have paid a little more attention to his hair, I found my fingers tingling to feel it.

"Don't do it." CJ had switched to bottled beer, and brought the opening to his mouth as he spoke, holding the neck with his thumb and first two fingers.

"Don't do what, exactly?" I leaned my elbows onto the bar in front of him.

"Regan."

I searched CJ's eyes and face for signs of humor, an indication that he was teasing. All I found was an uncomfortable severity.

"W...why?" I hadn't planned on *doing* anything with Regan, but CJ's caution had me curious. And, curiosity was a force all its own.

CJ set the bottle down and stared at it for a minute. When he'd gotten all he needed from it, he looked to me. "Just...come on. Argh!" CJ ran a hand over his hair and it was clear.

Secrets.

Despite every shortcoming one could easily find with my promiscuous friend, gossiping wasn't on the menu.

"I got it," I said, placing my hand on his. "And, thank you. You're an awesome friend."

He looked up at me from under his unfairly long eyelashes. "Don't go spreading that shit around. I'm only in town for a few more days."

"I wouldn't dream of it." Just then, Regan returned with his violin and headed for the stage. "Get up there, teddy bear. Rock it."

CJ leaned over the bar and kissed me on the cheek. "You got it, gorgeous."

After Regan tuned and CJ settled behind the set, I started for the stage to announce them. Applause from the crowd in front of the stage told me that wouldn't be necessary, however. And, even if I'd wanted to announce them, they took off in song before I could even reach the stage. And I was nearly knocked on my ass.

CJ struck the drums with vicious force as Regan ripped the bow across his strings. It was a full Irish jig, each Kane boy relentless in their pursuit of excellence from their instruments. I'd heard a song like this before. Celtic Cross did a cover of David Garrett's "Celtic Rondo" here a few weeks ago.

The duo I was staring at tonight blew that entire band out of the water.

Every once in a while, CJ would pull back, and Regan would play a complicated solo. The fingers on his left hand moved just as fast as the bow in his right. When I closed my eyes, it sounded like there were two fiddles battling it out—that's the skill he beckoned from his fingers. It made me want to dance. And, I don't dance.

As soon as CJ entered the song again, the crowd cheered, and Regan turned to face his talented cousin. With hands moving independently from the rest of their bodies, Regan and CJ's smiles invited the audience into their shared history. Their family.

"Let's go!" Lissa grabbed my hand and gave it a tug.

"Where?" I squealed as she dragged me to the front of the stage.

"Dance!"

I shook my head and shouted over the crowd, "I don't know how! Not to this!"

Lissa lifted her arms overhead and began jumping to CJ's off-beats. "Just...move!"

"Ahh!" I threw my head back, rolling my eyes for effect.

Then, I closed my eyes. And, I danced.

I was free.

Whirling with Lissa through the notes springing from Regan's bow, and jumping to the precise beats of CJ's bass drum, I was free-falling up. Up, not down. Falling up is a much grander experience when one can find the let-go-ness to do so. I'd feared I'd misplaced my let-go, but there I was, sweat splashed across my chest and dancing.

"Woohoo!" Lissa lifted her hands in praise as the boys finished.

I pressed my thumb and forefinger into the sides of my mouth and whistled, catching Regan's attention. When his sea-glass eyes found me, I caught the vision of his tongue darting quickly across his lips before he smiled. I gave him a single thumbs-up before CJ hollered the name of a song I didn't recognize and counted off with his sticks.

And away they went...

Though it'd only been a couple of minutes, my crash-landing back to reality felt a bit harsh. While the guys continued playing, customers continued ordering beer and food, and they required someone to deliver it to them. I'd have much preferred to stand in front of that stage all night. They were each lost in the notes, but still able to communicate with the crowd. I couldn't take my eyes off of them.

It wasn't just that CJ and Regan were both good-looking—okay, hot—in their own ways. But, I'd known CJ for a long time, and even when he was starting to really excel at the drums, I'd never seen him look like *that* on stage.

The way music can turn a person's hidden emotions inside out was fascinating to me. And, exactly why I stayed away from musical instruments.

Over the course of the next half hour, through songs fast and slow, modern and historic, CJ and Regan transformed Monday Night Football into something tolerable.

"I'm sticking my tongue down CJ's throat tonight, whether he likes it or not." Lissa spoke over her applause as the guys wrapped up their impromptu set. Savage determination marched through her eyes.

I snorted at her interpretation of the unknown. "He'll like it, Liss."

Apparently, I'd spoken too soon. As they were leaving the stage, a tall young woman with long, loose curls suspended perfectly around her face and shoulders, walked up to CJ. She seemed timid, as if she were approaching him on a dare, but the *hither* in his arched brow and crooked smile advertised their acquaintance. CJ had much grander modes of expression when trying to garner attention. It was clear he already had hers.

Lissa groaned. "And, would you look at her? What, is she from some mystical island of carmel-skinned, green-eyed people? How is that fair...in any interpretation of the word?"

She sulked into the kitchen to retrieve food as I watched. Lissa was right; she did have caramel skin, flawless under the tavern lighting. She was long and lean, and the longer I stared the more familiar she looked.

"Your eyes just got all bug-eyed..." Lissa's voice trailed off as I walked over to Regan.

"Hey," I whispered into his ear as CJ spun his sticks around, otherwise occupied. I grabbed his heated hand and pulled him into the narrow hallway in front of the back room.

Regan looked around, confused. "What?"

"That's Willow Shaw." I pointed to CJ.

"Wow, you're really a Six fan, huh?" He leaned against the wall and hooked his thumbs through his belt loops.

"First of all, get your thumbs out of there. This isn't a saloon in the Wild West. Second of all, yes, I'm a big fan, but everyone knows who she is."

"She's not in the band..." Regan looked back to Willow, as if to double check we were talking about the same person.

I slapped his arm, attempting to stop his open gawking. "No, but she's kind of a socialite of the music scene here. She's produced a few of her parents' solo albums, and has worked in conjunction with *major* labels on some chart-toppers."

"Okay, that's good...right?"

"I can't believe I'm going to say this, but we have to keep her away from CJ. She's famous for her abilities in the studio, but notorious for her activities...elsewhere, if you know what I mean."

Regan's lips pursed into an incredulous scoff. "Please, Georgia. We can't tell CJ a single shred of that. That kind of girl is his holy grail."

"I just don't want her to use her status in the industry to get him into bed."

"She doesn't have to *get* him anywhere."

Anxiety simmered in my throat. "I just don't like her."

I didn't like any girl like Willow, throwing their breasts around as often as their talent. I didn't understand why women had to do that.

"The way you're looking at her," Regan interrupted my thoughts, "that's the same way Ember was looking at you the night you almost kicked her ass."

I pulled my head back. "I didn't almost kick anyone's ass."

"You know what I mean."

"Well..." Shit. He was right. "Is that what Ember thought of me...wait...is that what you think of me?"

Regan shook his head. "I don't think anything, Georgia. I just met you. I do, though, want to apologize for this morning. I didn't mean to...you know...make it weird. I didn't mean to almost kiss you." He looked down, clearing his throat in the way guys do when they're uncomfortable.

"Great. You think I'm like her. Willow. Fan-*tastic*." I attempted to go back to the bar, but he grabbed my wrist.

"I don't think you're *like* anyone—"

"Ow." I couldn't help but wince as his finger pressed onto the edge of my bruise.

He lifted his fingers, looking at my skin and realizing his misstep. "Sorry. I..." He grabbed my arm a little further up, lifting my hand so the bruise was between us. "I don't know what to think."

"Stop thinking about me, then," I snapped, pulling my arm back.

"No," he retorted defensively. There was a devoted determination circling his words.

"Wh—"

"I'm your neighbor now, anyway. Look, I didn't mean to offend you, but just...be safe, okay? I'm keeping an eye on you." He smiled, and I was actually thankful he didn't have a single dimple. It would have distracted from the red scruff popping up along his jawline.

My mouth swung open for a few seconds. "I...don't know what just happened here, but let me try to recap. You don't want to kiss me, right?"

"Right."

"Good."

"You don't think I'm like Willow, but Ember does."

"I don't pretend to know what Ember thinks, and we don't gossip about girls." His eyebrow twitched up impishly.

"And, for some reason, you think you need to look out for me?"

He shrugged unapologetically. "CJ asked me to."

"Don't."

"I'm going to."

"Why, for the love of God, is the Kane family so fucking stubborn?" I huffed, placing my hands on my hips.

"Most of us were born under the sign of the bull."

"You're a smartass."

"I am." He nodded once, his smile widening, lifting the tops of his ears.

"Why don't you want to kiss me?" I challenged. I knew he was lying, but I wanted to know why. "Girlfriend?"

"No." The tops of his ears dropped along with his face. "I don't want to kiss anyone."

"Are you gay?" It occurred to me that I hadn't seen him checking out, or trying to pick up, any girls either night he'd been at E's.

"No."

"Ah, broken heart, then?"

He half-huffed, half-chuckled. "That's the G-rated version."

"What does the R-rated cut look like?"

"I'll tell you what my R-rated is, if you tell me yours." He swallowed hard, his Adam's apple bobbing several times.

"What do you mean mine?" I knew CJ hadn't told him anything, but I got goosebumps anyway.

"Everyone's got an R-rated version of their pain, Georgia."

He wasn't going to budge. It was something big. So was mine.

"Another time, maybe."

He squinted as he grinned. "Deal. I know where to find you."

I looked away. He wasn't going to get in there tonight. Or ever.

"Come on," I ungracefully shifted subjects, "let's go see what CJ's gotten himself into."

"Or who," Regan mumbled.

It was funny, and I tried to laugh, but I couldn't.

Laughter lets people in.

CHAPTER *Eight*

DRINK ME

Regan

I DIDN'T SEE A lot of CJ during his last days in San Diego, but I got to hear all about them when I drove him back to the airport. Evidently Willow was amazing. And loud. And CJ would be returning to San Diego as soon as he'd saved up enough money for another flight.

A week and a half later, things were well underway at Blue Seed Studios, and I felt my life settling into rhythm. I was sitting on the couch in the recording room, as the band worked over a track they'd been wrestling with for half a day. I wasn't slated to be in that piece, but according to Bo, that was about to change.

He scratched his head, taking a deep breath before speaking. Always the diplomat. "I'm just saying, Mike, we take out the vocal interlude, move it six measures down, and throw a fiddle in there. Five measures. It'll make a world of difference."

"I hear what you're saying, kid, but..." Michael and Bo continued their back-and-forth as Ember flashed me a "get me out of here" look.

Aside from their talent, the Six relied heavily on Bo and Ember, and myself and Willow, to make sure their sound held enough freshness to attract new listeners, while honoring their decades-long fans. That worked well, unless one of us "younger folk" disagreed with one of them. Especially Michael, Willow's dad. Hence, my silence.

"Regan," Bo waved me over, "take a look at this. I'm right, right?"

Shit, I sighed under my breath as I rose. Willow giggled in the sound booth. Guess that's the benefit of being on the receiving end of all of the microphones in the room.

Bo slid over on the piano bench and handed me a pencil. "Do something."

He tried to sound even, but aggravation held onto *something.*

I stared at the notes. They were beautiful. It was a new experience for me, looking at instrumental and vocal parts on a single score, but thanks to my time at the Boston Conservatory, it was a short learning curve.

"We don't have to separate them," I said after two minutes, all eyes on me. "We can blend them, punctuate vocals on my staccatos here, here, here...and here."

A collective sigh startled me.

"Fresh eyes!" Michael patted my shoulder. "That's all we needed. Let's try it."

Several minutes and only one restart later, the song was complete, and almost perfect.

"Let's call it a night." Raven, Ember's mom, stretched her arms up, leaning back in what I'd learned was part of a sun salutation.

I didn't ask for this knowledge.

The group agreed the song we'd just done was a good stopping point, and the older members fled with talk of going to bed. It was ten o'clock. I can't blame them, as even I was starting to follow their routine. We'd get to the studio at 6 o'clock and be off and running by 7:30. I was grateful I didn't sing, because I had no idea how they could get their vocal cords lubricated that early in the day.

"Want to come over for some wine, or something?" Ember asked as she picked up her bag.

"No, I think I'm going to E's. I told Georgia I'd stop by once in a while to play, but I haven't been since we started recording."

"How's she doing?"

I shrugged. "I've barely seen her. Our schedules are opposite. She doesn't finish at the bar until three most mornings, then I'm out the door by six...in order to be twenty minutes late here."

Ember chuckled. "Yeah, asshole. Fix that shit."

"Anyway, by the time we're done here, she's usually back at work."

Bo wrapped his arm around Ember's shoulders. "Two ships passing in the night, huh?"

"I guess."

"None of her late-night guests have been keeping you up?" Ember arched her eyebrow, but it wasn't bitchy. She was teasing. But, I took offense.

"Ember, why do you take her so personally? I haven't seen or heard anyone with her, and, really, it would be none of our business if I had."

"I'm sorry—"

"No, it's not okay. Your attitude has really sucked lately, and I'm kind of over it."

Bo called after me, but I ignored him as I fled the recording room and sped down the hall, exiting the building and slamming my car door shut behind me.

I don't know why I was so protective over Georgia's reputation. She didn't seem to care what the hell anyone thought as she strutted around the bar and flirted with anyone and everyone. Plus, I hadn't seen her since the night at E's when she told me about Willow.

Who was now at my car window.

Willow tapped her fingernail to the beat of the song we'd just finished until I turned on the car and pressed the button for the window to go down.

"What's up?" I tried to sound composed, and unlike the tantrum I'd just thrown.

"She's not mad about Georgia, you know."

"What?"

"Ember. She's not mad about that girl from the bar. She's mad at me."

I shook my head and shrugged. Male code for *I need more information.*

"I made a pass at Bo two weeks ago, and she lost her shit." Her tone was nonchalant as she picked at her fingernails.

"You what?"

"Oh for God's sake, Regan, they're not married."

"But...they're together."

She arched the same eyebrow Ember always did. "So. They're not married. Anyway, I tried; he declined the offer. We move on."

I had a million things I wanted to say to her, but nine hundred and ninety-nine thousand of them would have guaranteed my departure from the album project, given her parents were thirty percent of the band.

"Nice," I settled on. "Well...I'm heading out."

I drove away, as Willow stepped back and slid into her black Beetle convertible. I considered calling Ember to apologize for my outburst with her, but I couldn't deal with that right now. I hadn't played much in the studio over the last two days, and I was itching to get to E's and let some of my pent up energy out on stage.

A sense of relief overcame me when I reached the parking lot at E's, and saw Georgia's car there. I found myself missing her smile and her lack of apology for anything she said or did. She wasn't crass or anything, but she didn't waste time filtering through everyone's facades to decide what she should or shouldn't say.

The crowd was modest for a Saturday night, but that worked in my favor in terms of finding an open stool at the bar. I hadn't eaten anything but raw fruits and vegetables, largely in the form of salads, for lunch over the last week and a half, and I was dying for deep fried meat.

"Hey hot-shot recording star, I thought we'd never see the likes of you in here again." Lissa caught me out of the corner of her eye, not looking up from the pints she was filling as she addressed me.

"It's good to see you, too," I teased.

"What can I get for ya? You're playing a set tonight?" She leaned forward, and where her cleavage should have been I just saw pale skin stretched across visible ribs in the center of her chest. Far too skinny.

"Wings. Hot. And, yeah, if there's an opening."

"For you, I'm sure there will be. Celtic Cross will be in later to do an after-hours set, I think. Maybe they'll let you play with them."

I shrugged and she handed me a Guinness I hadn't ordered, but needed. Badly.

After a refreshing sip, a more satisfying voice came up behind me.

"Well, well, well. How's life at the commune?" Georgia sat on the empty stool next to me, setting the oversized food tray on the bar.

Her voice was bright and normal, but her eyes looked tired. More grey than blue, and dark circles were starting to form all around them. Not just underneath. I realized she could have been sick, or something, and I wouldn't have known. Not very neighborly, I thought. And, certainly not watching after her as I'd promised CJ I would.

"It's good. Long days, a lot of lettuce...and yoga breaks." Not that I participated in them. Neither did Bo. We usually took them as an opportunity to sneak a beer at the bar next door. "How are you doing? We're neighbors and I never see you."

She sighed while smiling. "Busy here, then when I wake up you're gone. Oh! That reminds me, the mail came yesterday and there was a large envelope they needed a signature for. I was on my way here, signed for it, and stuck it in my car. Let me go get it." A thousand words a minute and she bounded on short heels out the front door.

"Here." She was slightly out of breath when she returned, handing me the large thin envelope with David Bryson and his Concord, New Hampshire return address in the top left corner.

Instinctively, my palms began to sweat. It wasn't that it was David I was worried about. Bo's surrogate father and business partner was a hell of a guy. It was that I hadn't spoken much with him since Rae's funeral.

I remained silent, feeling Georgia's eyes on me as I ran my finger between the seal and the envelope. I felt something square at the bottom of the envelope, but I pulled out the larger single sheet first, setting the handwritten note on the bar as I read it.

Regan,

I hope this letter finds you well. As you know, I've been managing the Cavanaugh estate in Bo's absence. A box of Rae's belongings was sent from UNH at some point over the last few months, and it was set in the garage. Inside the box, among other things, was this envelope, addressed to you but never mailed.

Bo gave me your new address. I hope you don't mind. It's yours—you should have it.

I hope things are going well for you in San Diego.

Take care.

-David

My fingertips and lips went numb as I stared at the large manila envelope. Inside was something from Rae to me.

A piece of her.

"What's with you?" Georgia tilted her head to the side and looked between the envelope and me. "You look like you saw a ghost."

"Something like that," I mumbled.

Setting the envelope on the bar, I ordered another beer. I didn't know if I wanted to look. Pandora had gotten with the times and had stuffed herself into a USPS envelope.

"What is it?" Georgia crossed her arms over the bared skin of her stomach.

"Don't know."

"Who's it from?" She seemed hesitant in her questioning, but I was grateful for her voice. It kept the panic attack a few feet back.

"Someone back home." I kept it simple. Describing David would have meant discussing Rae, and the things I purposefully hadn't packed for my trip to San Diego.

"Georgia! Food!" The cook's voice carried over the sound of a ringing bell.

She jumped as we both shot back to the noise of the room. It was as if she'd been sucked along with me into the foggy silence of my impending slip into madness. She took two steps backward, keeping her eyes between me and the envelope, then turned and walked to the kitchen.

With another Guinness warming my veins and numbing my fear, I picked up the envelope again. David's words fell off the bar and wedged themselves between my foot and the bar when I stopped the paper from hitting the ground.

It's been six months, Regan. Just see what it is. It won't kill you.

It might.

Before I could talk myself out of it further, I reached my hand into the envelope, wrapped my fingers around the flat, square item inside, and pulled it back out and set it on the bar.

Yes...it might kill me.

It was a card. A square, sealed white envelope, with my old address in Barnstable written front and center, and Rae's Concord address written in the top left corner.

Her handwriting.

I'd always found handwriting incredibly intimate. Whether words or notes on a page, they were the visible expression of the emotional and internal life spilled out through ink for the eyes to witness. View. Study.

"Regan." Lissa stood behind the bar, knocking her knuckles in front of me.

My head snapped up. "Yeah?"

"Wings." She set the plate down and looked at my glass. "Another Guinness?"

"No." I shook my head. "Liquor. Something brown."

While I waited for her, I grabbed the edge of the envelope, standing it up and tapping the corner on the bar a few times. I watched Georgia carry food and drinks across the bar twice before Lissa finally showed back up. Looking around, I realized the bar was growing thick with customers seeking their own elixir. Some to enhance. Some to numb. Some to just...something.

I stared at the way Rae's R's curled up a bit at the tail. In my name and hers. Only, on mine, she hadn't taken her pen from the paper before sketching a tiny heart at the end of the letter. I dropped the envelope onto the bar and closed my eyes, pinching the bridge of my nose until I was sure it would pop off.

Then I looked at the liquor.

And that's the last thing I remember.

Georgia

The longer the night wore on, the worse Regan looked. A piece of paper, the first one he'd removed from the envelope, was held against the bottom of the bar by the tip of one of his worn Converses. The more offending piece, it seemed, sat in the form of a square card. One that he'd look at, pick up, and set back down again between shots of whiskey.

Lissa robotically poured another shot and placed it in front of Regan. I'd have done the same on any other night, with any other customer. Watching this exchange, however, made my skin crawl. I didn't know what was in that envelope, but I knew that I hadn't seen Regan drink more than a pint or two whenever he'd been in here. It's quite a gap between that and shots of whiskey without much of a breather in between.

I looked around at the cast of regulars surrounding the bar, wondering how many of them walked in here for the first time after a letter of their own. Sure, some were well-seasoned alcoholics, and the rest on their way. But, the first sip after a letter like that differs from the first sip ever.

My father had received a letter like that once. A goodbye letter from my mom, taped to the bathroom mirror one barren morning in January. As his feet screamed against the frigid tile floor, his world fell apart.

Followed 15 years later by his liver.

Sure, he'd been a heavy drinker before that. But...it was different after the letter.

A half an hour later, the last of my dinner tables left, and I watched Regan's forehead settle onto his fist as he leaned over the bar. I thought about calling CJ, wishing he were right around the corner as he'd always been on the weekends early in high school. Intuition whispered that this wasn't a common scene for Regan, though, so who knows what advice CJ could have offered. Three thousand miles away, no less.

I shimmied behind the bar and bumped hips with Lissa. Well, my well-fed hip to her hipbone. She looked down at me and I eyed the clock, which read 2:30 AM, glanced at Regan, back to her and ran my index finger lengthwise across my neck, telling her *no more* for him tonight.

"What's the big deal? He's really only had a few shots." She wasn't fighting with me, just fishing to what I knew that she didn't. Which wasn't much.

I nodded in his direction, whispering as if he could hear us, despite the fact he hadn't lifted his head in over two minutes. "Look at him. I'm going to have to take him home. I'd like him to have a few minutes to at least be able to walk out of here on his own two feet."

"Takin' him home, huh? It's about time. He's so damn hot I was waiting to see how long it would take for you to cave...especially with his front door like six feet from yours." Lissa's seductive smile annoyed me as she filled a white bucket with cleaning solution.

"It's not like I have time for this shit, Liss. I've got to get over to—"

Lissa cut me off with a slam of the bucket on the counter. "Would you live for once, for God's sake?"

Now was not the time to argue with her about my life choices. They weren't my choices to begin with.

I took a quick look around and saw the crowd was thinning. There were some who wanted to leave before the lights were turned on. Those who were still holding on to some sense of pride.

"I'm out. I'm taking him home. Don't let Donnie tow his car, K?" I untied my apron, made change for my tips, and changed in the back room, allowing Regan a few more minutes to sober up before I disrupted his self-loathing. Or pity. Or whatever that was.

I walked back into the bar and found Regan sitting up, looking around as if he'd just hit the snooze on his alarm clock. Or wished he could.

I set my hand on his shoulder. "Hey, killer, let's get you home."

"I can't drive," he slurred.

At least he still had some sense.

"I know. Thank you for recognizing that, though. You'll come with me."

Dead eyes lifted to my face. "She's gone, you know. Just...gone."

I let my eyes fall to the letter he'd left unopened, but thoroughly touched, on the bar. *Rae Cavanaugh* sat on the return address line. The name rang a bell, but too faint to figure out at that moment.

"Well," I sighed, "I'm here. And I'll get you home." Predisposed in the role of caregiver, I knew this particular assignment would be short-term.

Despite CJ and Regan looking nothing alike, the cousins seemed to posses a gene for mobility while intoxicated because he gracefully left his stool and began a wobbly but unassisted walk to the door. Empty handed.

He was making a slow go of it, so I took a second to sweep the letter off the floor and slide it back into the envelope, along with the unopened card.

"Just leave it," Regan mumbled as if he had eyes in the back of his head.

"Okay," I lied.

He'd have regretted it had I listened.

I didn't know who sent the envelope, or why. But anything worth drinking that much over deserves to be read. I quickly unzipped my backpack and placed the envelope inside, just where I'd put it when the postman dropped it off. Maybe I should have left it there, or told him there was no one by Regan's name at that address.

No. It deserved to be read.

If someone writes you words, you read them.

"Need some help, G?" Dominic, the larger of the two aging bouncers, lifted his thick black eyebrows.

I shook my head, adjusting the straps on my backpack. "Nah, Dom, I got it."

"Yeah, Dom...she's got it." Regan sounded almost mocking as he leaned against the door.

This kind of dialogue was commonplace for near closing-time, and Dom just shook his head and held open the door.

Once in the fresh air, Regan seemed to stumble a little bit more. Having used all of his ability to keep his shit straight, he sat on the seat of a bike that was locked on a bike rack.

"It'll take you a long time to get back to La Jolla on that thing. Let's go." I hooked my arm through his and tugged.

"I can't drive, though." He pinched the bridge of his nose, shaking his head as if he was just aware of this fact.

I fished my keys out of my bag and gave them a jingle. "I can. Come on. I know where you live."

He chuckled. "Barely. You're never home. Always out with your guy friends and shit..."

"What?" I crinkled my forehead as I unlocked the passenger door, depositing him inside after sliding the seat as far back as it would go. His knees still came close to the glove compartment.

"All the guys," he slurred, "that you're all over all the time..." He clumsily locked his seatbelt into place. And leaned his head against the window.

I tried to keep defensiveness out of my voice. I was the sober one. "What about them?"

"You go home with them. You're never home."

"I don't...what does that have to do with anything?" I pulled out of the parking lot, wondering where this conversation was going.

"CJ told me to look after you." Regan leaned forward, resting elbow on knee, head in hand. "It's hard to look after you when you're at other guys' houses all the time."

I suppose I could have told him everything right there, but he wasn't in the brain space to put it all together. I was more interested in the truths he thought he held about me.

"Is that the branch up your tree hugging friend's ass? She thinks I'm a slut?" I knew Ember had thought I'd fooled around with CJ, and she had some attitude a couple of weeks ago, but Regan's statements illustrated the crossover.

Slut.

"You're not a slut, Georgia."

I glanced over at him as I merged onto the highway because his voice sounded suddenly sober. Then he slurred. Again.

"You don't do anything different than CJ does all the time... that's what he says..."

"That's what CJ said? That I sleep around?"

Regan looked down as his eyebrows pulled in. "No...he didn't say that. He said you *weren't like that.*"

Way to go, Ceej. Defending me without giving the truth away. Half-truths, full protection. Realizing I had no use for a drunken conversation of this subject — me — I turned the tables.

"Who's Rae Cavanaugh?" I swallowed hard at the courage afforded me in the tiny confines of my car.

"How do you know her?" His head was still in his hands, but he rotated to face me.

"Obviously I don't since I asked you who she is."

"She's...Bo's sister."

"Oh...that's why it sounded familiar. Last name. Okay, so, why did she send you that note that had you all drinky-drinky?"

"She didn't."

"Well, the envelope—"

"She didn't fucking send me shit, Georgia, okay?" A deep tenor filled the car as Regan yelled.

I jumped, thankful to be exiting the highway and a few minutes from home.

I guess we were done talking about Rae Cavanaugh.

Keeping quiet for the remainder of the ride, I half expected Regan to break somewhere in the five minutes after his last word, but he didn't. I saw his lips moving once in a while out of the corner of my eye, but he wasn't making any noises. He hadn't shown signs of mental illness before, so I was chalking the self-talk up to the alcohol.

Once we were in front of our building, I guided my car into the garage, deciding to take the interior stairs, given the railings were sturdier than the wobbly split-rail ones along the outer stairs.

"And, by the way," Regan started mid-imaginary conversation as he got out and shut the door behind him, "why'd you get all weird when we played that Guster song the other night?"

I tried to silently clear my throat. Go ahead, try it. That's what I sounded like. "What do you mean?"

"CJ started singing, which he like *never* does, and you looked like he cracked open your chest and crawled inside." Regan wandered over to the door and knocked on it.

I took out my keys, shaking my head. "He kind of did." It was okay to be a little honest with a drunk person. They might not remember.

"He did?"

"Look. The PG-13 version of my pain? I had a complete shit childhood, and CJ, for all intents and purposes, rescued me from that during the time I still lived in Massachusetts. That song is just...ours."

I opened the door and Regan put his hands in his pockets and started up the stairs.

"Could you take your hands out of your pockets?" I held onto his shirt. "If you fall, we'll be able to better prevent both of us from tumbling down the stairs if you can at least catch yourself."

Regan snorted. "Sounds like you've done this before."

"I guess you could say that. Just...go. You're staying in my apartment tonight."

"I live five feet from you, I think I can find my way." He stopped halfway up the stairs to take a breath, then slowly jogged the rest of the way until he was in the hall between our two doors.

"Yeah, and I want to make sure you can find your way to the bathroom if you need to throw up. I'd rather you didn't choke on your own vomit tonight. Anyway, I have your keys." I dangled his keys in the air then dropped them in my bag.

"How did you..."

"You handed them to Lissa when you ordered your third shot. You're smart. I like you." I unlocked my door and led him inside.

Without further protest, Regan fell to my couch and was half asleep before I flicked on the light and re-latched my door. I sighed, took off his shoes, set a garbage can next to him, and posted up in the chair across from the coffee table.

Once I was certain he was out, I reached for my laptop and, like any good American, I opened my browser and typed: *Rae Cavanaugh.*

My assumptions about Regan and his insides were dismantled wrecking-ball style as the first item in the search results produced an obituary from last summer. *Shit.*

Rachel Vivian Cavanaugh

Rachel (Rae) passed away suddenly on Saturday afternoon.

A native of Concord, and the daughter of the late Spencer and Vivian Cavanaugh, Rae was full of life and loved by everyone she encountered. Her kind nature and silent resolve carried her through many difficult trials in her short life.

Rachel spent her last year as a student at the University of New Hampshire, and working Director of Public Relations for the family organization, Drug Resistance Opportunity Program (DROP).

An avid equestrian and a lover of nature, Rae spent her last day doing what she loved, riding through the trails of Southern New Hampshire with her boyfriend, Regan Kane.

She is survived by her older brother, Bo Cavanaugh.

In lieu of flowers, the family asks that donations be made to DROP in Rae's name.

I was speechless. I had no one to talk to at that moment, anyway, but my mouth hung open.

"Everyone's got an R-rated version of their pain, Georgia."

If that obituary was the preview, my guess was whatever was inside that envelope was the main attraction.

CHAPTER *Nine*

EAT ME

Regan

BLUEBERRIES…

What?

I peeled my eyes open, disoriented by my surroundings, and the smell. I checked my phone, noting it couldn't have been very late, given it looked like sunrise outside. And, I was right. It was seven in the morning, and I was in Georgia's apartment.

That's all the information I had. There wasn't even a sliver of memory in my head as to what I'd done, or drank, last night in order to end up in this position. Shoes off, clothes on, and in Georgia's apartment.

With a *killer* headache.

I groaned as I sat up, the back of my neck meeting the base of my skull with a sledgehammer. I still smelled blueberries, though, and Georgia's kitchen was empty. It made my stomach growl.

I stood even slower than I'd sat up, and shuffled over to Georgia's bedroom door. Knocking once, the door swung open slightly, but no noise came from the other side.

"Georgia?" My voice sounded like sandpaper felt. Hell, it felt like sandpaper felt.

I peered through the crack and found her bed made and empty. Feeling for my keys, I panicked at their absence from my pockets.

I'd assumed when I woke up that I hadn't driven home, but I wasn't looking forward to a key search either.

Walking back to the couch, I noticed the smell of blueberries got stronger as I got closer to the door. I opened the apartment door and was swaddled with the smell of brown sugar, vanilla and the suspect blueberries. I pressed my nose forward like a bloodhound and followed the trail of baked comfort down the stairs. Though I hadn't walked those stairs in all the time I'd lived there, they seemed familiar.

Flashes of last night came through in fuzzy form. Leaning against the railing. Knocking on the door. When I reached the bottom of the stairs I looked right, to the door I seemed to remember knocking on. I whipped around, but the pounding in my head reminded me to take things slowly.

There was another door, one I was *certain* I'd never been through, and the smell was coming from behind it. I slowly turned the knob, half-surprised to find it open. Georgia had told me that she only operated the bakery for special orders. Given it was Sunday morning, I figured maybe she had some brunch order someone was picking up, though she hasn't had anything else to my knowledge in the two weeks I'd lived here.

The door opened into a perfectly polished stainless steel kitchen, which, in turn, was largely open to a seating area that had all kinds of crazy colors and designs. I couldn't focus on any of them though, because through the large picture window at the front of the store, I saw Georgia.

She was standing on the rock wall across the street that was the only thing separating our apartment building from the ocean. Her face was tilted up, and her hands were down by her side with her palms facing forward, fingers spread out purposefully. I watched her shoulders rise and fall underneath a deep breath.

And then, she jumped.

"Shit!" Any thoughts of mulling around in my hangover were trashed as I pushed through the swinging door into the cafe and pulled the door leading outside so hard I thought I dislocated my elbow.

"Georgia!"

Without looking for cars, I took two strides to cross the street and gripped the edge of the wall, leaning forward, looking down, not considering what awful thing I might find.

It was a playground.

A fucking playground.

Over the wall, there was a four or five foot drop, then a sloping sand and grass hill that led to a small play structure in the sand right on the edge of where high tide comes in.

Having apparently heard me scream her name, Georgia stood a few feet from the swing set, looking up at me, shielding the sun from her eyes. I hung my head, trying to catch my breath and not throw up.

"Good morning, whiskey. Awfully early for you, isn't it?" She shouted over the wind and waves, and I hopped the wall and walked down to meet her.

"I smelled the muffins, or coffee cake, or whatever you're making in that bakery you say you never use."

She smiled, walking over to the swing. "Muffins. And I told you—I work for large orders and stuff."

"Do you have a large order today?"

"Yeah," she chuckled, "your hangover."

Georgia gripped the chains of the swing, walked it forward, pressing the seat against her belly, stuck her arms out, and let go of her arms and legs at the same time. I watched her for a few seconds, swinging on her belly, eyes closed.

"W...what are you doing?"

She opened her eyes, but kept looking toward the water. "See, when I was in elementary school, I heard all my friends giggling about how they were flying when they were swinging. I'd been afraid to use the swings before that. But flying sounded fun. So, I sat on the swing and was...underwhelmed. No animal on Earth flies in a seated position. So, I started going like this. This...this is flying."

"If you don't mind," I walked around and sat on the swing, like a normal person, "I'll sit like this."

"I don't concern myself with the flight of others, Regan." Her eyes were closed again, and I felt awkward. Uncomfortable, as if I'd intruded on some ritual.

"Before you jumped down, you were standing with your hands out...what was that about?"

She smirked, a hint of teeth showing on her right side. "Spying on me?"

"No, I—"

"Relax. I was stressed. I figured if headstands could help clear *Ember's* mind, maybe a little yoga could clear mine."

I pulled the elastic from my hair and retied my hair back into less of a mess. "So, what pose was that?"

"Fuck if I know. I was just trying it out."

"You know, Ember might be willing to show—"

"Take it easy. I don't even know if I like her."

"You might. You were right about Willow, by the way." I pumped my legs a little, thinking better of it after one stomach-dropping swing reminded me my stomach belonged to Jack Daniels this morning. "Apparently she tried to hook up with Bo."

"Told you."

"You did."

"Did he do it?"

I laughed a little too loud for my liking.

"What?" she asked, pushing herself higher.

"No. He didn't. He loves Ember. I haven't asked Ember about it, but that was part of why she was so pissed off a couple of weeks ago." I didn't normally gossip, if that's even what Georgia and I were doing, but it just kind of seemed natural.

Georgia sighed with a little groan tailing close behind.

"What?" I let my legs dangle as momentum carried me back and forth a few more times.

"Had I known *Willow Shaw* was involved in Ember's attitude, I might have cut Ember some slack."

I shrugged. "She didn't really cut you any." I thought briefly to Ember's assumptions of Georgia, and CJ's defensiveness.

"I don't really give people a reason to think otherwise, Regan. It's just...it is what it is." She shook her head and opened her eyes toward the sand.

More awkward silence.

"So," I started after what felt like two very long minutes, "those muffins are for me?"

She turned and looked at me, squinting a little as the sun was behind me. "Yeah, I figured you'd need them to settle the assault on your stomach last night."

"Oh God," I winced, "did I throw up?"

"No," she laughed, "but you drank more than I've seen you drink since I've known you."

"I really have no memory of last night after saying hi to y—" I dug my heels into the sand as more unfortunate flashes from last night flickered through my brain. The envelope from David Bryson. The card from Rae. I looked to Georgia, who appeared to be studying my internal playback.

"Don't worry, I have it."

I covered my mouth, certain I really would throw up. "Did I open it?"

I would have remembered reading something from Rae, right?

Georgia raked her fingers through the cold sand, bringing herself to a stop before adjusting to a seated position on the swing. "No, you didn't. In fact, you were going to leave it on the bar, but I put it in my bag."

"Thank you." Leaning forward, I took one deep breath and slowly stood.

"Come into the bakery with me," Georgia said, leaping from her seat. "The muffins will be done in two minutes."

"K."

I couldn't form thoughts. Still thoroughly hung over, with no recollection of last night, and no dreams to remember, I was left with the knowledge that somewhere in that building sat Rae's last words to me. I assumed they were words, though I hadn't opened the card, and wasn't sure I had any intention of doing such a thing.

Halfway up a set of stairs I hadn't seen on my way down, Georgia stopped and waited for me to catch up to her.

When she lifted her face, her eyes were misted over and her cheeks were pink. "I'm...I'm sorry about Rae." She extended her hand toward mine and gave it a small squeeze before letting go and resuming her hike up the crumbly stone steps.

Once at the top, while we waited for a few cars to pass, I asked, "What did I say about her?" My voice shook, and I knew it was less from dehydration of my body and more from the drought in my soul.

We crossed the street, and Georgia held open the door for me. "You told me she was Bo's sister."

"That's all?"

Georgia smacked her lips together. "Yep. That's it."

"Then how did you...why did you..."

"I Googled her. Her obituary was the first link I clicked."

"Oh..." I wanted to know what she read, what she was thinking, all of it.

But, when I stepped into the bakery I'd fled a half hour ago when I thought Georgia was leaping into nothingness, I was knocked over by everything I'd missed in my haste.

I was thrust into a whimsical space that left me turning in a few circles, wondering how I'd missed it all in the first place. The walls were a pale blue, and booths lined with black and white diamond pattered fabric lined two adjoining walls. Above each of the six tables were chandeliers. Well, chandeliers in the sense that they were lights hanging down from the ceiling. The main light source came from what looked to be a small teapot, surrounded by four teacups that had smaller lights shining out of the bottom of their attached saucers.

A large clock was hung on the main wall, but it was wrong. The numbers were in the wrong place and the hands of the clock were squiggly, not straight. The wall immediately to my left held what looked like a candy bar. Bright colored teacups that looked as if they were about to topple over held glass jars that were filled with candy and sprinkles and chocolate. Above that was a large painting of a playing card. The Queen of Hearts.

"The Mad Hatter," I whispered as I walked forward, toward the display case, which was a scene all its own.

"What?" The door closed behind Georgia, and she locked it shut.

"It all makes sense, now," I said as I stood in front of the non-sensical desserts.

"I doubt it. But, what are you talking about?"

"*Alice in Wonderland.*" I turned on my heels, holding out my hands.

Georgia lifted her chin a fraction of an inch, a smile starting in her eyes, but traveling no further. "How does that make sense of anything?"

"The rocking horse fly!" I shouted as recognition overtook my brain.

She jumped, and shouted back, startled, "What about it?"

I clapped my hands together once. "The tattoo."

"Which one?"

"The rocking horse fly, Georgia." I reached my hand out and spun her around, placing my finger on the spot under her shirt that held the tattoo.

"Okay, okay, calm down." She rolled her eyes, taking a step back. "Come with me into the kitchen before your head explodes."

"Jesus, G, this place is fantastic. Why isn't it open, like, all the time?" My eyes followed her all the way to the large stainless steel oven and watched her bend slowly over, pulling out a pan of muffins before closing the door.

"I told you. No time."

"This looks new, though. Why would you open a place you had no time to run?" I hadn't considered the personal nature of my questioning until I watched her face fall.

"Sometimes our intentions are roadblocked by life, Regan."

"So was *Alice in Wonderland* your favorite movie as a kid?" Since I kept screwing up socially with Georgia, I'd gotten better at changing the subject.

She set the muffin tin down on the stainless steel counter. She curled her hands around the edge of the countertop and sighed. "Still is. The books are incredible, too."

"Books? Plural?"

"You know, *Alice's Adventures in Wonderland*, and *Through the Looking Glass*."

Without much thought, I reached across the space and grabbed her hand, determined to examine one of the mystery tattoos I'd noticed during our first meeting. On the inside of her finger, *Who are you?* was scrawled in cursive black ink.

"Who are you? The caterpillar." I locked eyes with her and she smiled.

"Look at all of those adorable little light bulbs just bursting away over your head." She pulled her hand away from me and used it to mess up my hair more than the ocean wind already had. "Go. Wash your hands and you can help me with the next batch."

Over at the sink, I turned my head and looked over to the seating area. As people walked by, they stopped, looked in, smiled at their friends and pointed at things, and some even pulled on the door before walking away with an unsatisfied stomach.

"Do people always try to get in here?" I nodded toward the door as more people passed, a wounded look across their faces.

"Sometimes. The sign says *Open by chance,* so they don't usually get too disappointed."

Sure enough, just as she said that, I saw the rectangle sign hanging from the door, a large Cheshire-like smile stamped where the period should be.

"Wow, you've really committed to the theme, haven't you?" I dried my hands and walked back to the prep area.

Georgia set butter, eggs, and sugar onto the table. "If you're going to do something, you've got to do it right. Completely."

"I guess you're right. So, where's the flour? I can sift that."

She looked up in a flash, mouth opening slightly. "You bake?"

"Probably not well, but I know that my mom always sifted things. I wanted to sound smart," I admitted.

Georgia smiled and squatted down, coming up three times, placing a different container in front of me each time.

"This is..." I shook my head, my kitchen prowess fleeing by the second.

"Flour. Sorghum, tapioca, and white rice." She tied an apron around her waist and tossed one to me.

"I...um..."

"This is a gluten-free bakery. I don't use wheat flour at all. So, listen carefully, or you'll fuck it all up..."

Georgia

Keeping his mind off of that letter was working, even if it was at the risk of opening myself up more than I wanted to. More than I needed to.

The look on his face last night, and then again on the swings, was too painful to swallow. If he wanted to talk about my bakery and his reasoning for why the theme was what it was, I'd allow it.

"I'm listening." He didn't make funny faces or weird noises when I uttered the phrase "gluten-free," so we were seemingly off to a good start.

"How much do I use?" He tied his apron around his narrow tattoo-free waist and waited for instruction.

I placed the sifter and a large stainless bowl in front of him. "A cup of each, then add in a half teaspoon of baking soda and a half teaspoon of salt."

"Salt?" His lip curled up in question.

"You have to put salt in baked goods, or you won't taste it."

"But that's such a small amount for all of that flour." His eyebrows pulled in as if we were in a chem-lab. We were, sort of.

"Trust me. Add the flour and baking soda. Then I'll scoop out a few tablespoons and we'll make one muffin without the salt. After they're done, I'll show you the difference."

I take my salt seriously.

"Okay." He shrugged and started carefully measuring the flour, dispensing it into the bowl with equal caution.

I moved to the large stand mixer in the corner of the kitchen and began creaming the butter and sugar, adding the eggs one at a time.

"What's the name?" Regan asked.

"Of?"

"The bakery. There's no sign out front."

"Oh...there isn't one. I couldn't decide." I cleared my throat at the questioning of an interloper in my sanctuary.

One I'd invited in, but that doesn't always matter when your soul is inches away from total exposure.

"What about *Mad Hatter's*, or something?"

"Too obvious."

"Yeah. This is all sifted. Do you have coffee? I swear I smell coffee." The adrenaline rush of the ocean and the decor of the bakery seemed to be waning in his voice.

I pointed to a ledge behind him. "Right there. Cream and milk are in the fridge, sugar is over there."

"I think I need black today."

I chuckled. "I get it. I have days like that, too."

Most days, really.

"How long have you been baking?" Regan yawned as he brought the bowl over to where I was. He leaned against the counter and loudly slurped his coffee.

I began the process of adding the dry ingredients to the bowl, scooping in yogurt between additions.

"Forever, it feels like. My grandmother was always in our kitchen, especially on Sundays, and she'd make sweet breads, brownies, cookies, muffins, sandwich bread. All by hand. After church I'd spend all day planted on a stool next to our island."

"Church?" Regan tilted his head to the side. Interrogation was exhausting.

I nodded. "Yeah, you know, church. Sunday. Jesus. Crown of thorns and all that?" I drew an imaginary circle around my head with my index finger.

"I get it..."

"Anyway, baking has always been a meditative and especially rewarding escape." Once the ingredients were all combined, I went to the deep freezer to pull out a bag of blueberries I'd picked and frozen over the summer. "Like music for you, I guess."

Regan sighed. "Yeah. I don't know what I would have done most of my life without it."

"Did it start as an escape for you?"

His lips twisted. "What four-year-old needs to escape something?"

You have no idea.

"You know what I mean," I huffed, hoping he hadn't read too much into my question.

He didn't seem to. "At first I was really proud. Excited. I got a lot of attention because the violin came so easily to me. I worked hard because I wanted to be better. To get more attention."

Using an escape to get attention was foreign to me on every level possible. But, he'd just said he hadn't started out on the violin to escape.

"After a while," he continued, "it became a self-fulfilling escape, if that makes sense. All of the praise I'd received and all of the pride I had in myself grew to pressure in no time."

I pulled out a fresh muffin tin, handed Regan a small ice cream scoop, and took one for myself. I scooped some of the batter up, clicked the handle to pour it in the tin, and looked at him. "Like this. So, pressure?"

He mimicked my movements, studying my hands carefully before confidently filling wells on his own.

"Yes," he sighed, "I can't blame my parents. The pressure I put on myself they reciprocated, and vice versa. I think they saw how hard I was working and they wanted to support that, but it was hard to do that without pushing me a little harder than I was already pushing myself. It's hard to know where the pressure started. I think it's inherent, honestly."

"In you?"

"In anything anyone craves. You want it to be perfect. No matter what it is. It just has to be...the best. If it's not, what the hell's the point? There. Done." Regan stood back with a victorious grin on his face.

I took the tin and slid it into the oven. "Well, in half an hour, we'll find out if there's a point to all of this."

Turning around, I found Regan with an entire muffin in his mouth. One I'd taken out earlier.

"Oh," he talked with a full mouth, "there's definitely a point. These are delicious! Can I have another one?"

"Sure." I grabbed my travel mug, filled it with coffee, and turned back around. "Grab a few and follow me back outside."

Once we were outside, I locked the door and led Regan back across the street.

"I'm not jumping." He sat on the rock wall and swung his legs over the edge.

"Ha. Ha. It's not like I leapt to my death, or something. Dial it down a little."

We sat in silence for a few minutes, eating the muffins and sipping — or in his case, slurping — the coffee.

"These are gluten-free, too?" he asked after eating his third muffin.

"I told you, the whole bakery is." I snatched a muffin before he ate them all.

"Why? Do you have celiac or something?"

"You know about that? I'm impressed."

"I pay attention to news and shit." He nudged his shoulder into mine as he laughed.

The more time I spent with him, the more my assumptions of him were stripped away. Is that how it worked? Would it work the same with me? I couldn't decide right then if I wanted him to have his assumptions of me dismantled. Whatever they were.

"I don't have celiac, but I know people who do. And, frankly, you just don't *need* wheat for a number of reasons I don't want to get into at eight o'clock on a weekend morning."

Regan shrugged and continued slurping his coffee. Seriously, what was with that?

"Do you always drink your coffee like that?" I asked, clicking my tongue in irritation.

"Like what? With my mouth? Swallowing?"

I brought my cup to my lips and mimicked the slurping sound.

"That was a bit dramatic," he scoffed.

"You're right…it was." I raised my eyebrow at him and he lightly smacked my shoulder with the back of his hand.

"All right, all right. Sorry. I have no idea why I do that."

"Has *no one* said anything about it to you before? It's really quite offensive." I laughed, setting my mug on the wall.

Regan went silent for a minute. When I looked over at him, he was staring at his hands. *You've got to be kidding me.*

I cleared my throat. "Rae?"

He nodded. "It's okay."

"Doesn't look like it."

"Well, she died…" He winced through that whole sentence, nearly closing his eyes by the end of it.

I sighed, my window of distraction officially slamming shut. "Tell me."

"We were out on a trail ride," he started.

"No," I cut in, "I don't need to know about that. Tell me about *her*."

I knew how hard it could be to talk about how people used to be, but for me, it provided a sense of comfort that the memories existed at all. I'd take the bad if I got to have all of the good that came before it.

I think.

"I don't know if I can…"

In the span of my drift off into my thought process, I'd missed that Regan had taken down his hair and tucked it behind his ears, snapping the elastic around his wrist repeatedly.

"Just...just tell me your favorite thing about her." I leaned my shoulder into his and left it there. His muscles were tense. Hesitant.

He laughed sort of silently. "She came out of nowhere. Tiny, bossy, and full of certainties."

"Certainties?" I tucked my knees into my chest.

"Yeah, she was filled with this stone-solid conviction. When she was passionate about something, she wouldn't let go. It wasn't in-your-face...it was...this quiet resolve. She was ferocious. She'd been through more than you and I both before I'd even met her."

I doubted that, but let him continue with his story.

"I've been in love before, but with her..."

"You've been in love before?" I pulled my head back and scrunched my forehead.

He smiled. "Oh, of course. Love is great. Swept off your feet, and all of that? I love it. The first time I was in love was with Kylee Graham in seventh grade. She always wore flowery dresses, and I was certain I'd marry her."

I bit my lip as I smiled. A thirteen-year-old Regan Kane, in love and making plans to marry. His cousin would consider such thoughts treasonous to the brotherhood of men.

"Anyway," he sighed wistful thoughts of Kylee into the sea air, "Rae was the first time I felt *grown up* love."

"What's the difference?"

He looked up and then closed his eyes. "It rewired my insides."

A hole the shape of my mother's smile seared through me and choked the air away from my throat. I let out an exhale as though

I'd been punched in the gut. Because I had, by his words alone. I was left struggling for the comfortable air of my cynicism.

"I know. Intense, right?" He smiled and took a silent sip of his coffee.

"Keep slurping it," I blurted out.

I needed him to be real, still. Flawed in the volume of his drinking. Loud enough to override the palpable rawness of his allegiance to the doctrine of love.

"When I was in high school I pictured a future with a few girls. With Rae, I felt it here." He patted his stomach, leaving his fingers to bunch around the fabric of his shirt.

"How long were you together, again?" I couldn't remember if he'd told me, but I was losing traction on reality.

"Barely two months."

"Wow."

"Mmmhmm." He ran a hand through his hair.

"Did she feel the same way?" I knew I was trudging into mucky personal territory, but come on, we were talking about his dead ex-girlfriend as it was.

He shrugged. "I don't know. I never told her."

"*What?*" My shock offended two nearby seagulls, who flew away in a tizzy.

"What?" Regan cleared his throat, looking concerned at my sudden trip into intensity.

"All of that talk about being in love before you even knew what to do with yourself and you never *told* her?"

The pained look in his eyes signaled I'd done it. I'd pushed too far.

"Well...I didn't exactly get the chance to, Georgia. I felt it so deeply that I was afraid if I told her that soon then I'd push her away. Then—"

"I know."

Regan reached his hand across my lap, grasping my knee. "Let me talk about it."

"Okay," I whispered.

"Then...she died. She. Didn't. Make it. Jesus." He sniffed and inconspicuously wiped under his eye. "Words have never hit me like that before. I'd been shot, I was sure of it. Every time I took a breath it felt like the air was leaving my chest through a hole before it ever got to my lungs."

It was time for me to regain some emotional control over this conversation. We'd passed my comfort level at the intersection of love and certainty.

"Was there an exit wound?"

He turned to me with a perfectly quizzical look on his face. "Huh?"

"An exit would. From feeling like you were shot. Did the bullet leave your body, or do we need to go fishing for it?"

"I..." Regan shook his head slowly, looking between me and the ocean with his bottomless eyes.

"Sew yourself up if it's gone, Regan. That's the only way you'll move on. If you want to move on. Come on...the muffins are done." I stood, brushing crumbled gravel from my jeans, and walked back toward the bakery.

CHAPTER *Ten*

CURIOUSER AND CURIOUSER

Georgia

"AND THAT WAS it? That's all you said to him? And all he said to you?" Lissa shook a martini like her life depended on it as we navigated an annoyingly busy Friday night.

I shrugged. "Yep. That was it. Then he went back to his apartment and I haven't really seen him since."

"Did he take the card?"

"No."

"Do you still have it?" She slid the martini to her customer in an uncharacteristically impersonal manner, more interested in the mild excitement she judged in my life.

"Of course I have it. What the hell would I do? Throw it away?"

It had been an awkward week in La Jolla. Regan hadn't spoken a word to me since he left the bakery on Sunday. Well, actually, after our chat on the wall before the second batch of muffins was done, he never came back into the bakery. He got up, looked me up and down with a disturbingly unreadable expression on his face, and went back into his apartment.

Saying he hadn't talked to me was slightly dramatic, given I hadn't actually seen him. But I heard him. He'd taken to practicing his violin in the wee hours of the morning. On nights I came straight home after work, I could hear him. It sounded like the notes were crying. Given our conversation on the swing set, it was hard to tell if he was escaping from something or putting pressure on himself.

I determined I wouldn't push him about the card from Rae. He knew I had it, and that was that. I've found that if you push people, they have an uncanny tendency to push back.

Lissa slid by me, lightly smacking my butt. "You've got skills, sister."

"Skills?"

She chuckled. "You spent all that time with him inside the bakery and you managed to avoid all discussion about it, its theme, or your mother whatsoever."

I roughly set a rack of glasses at the edge of the bar. "It's not just him. I don't talk about my mom. To anyone."

"Why?" She put her hands on her hips, as though we hadn't had this conversation every few weeks for the duration of our friendship.

"You know why. No one gets close enough."

"You don't let them."

I growled under my breath. "Liss. You know why."

Visibly frustrated, Lissa grabbed my arm and pulled me into the small entryway to the kitchen. "You can't use circular reasoning, G. You keep people away because of your mom, and you don't tell people about her because no one is close. Then, this amazingly nice and clean-cut guy comes in here, is clearly interested in you, and you still insist on pushing him away."

"Who? Regan? You saw how he nearly drank his face off over his dead girlfriend the other night. I'd hardly call that a place of moving on." Crossing my arms, I leaned back against the greasy wall.

"Whatever. I haven't heard him mention her once. If he's opening up to you, he trusts you. And that look he gets around you? The one where his pupils double in size?"

"How the hell can you tell what his pupils do in this light?" I challenged.

"Because," she smirked, "I can't stop looking at them."

I rolled mine. "Lissa, I don't even know what the point of this conversation is anymore."

"Georgia," her voice lowered to a purr, "the first night he was in here with the band, I saw the looks you two were giving each other. I chalked it up to fresh meat, something new."

"Romantic," I murmured.

"Shut up. But, that night he played with just CJ on stage, when Willow Shaw came in after? You should have seen yourself. You let go, G. All the way."

"It was music. What's your point?" I looked up at her as my cheeks heated.

She took two fingers and ran them across the apple of my cheek. "It was his music. And, for Christ's sake, you told me he tried to kiss you."

I thought back to the night that he and CJ dominated E's for an hour. And I forgot about my life for fifty-eight minutes of that time.

"It was a fluke. And he didn't really try. It was just that tense, vibrating sort of pre-kiss moment." I cleared my throat, ignoring my lips' desperation to have his on them.

"A pre-kiss moment you bailed on."

My shoulders sank as I pressed my head back into the wall. "I'll just hurt him. It's inevitable."

Lissa grabbed my shoulders. "No, Georgia, it's not."

"Genetics are pretty cut and dry, Liss."

She sighed, keeping her eyes closed as she swallowed hard. "You know that's not one hundred percent."

"Whatever. I'm not going to pursue something with someone who isn't even sure how long he's going to be here, who has a dead girlfriend that's sending him mail, only to inform him he'll lose me when the white rabbit drops his pocket watch down the hole in my brain and I go in after it."

"You and that goddamn fairytale..." she trailed off in a whisper.

"It's no fucking fairytale, Lissa. It's just the sordid story of a lonely girl. And there's no prince."

Lissa dropped her arms from my body and stood back, knowing this was where the conversation ended. It's where it always ended. She had nothing to say. No charts to disprove the course I was on. No scissors to cut the strings that were tied around my wrists generations ago.

Just a lonely girl.

And no prince.

I remained quiet for the rest of my shift. Head down when behind the bar, smile up when dealing with customers. Lissa didn't try to smooth over our earlier conversation. Not that she had any apologizing to do, but she knew well enough to leave me alone for the rest of the evening.

When I got into my car, and onto the highway, I had about fifteen minutes to make a decision on which exit to take. Home, to my quiet and comfortable bed, or another twenty minutes north to anywhere but comfort. After a few minutes of indecision, I realized I couldn't bail on her for the third night.

The staff at Breezy Pointe was beyond accommodating to our situation, and I felt bad when I didn't use it as set up. Visiting hours were pretty strict and did not encompass three in the morning. But, given I'd be an orphan when she decided she couldn't take it anymore, they'd always let me work on a schedule with them. Okay, maybe I wasn't a minor anymore, as I was when I first came out here and started my twilight visits a few times a year, so orphan wasn't a technical term.

Especially since half of the time I already felt like one.

There was a woman at the front desk I'd only seen a few times before, so it took me a few extra minutes to get back to my mother's unit. As usual, Daniel was waiting to check me in and put my belongings behind the nurses' station.

"She's gonna be pissed," he mumbled with a slight snicker.

"Did you just curse?" I gasped and dramatically put my hand to my chest.

He shook his head as we approached her door. "You just can't take no for an answer, can you?"

Actually, I could. I'd heard that word for most of my life. No, things can't be normal. No, you and Daddy can't come with me to California. No, I can't promise you this won't happen to you, too. Still, for Daniel, I laughed at his attempt at camaraderie.

"I told you not to come here," my mother's voice, graciously playful with a hint of discipline, rang from the other side of the door before I even entered.

"Mama," I sighed, "you're awake, so am I—what's the big deal."

"The big deal, young lady, is you don't have a life."

Amanda Hall seemed back to her old self, whatever that meant, and had been getting there over the course of the last several days. She sat on the edge of the bed. No wheelchair, a real smile, and making eye contact with me.

Daniel dutifully stood in the doorway as I walked over to the bed and took a seat next to my mother, laying my head on her shoulder. "You're my life, Mom."

"No, Georgia. You're mine. I demand you go get one." She nudged my shoulder. "Plus, I'm leaving here as soon as the administrative cats crawl into the office in a few hours."

Out of habit, when she said something I hadn't heard from her doctor first, my eyes flashed to Daniel, who refused, it seemed, to look at me.

"You don't have to check with him, Georgia." My mother caught me staring. "I checked myself in. I'm checking myself out."

"No...I know that. It's just..."

"You're scared that if I leave now, I'll be back here in a few days, like I was last time."

I nodded, peering up at her as if I were a small child again, and we were in my room for a bedtime story. Those usually had happy endings, though. "Last time you were only out for two weeks, Mom."

"And it was several months before that." She gave a firm nod, as if to signal the end of the discussion.

Only, it wasn't. There was no end in sight to these discussions.

"Susan—"

She cut me off at the mention of her sister's name. "I have a condo. I don't need to stay with Susan, and I will not be staying with you. Also, I need to talk to you about a decision I've come to."

Her words didn't make me nervous, but Daniel taking a purposeful step toward me did. I looked at him for a few seconds, trying to determine the risk I was about to take simply by listening to her. His face was set like stone, though.

"Georgia," my mother confidently brought my attention back to her, "I've decided to go forward with the ECT."

"What?" I shouted, causing Daniel to take another step forward. My mother didn't flinch. "No. Absolutely not."

"Darling," she put her hand on my leg, "that's not a decision you get to make."

I stood. "Oh, so now it's not a decision I get to make, but you drilled into me for, like, five years that when it was my decision to make, it was to be a hard no every time? What the hell? What's going on?"

I knew my ability to make medical decisions for my mother was only covered insofar as she was incapacitated. Once she left the confines of the hospital, she could do whatever she wanted. Including zapping the hell out of her brain.

"It's my best chance against staying out of here for the long term. The medication and the talk therapy can only carry me so far, honey."

"But, you—"

"I know what I've said in the past. Things have changed. I'm getting worse."

"So you want to fry your brain to get better?" I stood, the vomit working its way up my insides, needing more room to settle, or else it was going to be all over my mom's room.

She sighed. "Georgia, you know that's not how the therapy works."

"No, Mom, I don't. You spent several years making damn sure that I knew the exact and horrific reasons you didn't want that therapy. Now you're asking me to forget it?"

"I'm asking you to think of the times where it works. This is the last solid option I've got. Come on, Alice, take a deep br—"

"Stop!" I cut her off with a garbled yell, prompting Daniel to put his hand on my back. "Don't start with that bullshit now. You can't calm me down by making me pretend, Mom. I'm not eight, and that was just a fucking story."

Of a lonely girl. With no prince.

My mother's face fell; her lifetime tactic with me no longer effective. She looked at Daniel, then at me, then got up and walked to the window, saying no more.

"Please get my things." I looked at Daniel's shoes as I spoke. Once they moved toward the door, so did I.

"Georgia, I want to encourage you to stay. Don't leave like this." Daniel's movements were slow as he gathered my bag from behind the nurses' desk.

Tears welled in my eyes and threatened to burst at any moment. Now wasn't the time for discussion. I sniffed as I snatched my bag from his hands.

"Sorry," I sniffed again, tears fleeing the pressure of my head, "I can't. It's just...I can't."

Once in my car, I let myself cry for exactly ten seconds before cranking the engine and getting the hell out of there. I'd been so tired when I got there, having lived off of three, or so, hours of sleep a night for the last several days. But, now I was drained and vibrating with angry energy all at once. Worst of all, it was three-thirty in the morning and there was nowhere for me to go, except home. To my empty apartment.

To fill the deafening silence of my car for the next twenty minutes, I picked up my cell phone. It was still drinking time on the East Coast.

"Hello? G? Everything okay?" CJ was in a bar, that much was clear based on his needing to shout over the noise around him just to hear himself. No matter that I could hear him just fine.

The panic in his voice was certainly justified. I would never normally call during hook-up-o'clock. But, I had no one else to talk to who got it.

"I...sorry to interrupt your night." I kept my voice quiet so he couldn't hear the trembling behind it.

"Give me a second to get outside. There," he said after a few seconds of human static, "now I can hear you."

"For God's sake, CJ, it's February. Get your ass back inside before you freeze!"

"I'm sober enough to listen now, G, and drunk enough not to care about the blizzard."

Sadly enough, I understood him completely. Still, I vowed to make it quick.

"I...she wants to do the shock therapy!" I didn't mean to shout, but when you're trying to speak through years of frustrated tears, yelling is the only way to hear your voice.

"Are you driving? G?" CJ was so loud, so intense; it was like he was next to me.

I nodded, because that's what rational people do during a phone call, and then said, "Yes, I just left the hospital. She's fine. She's checking herself out tomorrow and informed me she wants the ECT."

"Pull over."

"What?"

"Pull the fuck over and talk to me. I'm getting in my car."

"You're too drunk to drive!" My heart raced, wondering what the hell he was thinking.

"I'm not too drunk to operate the heater. Just pull over, G, and talk to me. Tell me what happened."

A few seconds later, I pulled over into the safe confines of a scenic overlook. I stayed in the car, though, because between the ocean breeze and the highway noise, I'd never be able to hear him.

"K. I'm off the road."

"Can you start over?" Whatever alcohol accent he'd had when he answered the phone was gone.

I caught CJ up on everything with my mom right through my storming out of the facility like a pissed off teenager.

"Sounds like she's going to do the ECT, then, right? You can't stop her, can you?"

Tears streamed down my cheeks as I stared, unblinking, into the light traffic passing by me. "No, I can't stop her."

"Do you think she's really going to go through with it?"

"I don't know. She didn't flinch at my reaction. Wasn't affected by my emotions."

"It does work for a lot of people, though, doesn't it?" CJ's words were softer and further apart as he asked.

"I guess! But, I was indoctrinated to believe otherwise. By her. Now she's asking me to rearrange my ingrained belief system. Not just for some random patient. For her!" I slammed my hand against the steering wheel.

"Stop punching your steering wheel."

I gasped. "Did you hear that?"

"No, but I've sat with you in your car a time or two when you've been pissed. If you're not driving, then the dashboard gets the brunt of it. I'm sorry I'm not there, G. I have no idea what to say. What does Regan have to say?"

His question confused me, causing me to look around. "About what?"

"Your mom."

"He doesn't know." My stomach dropped. "You haven't told him anything, have you?"

"No. Calm down. I told you I wouldn't tell. I just figured since you guys lived together, basically, he'd know by now."

"What has he said about me?" The question sounded juvenile, but I was still trying to get a sense for how he viewed me. Rae Cavanaugh aside, I could never get a clear read on him. He was reserved, each layer I peeled off—intentionally or unintentionally—only served to create more questions than answers.

"We haven't talked much. A text here and there. And, we've never talked about girls."

"Ah, yes," I laughed, "must be the different philosophies you operate under."

CJ scoffed. "And what the hell does that mean?"

I sighed, thankful for the shift in our conversation. "Oh, you know, he believes in love, and you were a signer of the declaration of one night stands."

He laughed, and I could almost see him throwing his head back. It made me smile. "Oh, G, how glad I am you're not here to mess up my game tonight."

"I kind of am, since you're not in pledging your allegiance to miniskirts right now and you're stuck in your car."

"So..." CJ hesitated for a moment. "He told you about Rae?"

"Yeah, a little heads up would have been nice before that letter showed up on his doorstep." I lifted off my seat to check my mascara train wreck in the rearview mirror.

"What letter?"

"Huh?" My heart actually skipped a beat.

"You said before that letter showed up on his doorstep. What the hell are you talking about?"

Son of a bitch.

I responded by not responding.

"G..."

"Please don't say anything to him, okay? Shit, I figured he would have told you. I'm sorry!"

"You know I'm not going to say anything, but, what letter?"

I groaned. "There was this envelope addressed from New Hampshire. It had a letter in it that I didn't read, but also it had a card addressed to Regan, unopened, sent from Rae Cavanaugh."

"Shiiiiiiit."

I'd bet anyone a hundred dollars that CJ's head was on his steering wheel.

"What did it say?"

"I don't know. He was going to leave it at the bar. He got shitfaced and walked away. I took it and put it in my backpack."

"Has he read it?"

"No."

"How do you know?"

"Because I still have it."

"He hasn't asked for it?"

"No."

CJ sighed. "Christ."

"Should I make him read it...or something?"

"God, I don't fucking know. But...if he does ask you for it, stick around while he reads it, okay? He went off the deep end in a flee-the-country kind of way when she died..." CJ trailed off, having expressed more concern over another human being besides myself than I'd ever witnessed.

"I promise."

"G?"

"Yeah?"

"Regan's a good shit. Tell him about your mom, okay? He's just...he's a good listener."

CJ hadn't ever suggested I tell anyone about anything. I started to protest. "Ceej—"

"Georgia, come on. It looks like your mom is going to do what she's going to do. You're going to need support. If Regan is trusting you with something from Rae, reciprocate it."

"Reciprocate? You okay?"

"Ha ha. Fuck off." His tone was playful, but a little flat. "Love you."

"Love you, too. Come back out here soon, k?"

"I'll try. Bye, babe."

"Bye."

I tossed my phone onto the passenger seat and eased my way back onto the highway. It was nearing four in the morning, and I was wired from all of the emotional electrocution. Sarcastic pun intended.

There was only one logical place for me to be at that hour, in this state, and Regan already knew about the bakery, so it was safe. As long as he stayed the hell out this time.

It wasn't that I couldn't tell Regan about my mom—that would be the easy part of the conversation. It was the ramifications of that that were strewn about my life that gave me pause.

Maybe it was his music, as Lissa suggested. Maybe it was the unfettered trust he'd shown me, and that I'd shown him earlier in blindly renting him my apartment. Whatever it was, I knew that I had to tell Regan something, so he knew why I wanted to kiss him.

And why I couldn't. Ever.

Regan

"That was perfect. Do it one more time." Willow clicked her mic off from the recording room.

I groaned internally. It was four in the morning and we had been in the studio since 9:00 PM due to some scheduling conflicts that presented recording problems. Last year I could have easily kept up a schedule like this, but Ember's parents and her friends had trained us to operate on a "normal" schedule, as they called it, and this all-nighter was bullshit.

"If it was perfect," Ember snapped, "why the hell are we doing it again?"

She chose not to groan internally.

"Ember," her mother, Raven, cautioned.

Ember sighed. Apparently she wasn't yet over Willow's attempt at seducing Bo. I didn't really know the details of it, and I hadn't mentioned to Bo or Ember that I knew about it, but it was clear that now wasn't the time to interject my opinion.

"Let's go, Em. We can do it one more time, even better than perfect." I elbowed her and smiled.

Bo mouthed a thank you to me as the rest of the Six let out a collective sigh of relief. The track we were cutting was one between just Bo, Ember, and myself. The band wanted to give us some space on the album, to highlight some of their new talent. Their words, not ours. I was grateful for the opportunity and didn't have any reservations about playing the song for the 900th time.

So, we played the song again. And, one more time.

I'd been drugging myself on rosin and Chopin for the last week. Drowning myself in my craft kept me deaf to the telltale heart thumping away somewhere in Georgia's apartment. A card. From Rae.

No, I couldn't do it. Not yet, or, maybe ever.

I was grateful to Georgia for hanging on to it. I assumed she still had it, but I honestly hadn't given much thought to if I cared what she did with it or not. As usual, I hadn't seen her much during the days following our talk in her bakery. I hadn't smelled anything signaling her use of the kitchen in a few days, and I'd long since finished the last of those delicious blueberry muffins. I wanted more.

Not even more of the muffins, though that was a sweet benefit. I wanted more Georgia. She didn't have a shred of innocence left in her eyes, and that made me trust her. I wasn't worried about harming her glittery view on the world, because it was clear she didn't have one. And hadn't for a long time.

Despite the whimsical appearance of her bakery, I sensed there was something dark underneath it...even if I hadn't been freaked out by the Cheshire cat eyes painted in stark green, above an equally jarring white smile, on the black crown molding in the cafe area. The desire to kiss her never really left me after the failed attempt weeks ago, even though I'd already apologized.

I didn't mean the apology. Because I'd wanted to kiss her in that moment. I shouldn't have taken the apartment, really, since I wanted to kiss her. That's a standard bad idea. But I just trusted her. And, she seemed to have exactly zero interest in me beyond friends. Really, I was fine with that. She had some heavy secrets that weighed down her smile, and even if she didn't want to tell me what they were, I had to be there for her. I'd promised CJ, if nothing else.

We finished our final cut of the song, and I played a couple more notes, lost in my swirling, exhausted thoughts.

Bo placed his hand on my shoulder, but all I heard was garbled noise.

I took my headphones off. "What?"

"I said, give it a rest, bud. We're done. Freed!" Though he looked exhausted, he managed a smile and a fist pump into the air.

"I'm sleeping from the minute we get home until the day after tomorrow." Ember yawned and lazily slung her backpack over her shoulder. "Let's go, Bo."

I cut off her attempt at hugging him. "Actually, can I take you home? I have some stuff I want to talk to you about."

Bo backed up in mock defense. "What? You can't talk to me?"

"This is..."

"Girl stuff?" he teased.

Ember smacked his stomach. "Shut up, ass."

Bo laughed and Ember did too, so things seemed okay there, I guess. Though navigating the complex knots of Bo and Ember's relationship wasn't something I had the time or training for.

After locking up the studio, Ember and I headed to my car. A few minutes into our drive, she yawned and looked at me. "I've missed seeing you every day."

"You mean you miss keeping an eye on me. Spying on my emotions," I teased.

"Regan, I couldn't spy on your emotions if you drew me a map." She knocked softly on my head. "Closed book."

I shrugged. "I'm not that closed off, I'm just not...Bo."

She chuckled and leaned her head back on the headrest. I'd intended to tell her about the card from Rae but was getting gun-shy.

"So...Willow..." I didn't have enough emotional attachment to the San Diego socialite to care that I was throwing her under the bus in my cowardliness.

"Argh! What about her?" Ember growled.

"Last week she told me about...you know."

Ember snapped her head back around, looking deadly at the side of my face. "No, I don't know. What'd she say?"

"She said you were all pissy at her because she put the moves on Bo."

"Is that all she said?"

Dear God, what did I just get myself into?

"Isn't that...all there is?"

Ember chuckled, but it wasn't the friendly kind. It was the kind that made you expect to see a crow on her shoulder, the way her eyebrow didn't arch, but pitched to a severe point. "I guess that's all there is."

"Okay..." I didn't believe her.

She continued, "Unless you count her telling me she thinks we're half sisters."

I swerved into the next lane, grateful that weekend traffic this early in the morning was nearly non-existent. "What?"

"Can you fucking believe her? Seriously! Always something to get attention."

"Did she...are you...do your parents—" Given my history with the emotions of Ember, she seemed to be handling this well. Maniacally, maybe, but well.

She reached her hand over and patted my leg. "Calm down. She's full of shit. No, I haven't said anything to my parents. Willow blurted it out one night when we were drinking when we first got here. She said we had to have the same dad."

"Had to?"

"She went on about how our families were always together growing up. Even when I pointed out that they were all fucking hippies who lived in co-ops together and shit our whole lives, she had to point out the vague similarities in our looks." Ember ran her hand through her hair and left it there, as if mentally comparing it to Willow's.

Vague was not the correct term to discuss the similarities between Ember and Willow's looks. Sure, Willow had darker skin, since her mom was black, but they had the same long wavy hair. Willow's was only slightly less auburn than Embers, but their eyes were identical. Not just the color—a striking jade that often had me staring at both of them for too long—but the same shape and same size. Slightly too big for their face by some standards, but breathtaking by anyone who could see clearly. It wasn't a far stretch to believe they were related, but I wasn't about to tell Ember that.

"What?" she cut into my thoughts. "You believe her?"

Shit.

"I...I don't have...any facts?" I shrugged, trying not to sound like a complete bastard. I knew that girlfriends were supposed to believe each other no matter what, but I wasn't her girlfriend. And, when I looked at Willow and Ember side by side, I saw two counter culture children who could very likely share DNA.

"Oh you know what, you and Bo can just go shove it, okay? There's no way that on top of everything else I went through in my childhood that my parents would have lied to me, too."

"Ember, your childhood wasn't anything to go through. Calm down. And, who's to say that even if it were true, which I'm not saying it is, that anyone knows about it?"

Ember rested her elbow on the tiny ledge next to the window. "Willow says she asked her parents about it when she was in college and stumbled across pictures of us as kids."

"That's bullshit."

"I know it is."

"So...why not ask your parents? I mean, seriously. Willow's one...interesting chick, but...why would she lie about this?" Ember glared at me, but I continued. "Think about it, Ember. She's got money, status, and plenty of family and friends. Why would she lie about this, but only tell you about it? If she wanted to make a thing about it, wouldn't she, like, I don't know, put it on Twitter, or something?"

Ember was silent for a few seconds, and when I looked over at her, I found her wiping under her eyes.

"Em, I'm sorry, I didn't mean to be pushy."

"No," she sniffed, "it's okay. This has just been really under my skin. I don't know if it's because I think it's true, or what...Bo thinks I should just talk to my parents and get it over with. I feel bad, though. I didn't mean to be so bitchy with Georgia, but this was just...taking up my brain space."

I pulled my eyebrows together. "This is why you were so... touchy a couple of weeks ago?"

"Yeah, why?"

Nope, not mentioning the pregnancy scare.

"Regan..." she prodded.

I shook my head and shrugged, trying for the standard non-committal response.

"What'd Bo tell you?"

Damn, she's good.

"He said you had a pregnancy scare, and not to mention it to you."

She threw her head back in full laughter. "That shit."

"It worked, didn't it? No one's asked you about your mood."

She yawned again. "God, I need to sleep. So, what did you want to talk to me about?"

It only took me a second to rethink the earlier decision I'd made to not mention Rae's mail to Ember. She was under enough stress, and I couldn't ask her to keep a secret from Bo. I wasn't ready to tell him, because I didn't know if I decided to read the letter if I'd want him to know what was in it.

"Nothing," I lied effortlessly. "I just wanted to sneak a few minutes of alone time with you. Good thing I did, or else I wouldn't have known what was going on with you. Talk to me, Ember. Any time, okay?"

I pulled into her driveway and put the car in park.

Ember leaned over and kissed my cheek. "I will. Promise. Don't say anything to anyone about this."

"You know I wouldn't."

"I know. See you the day after tomorrow. Hooray for a day off, huh?"

I agreed. The schedule had been taxing on all of us, it seemed.

I barely remember the drive back to my place, because I was so focused on just keeping my eyes opened. I needed sleep. Badly. Also, I needed some time to think about what to do about that letter.

When I pulled into the driveway at my place, it was a little after five in the morning, and I saw a light on in the bakery kitchen. The door was locked, of course, but I could see Georgia dancing along to music coming from her earbuds.

Her hair was tied up in the same bright red bandana that she'd worn the day we first met. She had on black yoga pants, an item I became familiar with during my time with people who actually practiced yoga, and a black and white plaid shirt, sleeves rolled to the elbows.

She looked happy. I couldn't see her face, but the airy movements of her hands as she poured ingredients into the large stand mixer suggested peace over angst. And, since I was doused in personal torment, I decided to leave her alone. She didn't use the bakery that much, for reasons that were still unclear, but what was clear was that it seemed to be a happy place for her. An escape. From what, I had no idea. Maybe from her dead parents? I knew her dad died recently, but had no idea what happened to her mom. The only time I tried to bring it up, her muscles froze before she told me she was just...gone.

My eyes lingered on the slow motion of her hips for a few minutes more, until I felt my eyelids getting heavy. I wanted to knock on the door until she heard me, to wrap my arms around her body and, moreover, have her wrap hers around mine.

I needed to be hugged. Held. Told it was all going to be okay.

I needed to be loved again.

Sew yourself up if it's gone, Regan. That's the only way you'll move on. If you want to move on.

Georgia's words from the week before echoed in through my ears as I trudged up the stairs and heaved myself onto my bed.

I wanted to move on, but was unsure if I'd be able to do that without reading that card. I fell slowly asleep, dreaming of Rae's laughter, Georgia's eyes, and the smell of cupcakes.

I slept through sunrise, my eyes peeling open around ten. In my sleep, it seemed I'd decided I'd get Rae's card back from Georgia, because the second my feet hit the floor, I slogged through my apartment, destined for hers.

I had to move on. It turned out that saying goodbye to Rae wasn't reserved for just the funeral. I wasn't ready to say goodbye then. But, I was getting there now.

Opening my door, I was startled by a petite woman with shoulder length brown hair who was knocking on Georgia's door. She turned around when she heard me, and the startle didn't stop there. She had a smile so similar to Georgia's, it made me almost uncomfortable to stare at it. I looked around, feeling out of sorts.

"Do you live here?" she asked in a soft voice.

I nodded.

"Do you know where Georgia is, by any chance?"

I took a deep breath, not sure how to answer that since I never knew where she was unless she was at E's. As I inhaled, though, I smelled freshly baked goodness. I was briefly concerned, adding up that she'd been in the kitchen for more than six hours.

"Smells like she's in the bakery." I smiled, and the woman's eyes widened as she smiled even bigger. I continued, "I can take you down there. She usually locks the door. But...can I ask who you are?"

The smile left her face as she looked to the ground, almost confused. When she looked back up, there was a vacant sadness in her eyes.

"I'm her mother."

So, there I stood. Six inches away from Georgia's dead mother.

CHAPTER *Eleven*

SENTENCE FIRST, VERDICT AFTERWARDS

Georgia

SIX HOURS LATER, and surrounded by more gluten-free muffins, brownies, and cupcakes than I knew what to rationally do with, I finally felt tired. Twice in a week being in this kitchen was a lot lately, and I loved how good I felt after several hours of work.

And hated it. Because it wouldn't last long. Late night freak-outs and phone calls, middle of the night trips to talk her off the ledge...that was all around the corner since my mother was checking herself out of Breezy Pointe this morning.

CJ was right. I needed to confide this to someone, and Regan was the best candidate. I'd have a lot of talking to do to get him caught up, but I was willing to forge through that discomfort in order to get to a place of peace about the situation. I needed someone.

Taking a deep breath as I frosted the last of my let's talk about my problems cupcakes, I heard a tentative knock on the kitchen door. I don't know when Regan got in, but I recalled seeing his car in the driveway sometime after dawn. Maybe the smell woke him. Given the last time we were together I told him to get over his dead girlfriend, I understood his hesitance in approaching me. I needed to apologize for that, too.

"Come in," I chirped, trying to sound a lot more awake than I felt.

Just as I suspected, Regan opened the door and slid through, leaving it cracked. He looked a little grey, and I chalked it up to exhaustion.

"Morning. Sorry if I woke you. Look, I'm sorry if I upset you last week when we talked, so," I held up a plate of chocolate and vanilla frosted cupcakes, "here. A peace offering. And, I was hoping we could—"

Regan put up his hand. "Wait."

I swallowed hard, his quietly harsh voice drying out my throat. "What?"

"Someone was looking for you upstairs. I told them I'd check to see if you were down here."

It wasn't what he said, but how he said it that sent my heart on the erratic flight pattern of a bat.

"Just send them—"

He opened the door the rest of the way, and there she was. My mom. Checked out of Breezy Pointe and standing next to one of the most decent guys I knew. One who knew nothing about her, most notably her alive status. My eyes flicked back and forth between hers and his, both sets filled with questions. Too many. I had answers for every one of them, but was running out of time as Regan folded his arms across his chest.

"Regan, I can—"

He pulled his head back. "Explain? No need. This is your mom, right? It's all good. I was going to your place to ask if I could have that envelope you were holding for me." His tone was flat. Cold.

"Just give me a minute. Um…Mom, can you give us a sec?"

My mom's eyes had been busy scanning the dining part of the bakery. She hadn't been by since I completed it. Her face was red with impending tears as she faced me. "Sure. Um…"

"Just, here, take this plate of muffins and go to a table, all right?"

As if choreographed by the biggest asshole in history, my mother and Regan moved at once, and in almost slow motion. She walked cautiously into the seating area, still taking in the decor, and he turned and made his way up the stairs without a word.

I took a deep breath before going after Regan, not sure what I was going to say since I'd never chased after anyone in my entire life. When I got to the bottom of the stairs, I realized what a chase it really would be, as he was taking the stairs two at a time in a slow, forceful motion with his hands in his pockets.

"Regan," I called, out of breath as I raced up the stairs.

He stood far enough away from my door that I could unlock it. "Just give me the letter, Georgia."

"I'm sorry. I need to explain about my mom. It's complicated."

"No, no. It's fine. You never actually told me your mother was dead. You just said she was gone. And never talked about her. And looked depressed every time I saw you, leading me to believe that you had a string of horrible luck, like Bo."

My cheeks heated in anger and guilt. "You don't have any idea what you're talking about. I was going to tell you. I called CJ and he said—"

"Yeah. You were going to tell me. You know what, Georgia? I was going to tell someone a lot of things. Now I can't ever again. Can I have my goddamn mail please?"

My chin shook as I nodded, tears clouding my vision. He was hurt, and thought he could trust me, and I screwed it up. I was too late to help.

Story of my life.

Regan didn't enter the apartment, choosing instead to stand in the doorway with his arms at his sides. I rummaged through the backpack on my couch, and pulled out the large manila envelope, feeling around to make sure the square card was still inside.

I cleared my throat in hopes that it would stop the tears. It sort of worked, but I had to walk half-blind back to the door, refusing to blink.

"Here," I whispered. "Just please don't do anything stupid with it, okay? I can tell how much it means to you."

Regan huffed as he took the envelope from me. "Honesty means a lot to me, Georgia. I trusted you. Even when you were harsh in telling me that I needed to get over Rae, and sew myself up, and all that shit? I heard you. I was processing it. I trusted that you knew what you were talking about—that you'd been all the way through something."

"I have," I cut in.

He held his hands out, never raising his voice. "How can I believe that? You tell me you're not hooking up with all of those guys from the bar, but you're never home after your shift. You tell me you don't have time for the bakery, but as far as I know, the bar is your only job and, come on, we both know this place could make you a hell of a lot more money than selling glimpses of your skin for tips."

I ground my back teeth together, reminding myself he was speaking from a place of anger and pain, but it still pissed me off.

"You never give me a clear answer. There's not one complete story I can remember about you. And, CJ's no help. He just tells me to watch out for you. Who the hell am I watching out for? It's all like mismatched puzzle pieces I'm expected to just put together without any questions."

The frustration on his face highlighted every person I'd ever pushed away in my life. In order to protect them, I thought. Regan's eyes, though, looked anything but protected.

"Can you just...hear me out for a second?" I grabbed the fabric of my apron, twisting it around my hands.

Regan shook his head and lifted the envelope. "I've got some wounds to go sew up. Right after they're torn the fuck open."

With that he vacated my doorframe and left out the back door. His footsteps clomped angrily down the stairs, and I didn't move until I heard his car start and the sound of the engine fade into the distance.

"Georgia?"

I jumped, her voice still out of place here. Turning around, I found my mom halfway up the stairs.

"How much did you hear?" I asked, crossing my arms over my stomach to prevent my guts from spilling out in front of her.

She closed her eyes, clearing her throat before ascending the rest of the way. "It wasn't what I heard, Georgia. It's what I saw."

"I don't have time for riddles today, Mom." I sighed, fighting tears with what little fight I had left in my body.

She shook her head, a small, faraway smile on her face. "It's what I saw when I told him I was your mother. He was confused, and, honestly, looked hurt. It was the perverse, horrified shock on your face when you saw the two of us standing in the doorway together. Did you tell him I was dead, like you told all of your high school friends?"

I pursed my lips, the last line of defense against my tears. "Mom..."

"Sweetie." She tentatively reached up and tucked some hair behind my ear. I let her.

"I didn't tell him you were dead. But—"

"You didn't exactly tell him I was alive and kicking."

"I hadn't gotten there yet. He's CJ's cousin. Remember my friend CJ from the Cape?"

"Ah yes," my mother smiled, scanning her memory by looking at the ceiling, "the underage boy who your father let play the drums at Dunes?"

I chuckled. "That's the one, though we're well past underage now."

"And he lives next door?"

I nodded.

She took a breath. "Go."

"What?"

"Go, Georgia. Go be honest with him."

"Mom, I don't have time for this. You just got out of..."

She gripped my shoulders, looking deadly as she caught my gaze. "I am not your responsibility, Georgia. You're mine. As your mother, I'm telling you, make amends with someone who means that much to you."

"Means that much to me?"

"That apartment has sat empty for six months. Go. We'll talk about the decor of your bakery when you get back. Let me into your apartment, I'll wait for you until you come back." She held out her hand, the arch in her eyebrow signaling the definite end of our conversation.

I handed her the key and headed for the back door, stopping to turn around when I reached it. "What do I say?"

My mom looked almost embarrassed as she spoke the words, "The truth."

Truth. A single word, whose antonyms underscored my entire life, was the only thing that could save my friendship with Regan.

Was it a friendship?

Truthfully—there's that word again—besides Lissa, who was a strict "work friend," Regan was the closest thing to a friend I'd had since CJ. So far, "things we knew about each other" sculpted the parameters of that friendship and, well, I was scoring a zero there.

Yes, he was my friend. And, I wanted to be his.

So, with a nod to my mom, I left the building and sat in my car for five minutes before starting the engine and heading to find him. Though, I had an idea where he'd be.

Twenty minutes later I was navigating the sandy neighborhoods of North Cove, in search of the Hippie Dream-house. Thankfully, the night CJ brought me back here, I had been sober enough to remember the general direction, but it was dark that night and I was tired, so that complicated things.

I recognized Regan's car as soon as I saw it, and I sighed in relief as I pulled in behind it. Getting out of the car, I saw Ember in her seemingly usual spot in the sand just beyond their deck, only this time she wasn't in a headstand.

I approached quietly, not sure what the etiquette was to interrupting someone's ohm, though I was pretty sure I wasn't supposed to at all. When I got within six, or so, feet of her, I stopped, looking around and playing with my hands like I was eight years old and waiting to be picked for a dodgeball team.

"Hi Georgia," she said in a seductively smooth exhale, while moving from one position I had no name for to another.

"Hi. Um..." Discussion between Ember and I had been tense at best, disastrous at worst, and I didn't know how to ask where one of her friends was so I could apologize for offending them.

"Regan went for a walk down the beach. I had no idea why he was here, and in such a pissy mood, but," she exhaled slowly and flowed into another position, this time facing me, "I guess I have more answers now than I did a few minutes ago."

I put my hands behind my back, then again in front of me. I never did know what to do with my hands. By my side, then.

"Yeah," I stammered, less affected by her grace than by my own lack of such.

"Come here for a second, do some with me," she said as if some were an obvious subject.

"Do what? Yoga?"

She nodded, her eyes closed as she seemingly breathed herself into another pose.

"No thanks." I shrugged, prying my hands into the pockets of my too-tight shorts. "I'm not all skinny like you are. I'd hurt myself."

Ember stood straight, breaking her flow, and looked at me. "It's not about being skinny, Georgia. It's about getting out of here," she pointed to her head, "and getting into here," she patted her bared belly button."

"Thanks, but I've clearly been here enough." I pointed to the softer skin around the bottom of my shirt.

She rolled her eyes, approached me and took my hand. "Good lord, come with me."

I had to give her credit. Not only did she not stand there in her slender glory and try to tell me she wasn't skinny, which is the single most annoying thing about some skinny girls, she also didn't try to lie to my face and say in a chipper kill-me-now voice, oh Georgia, you're skinny, too. Annoying skinny-girl habit number two.

Based on those two things alone, I allowed Ember to drag me to her sacred spot in the cool sand.

"Loosen up. Just shake everything out and hang like this." Ember folded forward and let her upper body hang as if draped over her own waist. "Make sure you keep your neck loose."

Uh, okay.

"Come on," she urged when I stood there for a few seconds longer than it should have taken me.

I did as instructed. "Just...hang here?"

"Yes. Let your upper body surrender to gravity. You don't have to hold yourself to the Earth. Gravity does a fine job all by itself and doesn't need our help."

Something in the words she said brought more tears. They dotted the sand before I knew what was happening and could try to stop it. The Earth didn't, in fact, need my help. An overpowering sense of humility pushed me to the sand and I sat there, my knees digging into the cool silk of it.

Ember kept her head down, but spoke as though she'd seen the whole thing. "It's a hard thing to get used to, sometimes. Not doing everything ourselves."

She had no idea. None.

"Bo and I have had to work on that with each other. Me, because I'm an only child of recklessly fantastic parents," she giggled before taking a breath and sitting next to me, "and Bo because, well, when his parents died—"

"Wait," I cut in, "his parents are dead, too?"

Ember nodded. "They died a few years ago. Before I met him. Car accident," she added quickly, as if anticipating my next question.

Okay, maybe she had some idea.

"Since you said too, I assume you know about Rae, his sister?" Ember's lips tightened to a close.

I nodded, looking over my shoulder.

"Did Regan tell you? Or CJ?" She took the elastic out of her hair and let the wild beauty of it fall all around her.

I didn't know why it mattered who told me, but I answered. "Regan."

She gave a side smile that made my insides hurt. "He doesn't talk about her much. With anyone."

Piecing together fairly quickly that Ember likely didn't know about the nuclear letter that showed up on his doorstep, I thought better about bringing it up.

"He must trust you," she continued, grabbing small fistfuls of sand and letting it drain between her fingers like an hourglass.

"Yeah," I stood, brushing the sand from my shorts, "I think I screwed that up royally this morning."

Ember stood, and though she was a few inches taller than me, she didn't make me feel that way with her smile. "Not likely. Regan's all brood, no bite."

"It was kind of big..."

Ember shrugged, looking unimpressed.

I tilted my head, scrunching my forehead. "Why are you being so nice to me?"

She sighed. "Because you deserve it. Everyone does. Kind of like innocent until proven guilty? We should all be nice, I guess, no conditions around it. I was a bitch to you before. And, I'm sorry. I just—"

"It's okay," I put my hand up, "I know all about the pregnancy scare and Willow trying to plant herself directly over your boyfriend."

Ember let out a fantastically airy laugh. "Do you know Willow?"

"I...let's just say I know how she operates."

A grey look passed through her eyes. Seeming to force a grin, she hitched her thumb over her shoulder. "He's probably that way. There are fewer houses down there, and a nice rock wall."

"Thank you." I smiled, put my head down, and made my way along the edge of the water.

I didn't have to walk very far before I saw him. Shirtless and shaking water from his hair, Regan walked over to the rock wall Ember had assured me was there, and picked up his towel. Before drying off, he tossed the towel over his shoulder and leaned forward and picked up an envelope. I knew it was the card from Rae based on the shape, and the reverence with which he was handling it, dutifully setting it back on the rocks before drying off.

Thank God he didn't toss the letter.

I hate being startled—life holds enough surprises—so I decided I should clear my throat, or something equally as juvenile to announce my presence.

I sniffed.

Of course, as intended, he looked in my direction, though I was embarrassed at my choice of greeting.

"Hi." My voice was shaky and I braced for his retreat. Certainly there was some hole behind that rock he could heave himself down.

"Hey," he mumbled back, wrapping the towel around his waist and sitting on the flat ledge of sea-bathed stone.

I made my way to the edge of the wall, keeping a five foot space of uncertainty between us

"I just wanted to say," I started, wanting to get out as much as possible before he decided he'd heard enough, "that I'm sorry about this morning. I wasn't...I wasn't all the way honest with you, and that wasn't fair. I'm...just...that's all I can say."

Regan stared straight ahead, watching the water, maybe, or the space above it. He nodded once, no change in his face to tell me if he accepted my apology or was just acknowledging that I spoke.

After a few seconds of silence, I figured it was the latter, and decided I should leave. Leave him alone with the grief of that still unopened letter splattered all over his face. He didn't want me, a liar, there to help him deal with what was the loss of a true love.

I took a few steps backward, sketching his silhouette into my memory so I could have a happy place to call upon in the days and months ahead. A friend. Even if it was all over. Finally, I turned, unable to keep my head up as a heroine might do in the movies, looking down at my chipping pedicure as I walked away.

"Georgia," he called out, sounding as tired as I felt, "wait."

Regan

Georgia stopped mid-stride, but didn't turn around. It was as if she were waiting to see if she'd heard me correctly.

"Georgia," I called again.

She turned around this time, her face caked in a shame I wanted to take away. It didn't belong there.

"Come. Sit." I moved over, patting the place next to me.

She tilted her head to the side, like she couldn't understand me, but she walked anyway. When she reached the wall, she put her palms behind her on the ledge and lifted herself so she was sitting next to me.

"I'm sor—" we spoke at the same time, both snickering nervously.

She put her hand on my leg. "Me first. I'm sorry about this morning."

"What are you sorry for?" I wasn't testing her. I just needed to make sure we were on the same page.

"Well...you met my mom. Because she's alive."

"You never told me she was dead." I'd come to that conclusion somewhere during my swim, but that was all just a technicality.

Georgia crossed her legs in front of her. "We both know that's bullshit, Regan. I don't know why you're being so decent about it."

"So, what's...the deal there?" I tucked my hair behind my ears and leaned back.

"Did you open your letter?"

"Uh-uh. We'll talk about that later, though. I think we can agree that I've shared a bit more than you have in recent weeks."

Her shoulders sank as she sighed. A long, thoughtful sigh.

"Schizophrenia."

She paused, looking up at me and squinting the sun away from her eyes. I didn't react. Not a twitch of a muscle or a blink of an eye. She expected me to, maybe wanted me to by the challenging look on her face, but I wasn't going to. She wasn't getting away without giving me some actual information.

I lifted my eyebrows, urging her to continue.

"My mother has schizophrenia, and she's spent the last few weeks at Breezy Pointe, an inpatient psychiatric facility north of La Jolla."

"I'm sorry. I didn't know," I replied stupidly. Of course I didn't know.

"That was by design." She seemed to echo my thoughts.

"Why?"

Georgia shifted so she was facing me, her bent knee resting warmly against my outer thigh. "Why what? Why she was at the Pointe or why I didn't tell you?"

"Both, I guess."

She cleared her throat. "My mother has catatonic schizophrenia. With the right blend of meds and therapy, she can function just as well as you and me. If something gets out of balance with the therapies or in her brain, everything goes haywire."

"She didn't look catatonic," I interjected.

"I was getting to that. It's kind of on a spectrum, erratic behavior on one end, and catatonia, like you're probably thinking, on the other. It's rare she has episodes like you're thinking, but when that happens she needs medical intervention. She's completely unable to take care of herself. Feeding, bathing, all of it."

Georgia's cheeks reddened as she spoke. I reached my hand over and touched her knee, but she bounced it, indicating she didn't want me to touch her. I pulled away before she did.

"Anyway, that's what sent her in a few weeks ago, then the weekend that I met you guys, I went to visit her and she had kind of a mental flare, you know, like a solar flare. She grabbed my wrist and had to be restrained, and that earned her another week and a half..." She trailed off and looked skyward, taking a deep breath."

"Shit..." I sighed on instinct. Then, I put it together. "Fuck, all the commotion about the bruise on your wrist. That wasn't about Dex at all."

She shrugged. "He's totally innocent."

"But," I started with further revelation, "you never actually said he did anything."

"Fancy, huh?" She gave a wry grin, but I didn't buy it.

"Why do you lie?"

"I don't fucking lie," she snapped.

"Then why do you...I don't know...craft a different reality?"

My words seemed to strike somewhere deep. Her eyes filled with thick tears and she slid off the wall and walked toward the water.

"Georgia!" I shouted, "I'm sorry, don't go."

"No, it's okay," she called over her shoulder. "Just walk with me."

I caught up to her and put my hands in my pockets. "So..."

"When I was little," she started after a quiet sniffle, "my mom was really honest with me about the schizophrenia. She was diagnosed when I was four, and left my dad when I was ten."

"Because of the schizophrenia?"

She stopped to pick up a seashell then kept walking. "Yes. Her father had it, too. Schizophrenia. Blew his head off in front of my grandmother when my mom was in elementary school."

My mouth opened but less than nothing came out.

"He didn't know he had it, though. My mom didn't figure that out until she was in college in an Intro to Psychology class. That's when she learned the symptoms and the epidemiology, and pieced together what she remembered of her dad with the stories she'd heard after he was gone. So, she changed her major so she could help people like him."

"She became a psychologist?"

"Psychiatrist. She was at the top of her field almost from the get-go thanks to her passion. She knew her symptoms right away."

I stopped and faced Georgia. "You've got to be kidding me." The thought of a daughter dedicating her life to her father's illness, only to be stricken with the same thing was enough to almost double me over.

"Yeah. God saves his bad days for her."

"W-what?"

She forced a smile. "Keep walking. It's easier to process when you feel like you can walk away from it."

I took a deep breath and tried to remember the woman I'd met in my apartment building hours before. She seemed normal, no signs of a lifetime of holy treachery staining her eyes.

"My mom wanted to make sure I wasn't in the dark about what was going on with her. She knew that days of erratic and unexplainable behavior were ahead, and, I guess, she wanted to prepare me the best she could."

"How do you prepare such a little kid for something like that?"

A cynical smile appeared on her velvety lips. "A different reality."

"Ah." I nodded, recalling the moment she fled our seated position and led me on this walk. "Explain?"

"My mom sat me down and," Georgia cleared her throat, doing a hell of a job retaining composure, "told me that sometimes she might say or do things that didn't make any sense, and it would feel like a fairytale."

"Uh, not like any fairytale I know." I twisted my lips in confusion.

"Wonderland," she sighed.

"W—oooooh. Alice in Wonderland..." As she nodded in the corner of my vision, my first memories of Georgia flashed through my brain. Strange tattoos, riddled speech. I looked at her again and she made sense for the very first time.

"Stop staring at me."

"I can't."

"What?"

"Tell me why your mother chose Alice in Wonderland." It seemed obvious, but I doubted that I knew it all.

Georgia stopped and sat, digging her toes into the cakey wet sand. "It was my favorite movie and book when I got old enough to read. But, she just used the movie when she explained her condition. She told me that when Alice fell down the rabbit hole and landed with a thump in Wonderland, she sometimes saw things that were pretty, and sometimes things that were scary or confusing, but always at the end she woke up from her dream in the field of flowers in which she started."

"So," she continued, "my mom assured me that if I felt confused or scared, it was no different than Alice, and when it was all over, everything would be normal and comfortable again."

I'd been standing as she was talking, but I sank on my heels next to her, wrapping my arm around her shoulder. She never settled into the embrace, but didn't flinch away, either.

"So, your tattoos, the bakery, the random things you say sometimes..."

She smiled. "All a part of my life. Who I am."

"Isn't that kind of more who she is?" I questioned, pulling my arm away and leaning back on it.

Her face went grey. "Same thing."

"I don't..." I wanted to say understand, but she didn't let me.

"That's enough, okay? I'll tell you more, just not right now." Two tears rolled down her right cheek, and she just let them. They bumped into each other at the edge of her jaw and fell as one onto her shoulder.

My chest ached for her. I didn't have all of the answers to her behavior I'd witnessed over the last several weeks, but it seemed they all lay in this story. This empty hole of a story that messed with her face and made it look older than her twenty-four years. The hostility I thought I'd observed in her eyes looked like pain in the light of personal tragedy. Maybe hostility lingered, though.

I had to touch her. To hug her. Never in my life had I seen a person who needed to be hugged as much as Georgia did. As she sat, her knees pulled to her chest, that half-assed excuse for a self-hug didn't seem to be taking hold in her soul.

"I'll shut up about it," I said as I slid closer to her until our sides were touching, "if you let me hug you."

She scrunched her eyebrows and looked at me like I'd just said the most absurd thing she'd ever heard. As ironic of a look as I'd ever seen.

"Please." I nudged her shoulder with mine. "Just let me hug you. I can tell you need it."

"I'll let you hug me," she straightened her face as she sat forward, "if you open that letter. Then maybe we'll both need one."

Feeling like I'd been tossed down my own rabbit hole, I shook my head. "I can't."

"That makes no sense. You have every body part necessary for the task."

"You know what I mean. I...physically can't."

"Why not?"

"What if it's bad?" I'd been tossing possibilities around in my head for a week straight.

"I'd say the worst is over, isn't it? The absolute worst thing has already happened. What the hell else could be worse?" Now her hand was on my leg, but I didn't move. Human contact was at a premium for me these days, and I needed it.

She was right.

The absolute worst thing had already happened. Rae died, then I did, and I was wandering the earth as an emotional zombie amongst the living.

I sighed, looking to the sky for some sort of sign. It was perfect and blue. Nothing scary.

"Okay, I'll open it."

CHAPTER *Twelve*

EITHER IT BRINGS TEARS TO THEIR EYES, OR ELSE

Georgia

"NOT HERE, THOUGH," Regan said of opening the letter. "Bo and Ember don't know about it, and I don't know if I want them to."

I shrugged, but my heart was racing as he stood and I followed him back to the wall where the letter sat. "When I said open it, you know I meant open it and read it, right?"

He nodded, but kept walking a good five paces ahead of me.

"Okay, because I know some people get real literal under stress. I don't happen to be one of those people…"

He chuckled. "Neither am I."

I was out of breath after speed-walking through the pillowy sand. Maybe I'd have to start working out with Ember.

Or I could just keep making cupcakes.

I shook my head, inappropriately light thoughts always invaded my head when catastrophe loomed. My mother had trained me as such, as I'd just finished explaining to Regan. I was one of Pavlov's dogs, salivating with mental escape tactics at the ringing of the emotional bell.

"Okay. I'm going to go back home. My mom's there waiting…" I nervously tucked my hands into my back pockets.

Regan held up the perfectly square card. "Take this."

Oh, hell no.

"Uh, no."

"Please." He pressed it into my chest with urgency in his eyes. "If I chicken out between here and the apartment, I'm just as likely to throw it out the window of the car as I am to read it. I have to talk with Bo and Ember about some band stuff, but I'll be back home in a little while. Just...please take it with you. Please."

I put my hands up, taking the offending parcel into my hand. "Okay, okay, I'll take it. I'll read it myself, though, if you don't come back."

His eyes lit up. "You could read it, then just...tell me?"

"You've lost your fucking mind." It was a phrase I didn't use lightly.

"Maybe so. Thanks. See you later." He leaned in and kissed my forehead, and then turned and jogged toward the house.

Did he just...

Never one to disassemble motives, I walked to my car like I was carrying a live bomb, briefly considered buckling it in, and drove back to the apartment.

It wasn't until I was a block away from my apartment that it dawned on me with a sickening sinking feeling. My mom showed up, and I never asked her how she got there, if she needed a ride back to her place, or if she wanted to stay with me. I was so wrapped up in the hurt on Regan's face that for the first time in twenty years I put someone before my mom. Me.

That was exactly why Regan and I could stay just friends. I had to keep my priorities straight. Well, it wasn't the only reason, but it was enough to get me through for now. My mom did have a point though. She didn't need me. There were great assisted living facilities throughout the area, and she knew exactly what she was looking for when that time came. Maybe I was the one who wasn't ready for that.

I parked in my garage and raced up the stairs, hoping my mom had actually waited for me. My door was unlocked, which was a good sign, but not an absolute.

"Mom?" I called before looking around.

When I finally paused and took a minute, I smelled fresh bread and turned and jogged back down the stairs.

"You're baking," I said as I opened the door, trying to sound nonchalant. Baking meant she wanted to talk. I forced myself to be ready to listen.

"You're out of breath," she observed. "Were you worried I'd disappeared?"

I shrugged, taking a seat on the stool nearest the stove. "I have varied success with my conspiracy theories. So..."

"So?" Mom put a loaf of bread on the counter to cool and began pulling out ingredients for what seemed to be cookies.

She put the ingredients down and looked me straight in the eye. "The board accepted my resignation this week."

I knew it was coming, but hearing the words caused the muscles in my abdomen to squeeze around themselves. I nodded, keeping my trained stiff upper lip in place.

"Did they, um, say anything?" I wrapped my arms around my stomach.

"They thanked me for my service, praised me for addressing my condition head on, and sent confirmation that my license to practice is now null and void."

"How are you feeling?" I slid off the stool and walked on shaky ground over to where she stood, unmoving.

"Twenty years as a board certified psychiatrist. When I started, I had a fire inside me, Georgia. A fire to help people like your grandfather. To heal families from all kinds of trouble. It was only in my worst nightmares that I'd turn into one of those people." She looked into the distance, smiling through barely visible tears.

I wrapped an arm around her waist, resting my head on her shoulder. We'd talked about her resignation for months. Years, if we were both honest with ourselves. She'd only been practicing for a few years before she was diagnosed. At the time, she took it in stride. She didn't crumble and try to run away, as I'm sure I would have. She faced it head on and turned her brain into a case study.

It wasn't until her first major catatonic episode five years ago that she started to question the ethics of her oath. Once she was regulated again with new medication, all was well. Until this year, when my dad died.

Though my parents had long been divorced, his death triggered a series of devastating episodes for her, starting with her yelling at a patient, and ending most recently with her crying in the fetal position under her desk. I had to go get her. That was the last time she was ever there as Dr. Hall. The next time she walked through the doors of the medical center, it was as a patient-only. I tried to encourage her to go somewhere else, somewhere she wouldn't feel so exposed, but she wouldn't have it. She reminded me that she worked at the best facility in California and intended to have her treatment carried out at the same place.

"Well," I sighed, pulling up my emotional big-girl panties, "let's talk about the ECT, shall we?"

My mom wiped under her eyes. "You're not going to yell at me and storm out, are you?"

"No. Promise." I took her hand and led her into the seating area, sitting us in a booth in the front window. "Tell me everything."

For years my mother had warned me about ECT, only having recommended it to her own patients in extreme life-threatening circumstances.

"The medication alone isn't working anymore, Georgia. You know as well as I do that there are triggers that can set off schizophrenia in someone who hasn't ever experienced symptoms, and in those who are already diagnosed, can trigger episodes like I've been experiencing. The therapy and medicine aren't enough anymore." She repeated her last line almost as an affirmation. Or surrender.

"So...what will this do, then? Have you been thinking about hurting yourself?" While she'd never exhibited suicidal ideation around me, terminology I'd picked up from years of studying psychiatry along with her, it was never far from my mind that her father ended his own life.

She reached across the table and set her hand on mine. "No. This isn't like your grandfather."

"But he had—" I started, and she cut me off.

"I speculate that he had schizophrenia, Georgia. All the signs were there, and had I read a file on him after I graduated college, I could have diagnosed him from that alone. But, he was never diagnosed. He didn't know what was wrong with him. Grandma only said he felt 'watched' all the time, like he was going crazy. He didn't have help. That's why he killed himself."

I nodded in understanding, and she continued.

"While I'll never practice psychiatry again, I need to be able to live as stable a life as possible. I want to enjoy life. You know me—I'm not going to sit in a rocking chair at Breezy Pointe until the day I die. The ECT can help my brain get out of the cycle it seems to have been in since your dad died."

"But, what about the side effects? What are they?" I hadn't done in-depth research on the subject myself. My mother had made clear with me where my position was: a firm no.

"Varied. There are some physical side effects that I'm not at high risk for. The main thing that's kept me away from it all of these years is the high possibility of memory loss." She bit her pinky fingernail and looked out the window.

I took a deep breath. "What kind of memory loss? Like, how much?"

"Usually it's only trouble remembering things in the weeks leading up to treatment, and trouble with memory during the three to four weeks it takes to complete a treatment cycle."

"So...like this conversation?" My chin quivered.

She nodded. "Maybe."

Couldn't it just mess with the bad and leave the good? Why did everything have to go...potentially?

"The benefit, sweetie, is that I might never need it again after this. It could completely reroute whatever's gone haywire and set me straight again. For a long time, if not forever."

For a few minutes more I listened to my mother, not an ounce of waver in her voice, discuss with me that treatment was to start in a week. She'd need my help to drive her to and from the hospital, and while the treatment itself only lasted a few minutes, they'd keep her in observation for a few hours afterward before releasing her. Two times a week for three weeks was the plan, evaluating progress halfway through.

"I'm getting a coffee, do you want one?" My mom stood and I nodded.

A moment later, she returned with two hot cups of coffee. We both drank it black, which allowed us to get drinking as soon as humanly possible in the morning.

"What happens if you get lost there?" I asked, staring into the steam swirling off my cup.

"Where?"

"In the...haywire. What if it doesn't work? What if you're stuck in that faraway place forever?" The end of my sentence was cut off by a rogue sob breaking through my restraint.

My mom left her seat and slid in next to me, bringing my forehead to her shoulder as she squeezed me closer and I continued crying.

"Then," she sighed and sniffed away some of her own tears, "we'll always have this moment. Right here."

She squeezed harder, and I cried harder. Until the sun went down in my little slice of the Mad Hatter's tea party, I cried in my mother's arms, certain these moments were on borrowed time.

Regan

It twisted my stomach watching Georgia's car drive away with Rae's letter inside, but I knew it was safest that way. I wasn't always levelheaded in the emotional department. I knocked on the doorframe to Bo's room, where he was sitting and strumming his guitar.

"Hey, bro, come in." Bo set his guitar down and smiled, waving me in.

I sat on the edge of the bed. "Your fingers have to be getting raw. This recording schedule is brutal."

He laughed. "It's definitely not for the faint of heart, but isn't it great to be creating on a regular basis?" He stretched his arms overhead and leaned back in his chair, cracking his back.

"It is. I'm happy we have today off, though. I'm exhausted." I knew better than to think it was from the schedule. It was from that damn letter, keeping me up at night with its endless possibilities. I wasn't telling him yet, though.

"Well you've been rock solid in rehearsals, dude. I'm psyched you agreed to come."

I nodded and he leaned forward in his chair. After some heavy silence, I took a deep breath.

"What's up?" Bo asked, scrupulously studying my face.

"I miss her, Bo."

Bo was understandably taken back by my admission. It was obvious, and expected, sure. But, I never talked about it. Not since shortly after returning from Ireland three months after burying Rae.

He reached out and put his hand on my knee, smile still on his face, but eyes clouding over. "I do, too."

"Of course you do," I stood, pacing the length of the room, "you're her brother. I shouldn't even be dumping this on you."

"Dude," Bo stood, crossing his arms and shrugging, "I don't own the rights to grief. Nor do I want to. We all lost someone when she died. The whole goddamn world did." He sniffed and cleared his throat.

I sat back down. "I know, man, but...damn. I go along thinking everything is fine, then I'll have a flash of pain, like real pain, like someone is stabbing me, or punching me, or kicking me, or all three at once..."

Bo sat next to me, his arms still crossed. "Yeah. Sometimes, for me, it's like someone's holding my head under water. When I finally fight my way up and catch some air, I look around and realize I'm alone in the middle of the ocean."

"You've got Ember."

"I do. She rows by in her boat every time. But, I've learned to swim, too, Regan."

I cracked a smile. "Did your therapist give you all of this water imagery?"

He punched my arm. "No, smartass, but it's true. You know she'd want more for you than for you to wade around just keeping your head above water."

I nodded. "You're right. I feel like I do okay with that most of the time."

"How's the place in La Jolla?" Bo was as stealthy about changing the subject as I was.

"It's great. But, you know how it is with our schedule lately…all I really do is sleep there."

"How's Georgia? I saw her here earlier. Everything okay?"

Not particularly.

"Everything's fine. We just had a misunderstanding, but it's all good now."

"Well, I think I'm going to catch some sleep now, but maybe we should all go down to E's tonight. I'd like to see her again—she seemed really fun. Maybe check with her to see if they have any sets available tonight?"

I shook my head. "You're a machine, dude."

"I've never been able to, like, do this for a living. I want to soak it all in while it lasts, you know?"

I don't know if he was aware of the double meaning of his statement as he said it, but he seemed to be about a second later. Time is not something to be wasted. Not a second. Rae lived her life with a precious urgency. I realized that in the time I'd spent replaying our relationship. It was injected in her soul to take each day and own it. I needed to get on with owning some.

"Yeah," I nodded, "I know. Give me a call later. I might be up for kicking back and watching you glorify yourself on stage," I teased.

"Get the hell out of my house." He laughed and gave me a side man-hug. "Let's talk more, okay?"

Sigh.

"Okay." He was right. We needed to talk more. "By the way... Ember told me about Willow...and the dad thing. I think you're right, she does need to talk to her parents."

Bo let out a long exhale. "I'm glad she told someone else. She's been carrying that shit around for weeks and it's pulling her down big time."

"I thought hippies were supposed to be drama free," I joked.

Bo yawned. "Looks like those girls are Hippie 2.0, the Gossip Girl edition."

I laughed. "I hate that I know exactly what you're talking about. Later."

"See ya tonight."

Walking back through the house, I found Ember sleeping on the couch. Clearly the taxing recording schedule was starting to wear on all of us. Just a few more weeks and we'd be able to take a break while Willow produced a chunk of the tracks. We could take a listen and decide how we wanted to continue.

During my drive back to my apartment I played a mental game of "open it" or "toss it" in regards to the letter. There was always secret option number three, I suppose, which was to save it and open it when I was ready, but I felt like a definitive decision was the only way to handle this.

It was just a letter.

Just a letter.

Just words.

Not just words. They were from Rae.

Shit.

Open the damn thing.

Back in La Jolla, I found Georgia wiping down tables in the bakery. I knocked on the door so she'd let me in. She did it with a smile, though she looked tired.

"Did you, uh, have people in here?" I asked as she locked the door behind me.

"No, it was just me and my mom."

"Oh, sorry I missed her. How is she?"

"She's good."

"Hey," I put my hands in my pockets and walked through the seating area, "how long has this place been open?" I put air quotes around the last word, given it wasn't open, as such, but just functional.

She chuckled. "About six months. I renovated this space at the same time I did the apartments upstairs."

"What was down here before?"

"Oh," she sighed and put her hands on her hips, "over the years it was a lot of things. My dad leased the space to a bunch of retailers. Clothing stores, a bait and tackle shop—that one was gross—and last year there was a coffee shop here."

"I know you're not, like, officially open for walk-in customers but...you should name it. Be proud of it."

"If I name it then people will have all kinds of expectations." She walked back into the kitchen and started washing dishes.

I followed her, digging a clean towel out of the drawer and drying as she talked. "What's wrong with expectations?"

"More ways for me to disappoint people in the end." She didn't make eye contact. She was good at that.

"More ways? What end?" I was pushing her a little, I realized, but I was taking slight advantage of my emotional upper hand given all the guilt she said she had. I wasn't doing it with cruel intentions, but this girl had some tightly woven layers.

"Regan..."

"All right, all right, sorry. Hey, those cupcakes are gorgeous. Did you make those?" I pointed to the counter, immediately realizing the idiocy to my question. "I mean..."

"Ha! Yeah. Well, my mom actually made the cupcakes. I made the frosting and decorated them after she left."

"She bakes, too?"

"That's where I learned. It was like therapy for both of us when I was little and things got tense. You have to concentrate to bake. Your mind can't wander. By the time you're finished you've spent lots of time thinking about something other than your problems and you get to eat something delicious. It really is the ultimate win." She smiled and carefully plucked two from the cake stand and put them on a plate.

"These are gluten-free, too?"

"Everything in here is. We've been over this."

"Huh. I didn't realize gluten-free stuff could look so...good. Smells good, too. I totally trust how it will taste."

She smiled. "Who said you're going to have any?"

"I did."

"The brilliance about gluten-free baking is it's even more complicated than regular baking. You have all different kinds of flours in varying amounts, and weirder ingredients like xanthan gum to contend with. In the end, though, the complicated equation gives the same beautiful product." She held one of the cupcakes in front of her, admiring it.

The back of my neck heated. "Just like you."

Her face flushed as she looked at me. "Complicated. Yes."

"And beautiful." My voice shook.

I had no idea why I just blurted that out. She was beautiful, more so with each minute I spent with her. Her gloves-off, unapologetic personality was laced around this hollow space she refused to let be filled with vulnerability, though it trickled in anyway.

"You think I'm beautiful?" She sounded put off.

I nodded. "You are."

"I'm a lot of things, Regan. Beauty is for the soft spirited girls, not the soft-bottomed ones."

"Take a compliment, will you? It won't hurt, trust me."

"It might. Let's go." She stuck a toothpick in the center of the two cupcakes she'd placed on a plate and pulled out plastic wrap.

"What are you doing?"

She wrapped the cupcakes in the plastic wrap. "You put the toothpicks in so the plastic doesn't ruin the frosting. It's not as fun to lick frosting from plastic as you might think. Kind of kills the mood."

"Where are you taking those?"

"With us."

"Us?"

"Yes. To the pier by the playground. You've got a letter to open."

My stomach dropped and writhed and dropped some more. "Now?"

She sighed a playfully irritated sigh. "This is the moment we're standing in, isn't it? Follow me."

Georgia picked up the cupcake plate and walked to the interior door.

"I thought you said the playground?"

"I have to get the letter from my car."

My heart did jumping jacks. "Oh…I'll…head down to the pier, if you don't mind."

She turned around and put her hand on mine. "Go," she whispered.

I walked through the garage and across the street, standing on the rock wall for a moment, the way I'd seen Georgia do a few weeks ago. I stood with my chin lifted high, eyes closed, palms open.

"Please," I whispered, "don't let this kill me."

I leaped down and walked down the beach and onto the pier. It was well worn, loved in its day, for sure, but that day had long passed. It seemed to only be suitable for foot traffic, now. Every muscle in my body shook with anticipation, dread, fear, and longing. That was the piece that had kept me from trashing the letter as soon as I received it. The longing. It was the last piece of Rae just for me. Once I read it, that would really be it.

"Hey." Georgia spoke as soft as she could to be heard over the buffeting wind.

I turned and found her setting the cupcake plate on the railing. "Hey."

She held the envelope in her left hand, and she reached out, holding it gently. I took it, the vibrato in my hand resonating through the starched and stiff square. I cleared my throat, never looking at Georgia, and turned to walk toward the end of the pier.

"Regan, wait!" she called after me when I was about twenty feet from her.

She caught up to me and before I could ask what she wanted she lifted on the tips of her toes and threw her arms around my neck, squeezing me in the tightest hug I'd had in a long time. My throat pinched shut as I was overcome with emotion. Human contact. And, she smelled like cupcakes. I hugged her back with as much strength as I could pull from behind the line of anxiety and breathed her in.

"I thought you said I had to open and read the letter before I got a hug." I smiled into the softness of her hair.

"Sometimes," she choked out, "you need to be convinced that it really will be okay."

She dropped her arms and I took a step back, taking her hand. "Will you sit next to me?"

"I—" she started, but I cut her off.

"Please?" I cleared my throat to avoid falling apart before anything happened.

She nodded, threaded her fingers between mine, and followed me to the end of the pier.

"You're not going to jump, are you?" She twisted her lips and cocked her eyebrow.

I appreciated her apparent need to cut through heaviness with humor. "We'll see."

She laughed, appreciating my identical need.

We sat with our feet dangling over the water. I looked at the envelope and before I could convince myself otherwise, I loosened my hand from Georgia's and ran my index finger along the sealed enclosure.

"That part's over." Georgia leaned into my arm.

I nodded, unable to speak. I pulled the card from the only home it'd had for the last seven months and immediately started laughing and crying at the same time. The front of the card had a cartoon violin with a face on it, and arms coming out of the sides, one hand up on the neck of the instrument and the other holding a bow and laying it across the strings. It was adorable, and funny, and thoughtful, and everything I missed about Rae staring me right in the face.

"She's too much." I wiped away tears, still smiling, allowing myself to speak in the present tense. Just once more.

Out of the corner of my eye I saw Georgia wipe some tears away from her pink cheeks. "I'm going to let you do this part by yourself. Is that okay? I feel like I'm intruding."

"You're not intruding, but it's okay." I knew she'd be only a few feet away. And, I had a letter to open.

Georgia squeezed my shoulder as she stood and as her footsteps grew softer, I opened the letter:

Regan,

Kind of looks like you, right? Kidding.

I was in the campus bookstore this morning trying to find a replacement book for that damn poetry class I'm taking, and I came across this. I just had to send it to you. I'll see you again before you get it, but there's something romantic about mail, isn't there? No one sends mail anymore.

Send me mail, sometime. Does chivalry mean nothing anymore?

In all seriousness, you're perfect, and that's the real reason for me sending this card. Violin Man was a bonus.

Well, that's not the *real* reason I'm sending this card. But I'm nervous to tell you the real reason.

With tears flowing freely down my face, I stopped reading for a second, my heart pounding out of my chest. I covered the bottom part of the letter so I wouldn't read anymore until I was ready. I took a deep breath and read on, nervous, too.

The real reason is...ugh, I'm so dramatic. Take a deep breath, Rae. Yes, this is my letter so I can talk to myself if I want.

Okay. The real reason for this letter is...I love you.

It's too soon and irresponsible and reckless and all of that, but, I don't care. We have fun, we laugh, and life is just better with you in it. I love you and I think you're wonderful and I'm going to stop writing now before I write myself into a hole. Or a corner. Or whatever it is writers write themselves into.

I'll see you this weekend. Because you likely won't get this letter before then, you won't think I'm crazy yet. I won't have the guts to tell you in person until after I know you've received this and then we can have that awkward moment where you say, "I got your letter," and I say, "Soo..." and we stare into each other's eyes, wondering who will say it again. Or first.

I need to stop this horrendous tangent.

But, not before telling you one more time that I love you.

I love you.

~Rae

I calmly set the letter behind me, sitting on the corner of it to prevent it from blowing away, and then, I stopped breathing.

CHAPTER *Thirteen*

WHO IN THE WORLD AM I?

Georgia

HE STOPPED ONCE at some point during his reading of the letter and looked up, taking a deep breath. I thought it was all okay, that he was getting through it just fine. When he seemed to finish, he tucked the letter behind him and sat very still for a few seconds.

I said nothing.

I took half a step forward, questioning even that, before he crumpled into the fetal position with his face pressing into the splintered wood, and began sobbing.

"Oh, God," I whispered, running down the uneven planks toward him.

His body was shaking and his wails were so loud I didn't know if he'd ever hear anything again. Or if I would. Like the EMT in emotional situations I'd been trained to be, I snatched the letter away from the cracks in the wood and tucked it in my back pocket before it could slip away and take him with it.

"Regan...Regan..." I didn't come close to matching his volume, but I was hoping a piece of him somewhere would hear me and allow his body to calm down to hear the rest.

He was coughing through thick sobs, the kind that make you feel like you're drowning from the inside. I looked around, trying to formulate my next move.

There was none. I shifted so I was sitting cross-legged with my knees up against his back so he knew I was there. It no longer mattered what the letter said, though I admit the past two weeks had allowed me to come up with all kinds of creative responses. What mattered was this...this mutilated soul who reached up behind him mid-sob and grabbed my hand.

For half an hour or more I was folded awkwardly over Regan's body in a broken hug as he clenched my hand to his chest. Where his heart once was.

Sometime after the sky turned grey and it started to drizzle, Regan seemed to recognize the precipitation from somewhere other than his eyes. He stood without letting me see his face, which I don't know if he meant to do, but he stood there at the end of the pier with his shoulders sitting unnaturally low.

Who was I becoming that in a matter of a few short weeks I suddenly couldn't push him away? Not only could I not push him away, but I decided in that moment that if he jumped into the freezing and shallow water below, I'd follow him. Not wanting him to jump, though, I tugged his hand.

"Let's get inside," I said as he lifted his head to the sky once more.

When he turned around, I wanted to jump. His face was splotches of red and misery, hazel eyes swollen, and even worse than if they'd been empty, filled with a pain that would have certainly driven a lesser person to their knees had they been staring at him.

He didn't say anything, but he held his other hand out when his eyes drifted to the card in my hand. I handed it to him and he squeezed his eyes shut, an impossible amount of tears wringing free. Pressing the letter to his chest, he followed slowly behind me as I led us down the pier and into the sand.

"You forgot the cupcakes." He spoke in a shaky, terminal voice.

I glanced behind us to the pair of cupcakes I'd abandoned on the railing when I'd gone down to the end of the pier.

"I know where I can get more. Let's get inside before it rains any harder, okay?" I winked and smiled the sweetest smile I could. I had to pull way back in my muscle memory for that kind of smile, but it worked.

He smiled, and chuckled once. A toneless breath of a chuckle that showed me his emotions weren't all swinging from gallows deep inside him.

He'd cried himself out all the way to his toes, it seemed, as tired footsteps lugged up the stairwell behind me once we were inside our building. Once at the top of the stairs, I hesitated. Deeply rooted instinct told me to open his door for him, close it behind him, and mind my own business for the rest of the day. But, this was Regan. If nothing else, he'd spent the last few weeks showing me that he needed people and he was okay with that need. Despite my discomfort in being needed beyond what I was certain I could give, I knew even deeper in my gut that I couldn't leave him. Not like this.

So, I opened my door and he followed without protest, crashing limply onto my couch, still clutching the letter for dear life. Within minutes, he was asleep. I might not have believed it if I hadn't, myself, fallen asleep during or immediately following an emotional catastrophe ending in tears, but I was thankful he did. It would hurt him all over again when he woke, but he needed the rest to be able to deal with that. Even when a wound is raw and exposed, it still needs to be covered in between exposure to dry it out. It was a delicate cycle, one I'd unfortunately become familiar with. Wound care, emotional style.

Once he'd stayed asleep for several minutes, I took a deep breath, allowing a few tears of my own to join the heavy party in my apartment. Regan let it all out there...his hurt, his internal homicide, in such a way I was almost jealous. I'd wanted to scream and kick and cry for as long as I could remember. Next week would bring a new wave of terror as my mother began shock treatment. Of that, I was certain.

I wouldn't tell Regan about that. Not yet, anyway. I knew I should, especially after the lack of communication surrounding the existence of my mother, but...no, not yet. Timing never had been on my side, after all. It was my problem to deal with and not burden the guy who just read a letter from his dead girlfriend. He'd want to help, and he'd be mad if he found out, but that was a risk I was willing to take to protect him.

That I wanted to protect him from anything was deeply disturbing to me, and further proof that I had to keep him at forearm's length at the very least, since full arm's length was not kosher with him.

As he slept, I picked up my cell phone and did the most unthinkable thing.

"Hello?" Lissa shouted over jukebox music.

"Liss, it's Georgia. I can't come in tonight, okay?"

"Is it your mom? Is everything okay?" I so rarely called in, I understood the worry in her tone.

"She's okay. Thanks, though."

"Uh...okay. It's slow tonight, anyway. I've got you covered. Keep me posted if you need anything, K?"

"I will."

I hung up the phone and watched Regan sleeping curled on his side on my oversized couch. With more tears streaming down my face, I shuffled over to the crescent shape formed by the curve of his body, and curled myself into it, my back to him, and cried into the couch cushions until I drifted into a dreamless sleep.

No white rabbits.

No Red Queen.

Just a lonely girl.

Who needed a friend.

Regan

I slept for what felt like three days. Before I opened my eyes, I took a deep breath and was surrounded by warmth and vanilla. Not the kind of vanilla girls can buy in a spray bottle, but the kind that comes from the actual bean. Madagascar, I think they're from. It was sweet and comfortable.

It was Georgia.

Georgia?

My back and arms stiffened as I mentally assessed the situation. Like a tsunami, it came back. There was Rae's letter, Georgia's cupcakes left on the dock, and...I was asleep on Georgia's couch. Rather, had been before I opened my eyes and found myself nose to a button-nosed sleeping Georgia.

Her arms were curled up against her chest, which was pressed against mine, and her features were soft. There was no ridge between her eyebrows from her ever-present cynicism. Her cheeks were pink and her lips were soft and warm. And, I know that because they were touching mine. Touching. Not kissing. Not moving. Just resting there with each other.

If I could have frozen my muscles any further I would have. As it was, my arm was draped over her waist and my back was pinned against the back of the couch. Before I could think much more about what we were doing in that position, and why, I heard Bo and Ember's voices across the hall.

"Regan? You there, man?" Bo's voice had an anxious edge to it that was rarely present in him. "I'll call him again."

A few seconds later, from the table by the door where I must have discarded my things, my phone started to ring, and their voices stopped outside.

Great.

I shifted slightly, needing to get to my phone and the door and Bo and Ember, but not wanting to roll Georgia onto the floor. I didn't need to be concerned about that for too long, because as soon as I moved some more, and a soft knock sounded on her door, Georgia's eyes shot open.

"Shit!" Her blue eyes widened in apparent horror as she shifted backward and landed on the floor with a thump.

"Georgia?" Ember sounded concerned as she knocked faster. "Are you okay? It's Ember. We're looking for Regan."

"I'm fine. Just a sec!" Georgia looked between me and the door like we were all on fire. I chuckled as I stood, reaching down a hand to help her.

"This isn't funny! What the hell is the matter with you?" Her voice was deep and raspy from the sleep. She refused my hand and stood, wiping her eyes and looking around.

I looked out the window and saw it was far darker than it should have been after a little nap. Once I reached my phone I saw it was past ten, meaning I was late for my drink with Bo, explaining their presence here.

As I placed my hand on the doorknob, Georgia snapped her fingers.

"What are you going to tell them?" she whispered in panic.

I shrugged. "Let's find out."

I wasn't thinking clearly, and that was the only thing that was clear as I opened the door and found Bo and Ember standing there, looking around like they were playing a game of Marco Polo.

"Hey guys." I yawned and stretched my arms overhead.

"Hey...Regan." Ember craned her neck and peered into the apartment. One look over my shoulder and I saw Georgia busying herself in the kitchen.

Bo leaned against the doorframe. "Everything okay? You were a no-show for our beer, then we couldn't get ahold of you and Lissa told us Georgia had called in..."

I looked behind me again and found Georgia blushing as she seemed to move pans from one shelf to another. When I looked back at Ember, her eyes were deathly focused on my face.

"You've been crying," she said flatly. "What happened?"

"What?" I waved my hand dismissively. "I'm fine."

"You do kind of look like shit, dude. What's up?"

I had to close my eyes and take a breath. I was certain it was inappropriate to still be feeling the heat from Georgia's lips against mine as I was staring at Bo.

Rae.

The letter.

I winced, feeling like I was being kicked in the stomach all over again. It really hadn't been a dream. She sent a letter. And told me she loved me. Georgia seemed to sense my stumble because she was right behind me within seconds putting her hand on my back.

"Sit." She led me over to the couch, where I started to panic.

"Shit...where's the..." I patted my chest all the way down to my waist, and felt around my pockets for the card.

Georgia knelt in front of me and picked the envelope off the floor. "It's right here." There was a kindness on her face that brought tears to my eyes.

"Guys?" Bo entered the apartment, with Ember oddly silent next to him. "What's…going on?"

Thoughts of the beautiful and secretly sweet girl in front of me were pushed far away as the last piece of Rae dangled from my fingertips. I motioned for Bo to sit next to me, my heart racing a million miles a minute. If he'd received something like this, I'd have wanted to know. That's what I kept telling myself as I slowly handed him the letter. Ember took a seat on the arm of the couch next to him, looking over his shoulder.

"What's thi—" Bo looked at the return address and brought his hand to his mouth. His eyes watered as he took a long, slow breath, exhaling into his palm.

Ember's head tilted to the side, and she carefully read the front of the envelope, her cheeks growing red as she stood. "If you don't want me—"

I held up my hand. "No, go ahead."

Bo kept his eyes on me as he pulled out the card. "When did you…how did you…"

"David Bryson sent this to me. He said it was in a box of her things from school." I chuckled. "She'd never asked for my address, so that will explain why there's a stamp on it and only my name."

Bo smiled. "When did you get it?"

"A couple of weeks ago."

Ember's eyes shot to me. "You didn't tell me."

I shrugged rather unapologetically. "I couldn't, Em. I didn't even know if I wanted to open it. Go ahead," I nodded to Bo, "it's so Rae."

Bo's hands trembled as he ran them over the inked words like he was trying to hold hands with his sister. The more flooded with tears his eyes got, the wider he smiled. His eyes were moving slowly over the lines, like he was trying to savor every second of Rae's presence. As he reached the end, at the same time as Ember it seemed, he chuckled, a mix of laughing and crying that brought the heels of his hands to his eyes, wiping away a mixed bag of tears.

Ember's arm was immediately around his shoulder, her lips went to his temple as if it was an emotional fire drill and she was taking her position. Only this wasn't a drill. Tears streamed down her face, and I watched her bite her lip, keeping her emotions silent and letting Bo work through his. She squeezed him harder as she kissed him on the cheek, then the head before resting her chin on the top of his head and taking a deep breath of her own.

I cleared my throat, not having the energy to cry anymore today. "So, I wasn't sure if I wanted to open it, or what, but Georgia encouraged me to. We went down to the pier and...long story short, I passed out on her couch."

Looking into the kitchen, I found Georgia leaning against the island, watching all of us with a lost and sad look on her face. I got up and walked over to her.

"Thank you." I took her hands in mine and dipped my head so she was forced to look at me. "Thank you for being there for me today."

"Of course." She tried to sound nonchalant as she looked over her shoulder at Bo and Ember in their embrace. When her eyes came back to my face, she drew her eyebrows in for a moment before wrapping her arms around my neck and exhaling, "You're welcome," into my ear.

I squeezed her back. The warmth of her body was intoxicating. "I'm sorry about your cupcakes."

"Did someone say cupcakes?" Bo's voice chirped like a teenage girl and we all laughed.

Sometimes, you just have to laugh.

I nodded. "Georgia's got a bakery downstairs."

"Oh?" Ember walked around the back of the couch. "I was wondering about that. It's adorable. There's no sign, though..."

Georgia shifted on her feet, wringing her hands. "Yeah, it's not technically open, but I fool around down there a lot."

"You did say cupcakes, though, didn't you, Regan?" Bo stood and wiped under his eyes a final time.

"They're delicious, too."

Georgia slapped my shoulder. "How would you know? You haven't had one."

"Well, I've had those blueberry muffins. I trust your talent transfers from baked good to baked good. Let's take these two downstairs, I know you have all of those cupcakes left from this morning." I don't know what I wanted more, to see Georgia in her element, or to step away from the letter for a few minutes.

Before she could answer, Bo was already at the door. "You said cupcakes. I want cupcakes. I might not always verbalize my feelings—"

"Yes, you do," Ember cut in with a smile.

"Whatever." He rolled his eyes as I chuckled. "Fine. I might always verbalize my feelings, but whatever they are, cupcakes make them better." He rubbed his hands together in anticipation.

"What's with his sweet tooth all of a sudden?" I asked Ember.

"You know...I don't bake, my parents used to think sugar was evil, I just...there are no cupcakes in my life."

"None?" Georgia nearly shouted.

Ember shrugged. "I try. I just...can't"

"That's the most ridiculous thing I've ever heard." For someone who said more nonsensical things than anyone I'd ever met, Georgia sounded serious about this. She breezed past Ember, and then stopped in front of Bo at the door, putting her hand on his shoulder. "Let's go get you a cupcake."

Georgia

It was innocent at first, bringing the grieving friends into my bakery for some confection-type comfort. But, as I watched the three of them eating cupcake after cupcake in one of the booths, laughing their way through memories of their lost sister, friend, and girlfriend, I started to feel like my own skin was too tight.

I didn't belong here. With them. It wasn't my scene. Friends. Laughter. Especially not given the fact that next week I'd start taking my mother to her shock therapy a few times a week. I was built for solitude, though the structure around me suggested that, at least at one point, I'd wanted this.

Life...around me.

"Hey, you." Regan walked into the kitchen, fetching the last of the cupcakes from the porcelain cake stand. "Told you they were delicious." He took a gluttonous bite and smiled.

There were no butterflies in my stomach as I watched him smile. No thumpety-thump of my heart. When I watched the tip of his tongue snag a stray drop of icing from the corner of his lips, there was none of that light and bubbly flirty feeling. It was heavy. So suffocatingly heavy was my need to be curled up on the couch with him again that I had to get out of there. It was too late to make a graceful exit, though, since Regan seemed to see my cheeks go flush.

"What's the matter?" He set the cupcakes down as Bo and Ember laughed softly in their booth and walked toward me.

I swallowed hard. We had to have the conversation. "I'm sorry about earlier."

"About what?"

I wiped my palms on my jeans. "The couch...I—"

Regan shook his head. "It's okay. It felt...nice to wake up next to you."

"Nice?" I pulled my head back and scrunched my forehead. After the reading of the letter from his dead girlfriend, how could he... just...how?

He swallowed audibly and took a deep breath. "Yes. Nice. It was nice to wake up next to someone. To feel the warmth of another body next to mine..." He ran his hand up the top part of my arm.

"But...Rae. Your letter."

He nodded. "Rae wrote a letter to me. It's not like she wrote it from beyond the grave, although it felt a hell of a lot like that as I read it. I just need to process what she said, and make peace with it."

He squeezed my arm a little as he said the words, like he was trying to say something else, but before I could interpret anything Ember stuck her head into the kitchen.

"Georgia. These cupcakes are so good. Can you give me the recipe? Bo's already sad that he's about to eat his last one."

I stepped back from Regan's hold. He didn't seem to give a shit what Bo and Ember thought about his boundaries with me. It was uncomfortable for me to be around someone so unashamed of every action, with no apparent need to cover anything up. He twisted his lips a little as I moved around him, but he dropped his hand without a fight.

"I can give you the recipe but you'll probably have to spend some time at the grocery store. I'm not sure if Regan told you, but everything is gluten-free."

Ember's mouth dropped open and she shouted to Bo. "Did you hear that, Bo? She said everything here is gluten-free! My parents would have a field day!"

"Excellent, where's my gluten-free goodness?" His impatience made me smile inside.

"Calm yourself, sweetie. Georgia," she turned back to me, beaming, "you have to make some of these for our recording session. And some muffins. And bread. Do you make bread?"

"Yes," I chuckled, "I make bread. Do your parents have Celiac or something?" Her enthusiasm over my ingredients was intriguing.

She waved her hand. "I ate homemade wheat bread from the fields of the farm we lived at most of my childhood. Made by my mom. All of a sudden it's an issue for them. Whatever. It's more my mom than my dad. He'll be thrilled to have something sweet."

"Oh, Georgia, that would be wicked. Please do it." Regan shoved the rest of the cupcake into his mouth.

"Okay. What time do you record tomorrow? I'll make some of the stuff tonight and the rest in the morning." It felt good to be wanted rather than needed.

Ember picked up the last two cupcakes. "I'm going to bring these into the other room. Regan can just bring the goods with him when he comes tomorrow. Regan," Ember raised an eyebrow to him, "be nice to her. This food is delicious."

I felt worse by the minute for having misjudged Ember's character due to a few shitty days she'd had. While I didn't envision us ever sitting around painting each other's nails, I no longer wanted to claw her face. It was progress.

"They'll pay you, too, you know." Regan wiped crumbs from the counter and tossed them in the trash.

"Oh...that's not why I said yes," I spoke quickly, not wanting him to misjudge my intentions. Especially since I didn't even know what my intentions were.

He laughed. I could get lost in that sound. It was deeper than his speaking voice, but full of this mouthwatering joy. "I know that's not why, but I'm just saying...maybe if you do it regularly enough, word will get around and you can, like, run this place full time."

I looked through to the seating area and watched Bo and Ember. They looked noticeably more relaxed than I'd seen them even in their own oceanside environment. My mom and her mom had been right; food brings people together, and sweet food is even better.

"Maybe." I shrugged, glancing up at Regan's face.

"Why haven't you opened it? The real reason." He leaned sideways against the counter and crossed his arms in front of him.

I wanted to make something up. But, given the events of the day that had him crying in front of me more than once, lying to him seemed particularly horrendous. I couldn't get in to it with Bo and Ember here, though. They were surrounded by hippies all day and took no issue with weeping in front of strangers. It wasn't that I planned on crying, but I'd have to be more honest with them than I'd ever even intended on being with Regan in the first place.

"We can wait till they leave, if you want. But, I want you to talk about it, okay?"

I hadn't realized I'd been staring for so long at the loving couple until Regan spoke.

I nodded. "Yeah. When they go. Go hang out with your friends. I'll clean up in here."

I bought myself some time. Time to come up with a story. One that would have been a lot easier to come up with had I not curled up on the couch with him, and inhaled the saltiness on his skin that made me miss home. And his lips. God. It had been so long since I'd felt lips against mine, I was certain they'd burst with eagerness.

Looking out at their booth, I caught Regan mid-smile and it honestly took my breath away. Hours earlier he'd been the saddest human being I'd ever seen in the flesh. How could he turn it around so quickly? How could he move forward—so open and not boxed in by his pain?

Maybe I wanted that. That was the only explanation for why I was turning over in my mind ways to keep him around.

After another half hour, Bo and Ember said their goodbyes to Regan and me. Bo made sure that I was serious about sending baked goods to the studio tomorrow. I assured him I was and laughed as Ember poked at Bo's rock-hard stomach and begged him not to get soft. I'd soften him up just to spite the skinny bitch. I said I no longer wanted to claw her face, not that I was going to sympathize with her ever running into the issue of bringing something into a dressing room, only to find out it's too big.

Regan locked the door behind them, without me asking him to, and came back into the kitchen, leaning against the counter with his hands in his pockets and smiling like I was holding a camera. "Thank you for letting me just bring them down here like that. I wasn't really thinking..."

I was about to make a snarky comment about his supposed thoughtlessness, but when I looked up, he was looking away. Not down, not off into the distance, but to somewhere no one else around him would ever be able to see.

"It's okay. I was afraid they'd be upset about you being in my apartment, or something." I realized how stupid it sounded as soon as I said it. We were two adults and we weren't found in bed, so to speak. And, really, even if we had been, what would anyone say?

I was too unsure of the ghost of Rae to know exactly what anyone would have really said.

Regan shrugged, allowing his vision to come back to the present. He opened his mouth to speak, but closed it once before opening it again. Then, he took my hand. "Come in here and sit for a minute."

I followed without argument, because you follow someone who looks that sad when they ask you to. As a matter of practice, someone should really always just follow someone around who looks that sad. He brought me over to the booth he'd been sitting in with his friends. A few cupcake wrappers and errant crumbs were young fossils of the happiness that briefly inhabited this space.

In the looming greyness that tomorrow would bring, those crumbs gave me hope.

"So," Regan started, "I'm sorry if it was weird for you up there in your place...all that crying and stuff. I didn't know if I was going to show Bo the card, and I certainly didn't plan on doing it in your apartment."

"It's okay." I shrugged. "It was a little jarring, obviously, since I haven't had that many people in my place, like, ever, and certainly not for anything so emotional."

"Do you always keep to yourself because of your mom?" His question was as direct as his eyes were. Unflinching. Bold.

"It's not really like that." I shifted in my seat, picking up the crumbs one by one and placing them on an empty cupcake wrapper.

"What's it like then?"

My eyes shot up. "What's with the inquisition, Regan?" I stood, but he lurched across the table, capturing my hand.

"Sorry. Please sit?"

I sat, but only because I swear I could hear a flicker of Irish accent in his voice, and I wanted to hear it again.

"Let me try this again." He cleared his throat. "What I meant to say was thank you for being so cool. Upstairs with Bo and Ember, and earlier today with me."

A few seconds ago I was uncomfortable with what seemed to be an interrogation, but that swiftly morphed into me viewing his own uneasiness. Then I felt like a giant ass for assuming it was about me at all. Regan picked at something invisible on the table, looking down, and lost again.

I put my hand on his to stop the maddening noise. "Hey, it's okay. She was clearly really special. Rae, I mean."

He released half his mouth into a smile. I needed to give him more.

"Tell me about her."

He looked up, seemingly startled. "Really?"

I nodded. "Really."

For the next several minutes, Regan told me the story of his star-crossed romance with Rae Cavanaugh. He had a dumbstruck grin on his face, but the wear around his eyes highlighted the unhappy ending that awaited me. I always read the last page of books first, anyway; it gives more guts to the story. It was no different here. Knowing the ending made Regan's smiles brighter. Tragedy has a way of amplifying the good and smudging the bad. When he finished the story of his spunky, tough as nails girlfriend, he sat back and took a weary breath.

"I like her," I whispered.

"I loved her. And," he cleared his throat but that did nothing to stop the tremble in his voice, "I never told her."

Regret is ugly. A pus-filled boil ready to break open on the face of your soul. As soon as I saw it forming, I stood. "Come to the kitchen with me. I need your help for the stuff I'm sending with you to the studio tomorrow."

"Really?" His eyes lit up and the boil faded into hiding.

"Really." I chuckled, mocking our identical conversation from minutes before.

Tomorrow I would tell Regan anything he wanted to know, because I knew he wouldn't forget to ask. For tonight, though, I'd let us get lost in the sweet escape of this confectioner's wonderland. A place where nothing was sour.

CHAPTER *Fourteen*

WHY IS A RAVEN LIKE A WRITING DESK?

Georgia

REGAN AND I had stayed up well past midnight making a mix of cookies, cupcakes, and muffins for him to bring to Blue Seed Studios with him the next day. While he'd seemed excited at the prospect of helping me, we completed the project in near silence. It wasn't heavy, by any means. It was more meditative. We didn't ask questions of one another; rather, we just seemed to enjoy the company and the silence.

I'd received a text message from my mother, reminding me to pick her up at ten in the morning to take her to her first ECT treatment. Regan asked what was wrong when he saw me check my phone, but I brushed it off as nothing. Just work, I'd told him, making sure I was okay. It was a small lie, but we'd had so much heavy crammed into one day, I wanted to spare us both from the "mom getting her brain electrocuted" conversation.

Once the goods were done, cooled, and wrapped, I sent Regan back to his apartment with bags filled to the top and I sank myself into a restless sleep.

The truth is I'd spent several days trolling the Internet for information on the effectiveness of Electroconvulsive Therapy. As I sifted through the horror stories and testimonies of support, I learned that the treatment had come a long way since the days of

One Flew Over the Cuckoo's Nest, and the reality was—my mother was the perfect candidate.

Years of successful pharmaceutical and talk therapies carried her this far, and there was literally nothing left to try on those two fronts. With the ECT she even had a chance of lessening the medication she was on. She also had a chance of forgetting large chunks of her life. Typically, the risk of memory loss surrounded the days and weeks preceding the treatment, but risks of darker holes in memory remained.

Frankly, I wouldn't blame my mother if she welcomed some of that memory erasing power. There were some hard years that dotted the score of her life like bullet holes. As I drove my mother to her appointment, I felt myself hanging onto every word she said as if I were the one at risk of forgetting everything. I couldn't figure out why I wanted to hang on to any of it, though.

"Georgia," my mom cooed from the passenger seat. She always had a therapist voice. Sing-songy and soft. Like a blanket.

"Sorry, I was just daydreaming."

"About that boy?"

"What boy?" I asked out of procedure more than necessity.

"The one with the penny-colored hair."

"Copper."

She rolled her eyes. "Same thing."

"Well, he's not six, so let's use a grown up word," I teased. "Penny-colored sounds like something said to or about a little kid."

"For goodness sake. Fine. The copper-haired breezy boy. What's his name again?"

"Regan. Not like the president. Like there should be two E's there, but there's not."

"I don't want to discuss the formation of his name, dear." She grinned and tucked her hair behind her ears.

I took the exit for the hospital, my heart starting to race. "What do you want to know?"

"How he manages to make you smile like you used to when you were a little girl."

"He doesn't." I couldn't have sounded more offended if I tried. I drew my eyebrows together and bit the inside of my cheek to combat the Regan-esque sensation overcoming my lips.

"You act like smiling's a bad thing."

"It's a lying thing," I mumbled.

"Pull over." My mom's voice was sharp.

I looked at her and she wasn't joking. Her eyes were on me and her finger was pressed against the window as if I didn't know where over was. Without a fight, I pulled over along the wide shoulder and put the car in park.

"What?" I looked around, trying to find the source of her sudden panic.

"Don't do this, Georgia."

I opened my mouth to accompany my sudden need for more oxygen. "Do what? Take you? We can go—"

"No." She put up her hand. "Don't throw away whatever is happening with Regan."

"You made me pull over for this?"

"You need to stop and listen to me. And to yourself. I know what you're doing."

"I'm not doing anything, Mom."

I sighed and put the car in drive, merging back into the thickening traffic. Everyone in the area worked at the hospital and the road swelled like grease-fed arteries during the day. I was annoyed at having left my spot in the line of cars to listen to her chastising.

"I just think—"

"Stop!" I cut her off, the stress of her impending appointment boiling over into my speech. I took a deep breath. "Sorry. I'm just trying to focus on you right now, okay?"

My mom sat back and crossed her arms in front of her. "For such a tough little shit, you sure let fear drive your decisions an awful lot."

My throat tightened. I tried to swallow it open, but it didn't work. I knew my mom was probably as nervous about her appointment as I was, and I'd just yelled at her so I couldn't very well do it again. Even if she was right.

Given the last time I'd seen Dr. Carver was when I was in his office stomping my feet like a sugar-crashing toddler, chatting with him before my mother's procedure was awkward at best. The nurse had taken my mother back to do all of her vitals, and things of that nature, while Dr. Carver discussed what to expect during and after the minutes-long procedure.

I sat at his desk, in an office I'd never been to before. We weren't at Breezy Pointe, which was nice on a superficial level. This office was more clinical. Sterile, with mock 1940's Coca-Cola advertisements on the wall. Bizarre, I thought, given the obesity crisis the medical community rants about. Though, I suppose if you have someone in front of you who is literally losing their minds, offering them a Coke is the least you can do.

"Georgia." He nodded, the way a principal might. Then he took a casual seat and fussed with his lab coat. His next lab was my mom's brain. I wanted to burn the coat.

"Hi, Dr. Carver. How long will the procedure last?" I didn't need him to retell the tale of why they were doing the procedure and what the procedure consisted of, or a discussion of why were incessantly calling it a procedure.

When people go in for most other procedures, they outline the parameters. Not here. Here, it was a procedure, because no matter how you sliced it, you couldn't keep the electro out of the conversation.

"Just a few minutes."

I knew how long it would last. As I said, I'd been doing my homework. I just felt the need to act like I gave a shit about what he said. Maybe my attitude wasn't fair. He'd been an exceptional doctor to my mom, but he was still the one who was going to be zapping her brain. There are some things I just can't look past in a person.

Procedure will last a few minutes.

Procedure.

She'll be monitored in recovery for a couple of hours.

Go home.

Those were the highlights of the conversation. I couldn't be in the room for a number of reasons, all of which prevented me from having to scream, I don't want to be in there.

So, I waited. I didn't count ceiling tiles or entertain the fish in the oversized tank with my longing gaze. There was no playing around on my smart phone, because if it were so smart, it would transform into a portal through which I could escape. I didn't want to be angry at my phone for not existing outside of reality, so I left it in my backpack.

"Georgia Hall?" The pleasant nurse who wasn't much older than thirty had a calm smile on her face. Not an overly enthusiastic one. I appreciated the common sense of her facial muscles.

I flowed from sitting to standing in one overly graceful motion. One that I'm sure made it look like I was trying not to look as twisted up inside as I felt.

"That's me," I chirped. I was done trying not to seem anxious. I needed to let it all out before I saw my mom.

"Everything went well. She's still coming out of anesthesia, so we can't let you back yet. Did you and your mother discuss you going home before she was released?"

My ears got hot. "No...why would I go home?"

The nurse tilted her head. "It might be a few hours before she's ready to go home, and we won't be able to let you back to see her for quite some time. You might want to go get food or something?"

I looked around, not having an answer. Not having a place to go, really. "I'll stay here."

I put enough conviction behind it that she didn't try to encourage me again to leave. "Okay. Well there's a deli two buildings down if you get hungry. Other than that, just make yourself comfortable, and we'll be out to get you as soon as we can."

"K..." I trailed off with a slight shrug. I'd hoped to be there when my mom came out of anesthesia.

Who am I kidding? I'd hoped not to be here at all. Once those expectations were blown, I didn't bother forming new ones.

I shuffled back to my seat and took out my cell phone as a matter of procedure. There was no one I had to notify about how it went or how long we'd be. I did a double-take as I was about to slide my phone back into my bag. I had a text message. Tapping on the envelope icon, I noted a message from a number I didn't recognize. Because I didn't keep any numbers in my phone besides my mother's. It was too risky, putting someone's number in your contacts like you were going to let them stick around enough to be "tapped" for a phone call one lazy Sunday.

Hey, the message started, the food was a hit! All gone within the first half of our session.

Regan? I typed back.

Are you handing out baked goods anywhere else? Any black market I should be aware of? Bo would raid it.

I smiled. The little girl smile I mocked with an eye roll. It seemed Regan really did make me smile like I used to. And he made me smile even when I was doing that slow lazy fall like Alice did through the rabbit hole. The one my mother trained me to parachute through. People refer to it as a fast, velocity-hungry descent. It's not. It's slow, and you get drunk on too much time to think while you beg for the bottom. Still, I smiled.

No, no black market. I forgot I gave you my number.

I didn't think I had.

You didn't. Lissa did.

Fucking Lissa.

Fucking Lissa. She can't keep a secret to save her life.

She really couldn't. Which is why she didn't know any of mine.

She put up a good fight, but I wore her down. I told her there was a leak in the apartment and your bakery was starting to flood.

I smiled again. Crafty, Kane.

Thank you. So. Can we have more of your goodies? Like tomorrow. Or...every day?

No. You can't possibly appreciate it every day.

I appreciate everything every day.

Damn him. I knew he did, too.

Come on, he cut in front of me, please? They're so good. The hippies are in love. Do you use organic ingredients?

I rolled my eyes. Tell them yes.

It wasn't them who asked. It was me. ;)

I chuckled out loud, my bitter exterior fading, peeling like old paint.

Still yes.

You're lying.

What do you care?

I don't want to die from pesticide-laden food.

Regan, I think the three cigarettes a day you think I don't know you smoke will kill you faster than processed tapioca flour will.

My smile took over my full face. Once I knew his recording schedule, I'd watch him leave sometimes. You can tell a lot about a person by how they leave a place in the morning. He was someone who wasn't at all convinced that mornings should exist.

Now you're the crafty one, Hall. Won't you be sorry when you're wrong. My tombstone will read "For the love of Tapioca."

I laughed out loud. An elderly man with his hand on a cane as he sat across from me looked up and smiled, too. I bit my lip and formed my response.

With a capital "T"?

Well, if it was the death of me, I'd say it's important.

I'll allow it.

Are you working at the bar tonight?

Yes.

Hmm. I'm coming. Let me play, too. Also, I'll stay till close and then we can go back to your bakery and make more muffins.

And cupcakes. I swear Bo has to shut up about the cupcakes. It's like he grew up in an Amish household the way he's carrying on about them.

You won't get any sleep if you do that.

Trust me, I don't need sleep. Baking that stuff keeps Ember and Willow from an MMA fight.

The power of food.

"Georgia?" The real-life voice sounded out of place in my ears. I'd spent the last half hour with Regan's muddled Bostonian-Irish mashup flowing through my brain.

Brain.

Shit.

I looked up to find the same pleasant nurse with the rehearsed smile and precision head tilt standing in the doorway.

"You can come back with me, now."

I stood. Smiled. Walked forward. Rehearsed.

We were all actors here.

Regan

I walked into E's promptly at 9:00 PM. That wasn't a time Georgia had told me to come. In fact, she never texted me back with confirmation of my request to come and play, and then to bake with her. No response at all even after a series of cheeky texts designed to make her smile. I know I couldn't actually see if she smiled or not. But the thought of her smiling was reason enough.

Bo and Ember were going to be coming in later, a make up of our cancelled date last night when we'd all ended up in Georgia's bakery for a couple of hours, openly processing Rae's letter.

As I approached the crowded bar at E's—a place just as crowded on a Monday as a Saturday—I was giddy for the first time in a long time. Baking with Georgia last night gave me direction and focus with a direct result. No waiting for an album to be cut, the results were immediate and delicious. Georgia's back was to me as she was waiting on people a few tables away from the bar. I hopped—literally hopped—onto the last open stool and ordered a Guinness from a male bartender I hadn't seen before. I always felt like they gave way more attitude than necessary. Maybe that was their schtick, like the women dressing the way they do.

"Here ya go, man." With triceps that tried too hard, he set the beer down without looking at me. That's the problem with young bartenders, too. They miss out on the stories around them while they're too busy flexing their egos. Too busy to hear what people are drinking to remember...or forget.

"Thank you. Do you guys have anyone playing tonight?"

"Nah." He shook his head with an authority that would have made you think he'd just said an actual word. "Football season just ended, though, so maybe they've got someone soon. Why?"

I looked over my shoulder to find Georgia, but she was nowhere to be seen. Surely she'd seen me by now. I wanted to ask her about playing and not submit myself to this guy's decision making.

"I brought my violin..." I started, but he stopped me.

"Oh, you're Georgia's friend, right?"

The word tasted like burnt coffee. Friend.

"I am."

"She said you'd be in and you could set up whenever."

"Oh," I hesitated, looking around once more for her, "did she go home, or something?"

He shook his head. "Nah, she's just in and out all night. Some family stuff to take care of."

CJ said nah all the time, but when this guy said it I wanted to grab him by the collar and scream, Please just take the time to form the word! I would have pressed him for more information, but I actually thought he would give me what he knew, and if there was anything for me to know, I'd want to hear it from Georgia.

I was a little concerned, given she dropped out of our text conversation without a goodbye. She hadn't told me about anything in particular going on with her mother, but there was no one in here I could ask about that, given I was under the impression no one else knew. Or, at least, knew as much as I did.

Just as I was spinning in a junior high blender of self pity, swirling with the word friend and my apparent insecurity, a hand landed in the middle of my back.

"Did Devin tell you it was okay if you played tonight?"

She smelled like almonds tonight.

I turned with a smile, which vanished as I studied her eyes. She'd been crying.

"What happened?" I ducked my head and whispered into her ear.

She shook her head. "Nothing, why?"

"You look like you've been crying."

Her eyes flicked to the guy behind the bar, then to the floor, before back to me. It was fast, designed to escape my notice, I'm sure.

"I'm fine."

"Are you sure?" I reached my hand out to touch her arm, but she took a step back.

"Can you play that song you were practicing the other night?" She took a deep breath and squared her shoulders, seeming to steel herself from whatever was happening in her eyes.

I shrugged. "Which one?"

"I obviously don't know the name but it sounded like...like birds weeping on a branch over a funeral service."

I brought my hand to my mouth and close my eyes for a split second. The collision of her description of the song—which was so spot on I almost stopped breathing—and her specific request that I play it was overwhelming. It was the Chopin Nocturne that I'd played the day I brought CJ to Blue Seed Studios.

"Why? Why that song? It's so..."

"Guttural." Her voice was as flat as her eyes had gone.

I nodded. "Guttural."

She shrugged. "I think sometimes the people in here need to hear what their problems sound like coming from your violin."

We were clearly not talking about anyone else in the room, but I nodded, knowing her emotional limits. And mine.

"I'll play it...if you'll tell me why that guy said you're going to be in and out all night for family stuff. What's going on?"

Georgia glared at the empty space behind my shoulder. "I'll tell you if you leave it alone for now and wait till the bar closes."

My nostrils flared as I took a frustrated breath. She didn't give anything away easily. "I'll leave it alone for now if you let me come bake with you when we're both done here."

She rolled her eyes. "Whatever. Just play it, okay?"

"Any other requests?" I slid away from the bar, violin case in hand.

She bit her lip and looked down for a moment. "Just one," she said as she looked up, fresh pink in her cheeks.

"Shoot."

"Play for as long as you can. Don't stop."

I frowned slightly. "Why?"

She let out a sad chuckle. "Why is a raven like a writing desk?"

I actually did recognize that quote from Alice in Wonderland. But, why? "What?"

She put her hand on my forearm and looked at my mouth. Her eyebrow arched as if it were trying to pull her gaze toward mine, but failed. "Sometimes the question is as complicated as the answer."

I settled myself on stage and looked into the moderately inhabited bar. The pit I had in my stomach had nothing on the look on her face as my bow and strings embraced, and wept as if separated by the war of emotions. The stubborn part of me wanted to stop playing right then and rush over to her and find out why she wiped under her eyes every few measures. Why she smiled through those tears. Moreover, why she requested the song in the first place.

The musician in me, though, ordered me to keep playing. To let her feel what she needed to feel. In time with the music. In the confines of the score. I couldn't move my eyes from her. Not during that song, or the rest of the songs I played over the course of the night.

As promised by the nameless bartender, she would disappear for ten or fifteen minutes at a time through the night, returning looking a little more broken than she'd left. As far as I knew, her mother wasn't at the facility, though I don't know that she would have told me if she'd had to go back, given I was led to believe the woman was dead in the first place.

I got the feeling that I thought more of my relationship with Georgia than she did. I felt like she was erecting new walls as quickly as I broke through long standing ones. Maybe I wasn't breaking through any at all. That seemed almost more likely as I watched her zip up her feelings and circle through the rest of her shift under my soundtrack.

At closing time, my fingers were sore, and my brain hurt from trying to figure out someone I thought I was getting to know. Georgia cashed out, cleaned up, and nodded to me when she was ready to leave. I followed her to the parking lot.

"Ready to go bake some hippie love?" While the words were light, her tone suggested she was psyching herself up for the night.

I shrugged. "We can wait for another day if you're tired."

Please don't be tired. Please don't be tired.

"No, I'm not tired."

Thank you.

"Ok, then. See you at home."

Her eyebrows pulled in a little. I immediately regretted calling it home, but what else was I supposed to say? I didn't want her thinking I thought we, like, lived together, but, for God's sake, we shared a roof. We gave each other tight smiles as we got into our cars and drove.

Home.

"Time's up." I whisked egg whites in a large stainless steel bowl, while Georgia sifted various flours that sounded like they should never go together. Garbanzo. Sorghum.

"Huh?" She turned for the oven and back to me, looking confused.

"You need to tell me where you were tonight. You promised."

She arched an eyebrow. "I never promised."

"Well. You said."

She softly bit the inside of her lip as she shook the last of the flours through the fine metal mesh.

"Something with your mom?" I encouraged.

Georgia took the bowl from me and poured the egg whites into her mixture. "She just got out of the hospital over the weekend. I was just checking in with her."

I didn't buy it for a second.

"Georgia..."

She smiled. "Look, Regan, there's nothing grander here. I was quiet about it at work because no one knows about what's going on with her. I can't stand the taste of pity."

"Why do you assume people will pity you?"

She looked startled. Her mouth stuttered open and closed a few times.

"Just because people care about what's going on with you," I continued, "doesn't mean they pity you. I didn't feel a single shred of pity from you when I read Rae's note. I felt supported and cared for."

Georgia sighed. Labored and through her cheeks, I watched her stubborn and self-mutilating resolve fade away.

"I've been thinking..." She cut herself off, grunting almost silently, like the words were too big to fit out of her throat.

"What?"

"I...I think it would be good to open the bakery. Like...for real." She placed her palms on the cold steel workspace and looked at me with her indelible poker face.

My eyes widened. "Really? That's fantastic, Georgia!"

"It's not as easy as it seems. I know I've got the space here ready to go, but I need to get permits. That won't be too hard, but, then...I need customers."

I playfully slapped the counter. "That will take less than a second. You're a genius in here."

A smile fluttered on her face for a split second before disappearing just as quickly. Like a hummingbird. "I need to spend a couple of weeks baking everything I know how to bake and delivering them to businesses. You know, like advertising. I need to get a spot at the farmer's market, get business cards made…I can't think about leaving my job at the bar unless I'm making enough here. And, I can't make enough here if people don't know about it."

Her hands were rolling around the air like she was listing an impossible number of obstacles. Excuses. But I stopped her.

"I'll help you."

Damn it if she didn't work those facial muscles to prevent a full smile. "You will? I mean…do you even have time?"

"I'll make time. Look. I need something to do when I leave the studio, something so nonmusical I can forget what the violin is for a while."

She smirked. "When you say violin…and some other words…you sound like you have an Irish accent. What the hell is that?"

I laughed, watching the way her eyes studied my mouth, as if the answer were written on my lips. "It's kind of…God, you caught me. I just like how it sounds. I'm not conscious of it all the time…"

She smacked me with a white dishtowel. "I knew it!"

I put my hands up. "To be fair, my grandparents have Irish accents as thick as fog."

"Just your grandparents? Not CJ's?" Georgia went back to her mixing.

"Other side of the family. My mom's parents. I'm nearly one hundred percent Irish." I pointed to the reddish and unruly hair on my head.

"So you just…like it?"

"Well, I spent a lot of time with my mom's parents when I was in high school. They lived closer to the boarding school than my parents did. They're the reason I decided to teach in Ireland when I was done with college. Being a musician, my ears are always training me to match pitch, so when I'm around lots of thick accents I just kind of...adopt them."

"Ah," she nodded, "so if we stuck you in Texas for a while—"

"My head would explode. I don't...do the south."

She snorted, a sound so perfectly unguarded it made me laugh louder than I had in a long time. And it felt good. She didn't know it, and I had a feeling I couldn't tell her—at least not yet—but Georgia had the captivating ability to make me feel better. Not by forgetting anything, because everything was at the forefront of my mind. Rae. The loneliness. But Georgia had this way of making it bearable. I knew she wouldn't try to throw loads of inspirational quotes at me, because she'd been there. The bottom of the barrel. She knew that those quotes were designed more for the talker than the listener. A tool to help people feel useful.

I had no idea why a guarded, spiky-skinned Georgia would ask me with help on something so personal as her bakery. Maybe those prickles were just origami spines, after all. It was clear that she trusted me, but what was clearer was that she didn't want me to vocalize it. To make real the trust she so rarely doled out. I didn't even want to call CJ about this. It felt like a perverted thought on its own. No, this would be just us.

I would take her up on her offer to help get this nameless bakery off the ground. I needed time. Around her. To see if a rewiring my insides was, in fact, what I was feeling, or if it was just the hopeless romantic in me.

She felt anything but hopeless, though, and that scared the hell out of me.

In my mind I pictured Georgia standing on the rock wall. Her face lifted to the sky and her palms forward in a peaceful second before she jumped.

I wanted to jump. I didn't know how far down the bottom was, but as I poured cupcake batter into the twelve perfect circles of the tin, I found myself hoping Georgia would be waiting for me down there.

Our eyes met as she closed the oven door and set the timer.

"Are you feeling okay?" She didn't make a move to put a comforting hand on my arm like Ember would have. Georgia knew her words were enough and didn't ever try to suffocate me with more than the situation called for.

I put my hand over my mouth, a throat clearing effort to cover a pending sob with a laugh. "No. Not at all." I shrugged and smiled.

And she did too.

CHAPTER *Fifteen*

ADVENTURES FIRST

Georgia

So, Regan said he'd help me. I can't say I was surprised by his reaction—it was the one I'd hoped for—but there was still an overexposure at his words. He really wanted to be here, with me. And I had no idea why. Or, really, why I wanted him to want to be here.

That's a lie. I wanted him to want to be here. I needed him to want to be in the bakery. With me. After long nights and days of sitting by my sobbing mother's side, I needed an escape. I needed to be able to make someone feel better. Customers with my food. Regan by helping me. He seemed to need to be needed.

Oh, the sobbing mother? That's just a fun side effect of the ECT. I haven't teased out if it's a direct side effect, or if it's residual from some of the other ones, but during the several hours following her release from her first two treatments, she cried. Just cried and sobbed, and sniffed, and cried some more. There were no words or acknowledgements of my presence. It was such a heavy sob I almost felt bad for not joining her.

I don't know if she was having regrets about the procedure because she didn't want to talk about it during the days in between appointments. Maybe she wept over memories she thought she lost, or hours or days in the vortex of potential memory loss.

Yeah, last week was a goddamned doozy. I was able to distract myself in the bakery with Regan, and I was back for more distraction tonight. We were doing a late-night session. Him because of some rearranging of the recording schedule, and me? Well, I told him I switched days off with Lissa. That wasn't a lie. What I wasn't doing was talking about the ECT. I wasn't talking about it with my mother, and I certainly wasn't talking about it right now with Regan. I needed to see him smile. I needed to get lost. Forget.

"I have to be honest with you, Georgia. I was afraid that after a few days of this, I would get bored, or something. I was thinking, Okay what's the big deal? There are muffins, breads, cupcakes, just different flavors. How exciting can that be?" Regan rambled as he flipped through my recipe book.

"That's...honest of you." I was trying to search his face for further information, to see if there was a but coming.

"But," there it was, "what I realized is...it's just like music. There are only twelve notes on a musical scale. Period. That's it. Sure there are octaves and other minutely measurable frequencies. But, the point is...all the music you've ever heard is based on twelve notes. Twelve!" His eyes lit up as he held out his hands, like he was presenting me with this gift of twelve.

"Right...twelve..." I smirked as he slid the book back to me. I thumbed through the pages to find my chocolate chip cookie recipe.

"People search for variety everywhere. With everything. In music and in here, in your bakery, we make variety. We are the masters of variety." He seemed quite pleased with himself, leaning back against the painted cinderblock wall and folding his arms across this chest.

"It's like colors," he continued. Dear God, he continued. "Primary colors. Red. Blue. Yellow. Boom."

"You've gone mad. And that's not a title I dole out to just anyone." I laughed and pointed to the recipe on the page. He dutifully began gathering flours as I pulled out the wet ingredients.

"I just mean, Georgia," he teased, "people generally take the few basic and bare things afforded to us in this world and make them as complicated as possible. Us, though? We complicate it in beautiful ways. We have fun with it. Basically, we're awesome."

He grinned. To call it a grin wouldn't do it justice, really. It was like one side of his face was sneaking up on the other side. Waiting to jump out and say Surprise! Both of his eyes lit up. He really was quite...I have to say it...beautiful. He was rugged and elegant. Traits that I'd been hard pressed to find on the men in my life anywhere. The way Regan carried himself made you think he could just as easily fall over as he could sweep you into a ballroom dance. Long, lanky limbs that moved in tempo with the earth on a frequency shared between him and Mother Nature alone.

Still, it was sexy. There, I said that, too. Regan was sexy and beautiful and he was helping me bake and I listened to him play his violin and we just spent time with each other. Few questions and fewer answers. I still didn't even have an idea what Rae said to him in that letter he carried around with him in his back pocket every day.

"How's your mom doing?" Regan asked so nonchalantly you'd think he was looking at me as I read the thermometer on the window, waiting for news on the weather.

We hadn't set rules on what we would and would not talk about with each other, but this was the first time he'd mentioned her. I panicked a little, thinking maybe he'd found out about the shock therapy and was preparing for a grand sprint out of my life.

"She's fine. Why?"

He shrugged. "I care about the people in your life. I haven't seen her around since the first time I, uh, met her. I feel bad about the way I hand—"

"Don't apologize." I held up my hand. "She and I talked that day. She knows you didn't mean any harm."

"Was she mad about me thinking she was dead?" He winced like a child trying out a swear word for the first time.

I smiled. "No. She wasn't even mad at me for making you think that. She's very forgiving."

"Is she excited about you opening the bakery?"

No, because she doesn't know.

"She's wanted me to open it for a long time. That whole binder there is filled with family recipes. Most of them I modify on the fly for this bakery, but they're all hers and my grandmother's."

She had wanted me to open it for a long time. I was trying really hard not to lie to Regan, as had become customary for me in nearly every close relationship over the last decade. Still, the full truth was too new, too infantile in its resilience to the rejection I knew would chase after it.

"Well, let me know when she's coming in again. I'd like to meet her, like, for real."

"Will do." I nodded. The fatigue of the last week and my mother pressed on me like a brick between my shoulder blades.

Tomorrow was another treatment. Another lie I'd have to tell Regan. Another reminder why I couldn't feel about him the way I was feeling. Because the last thing I wanted was to watch his smile fade as he drove me to my own ECT appointments.

To watch the brassy sheen in his hair turn white with the stress of watching his girlfriend, or wife, or whatever I could possibly become, have her brain rewired over and over. His wife, because that's what Regan would want, being the all-the-way romantic he is. His wife would forget little things at first. What she had for breakfast that morning, what movie they saw a few days ago. But, how long until she forgot about the way they met? The reasons they fell in love. How long before he looked for my eyes and found two empty wells? The deep kind. Not the wishing well kind.

There aren't enough pennies in the world to cover the cost of that wish...the wish that things would go differently for me.

"Georgia?" Regan ducked his head into my line of vision, grinning cautiously.

My face had grown hot, my breathing unsure. Coming out in the broken sounds of someone tripping in tap shoes.

"Are you okay? You look..." Regan's forehead bunched up as he walked toward me.

"Hey," he tried again, softer, touching my shoulder.

I looked up at him. Those eyes. The ones that watched me move around the kitchen and when he thought I wasn't looking. The ones that promised me, without his words, that he was genuine.

"I..." I trailed off, looking around the room for a reason not to. There were hundreds.

I ignored them.

I jumped.

I kissed him.

Holy shit, I kissed him.

I stood on my tiptoes, put my hands on his cheeks like every cliché I hate, and pressed my mouth hard onto his. My height made me fully commit to the kiss. I couldn't just give him a peck in passing. I had to get all the way up on my toes.

Then he moaned a little. Louder at the beginning than the end, like he hadn't intended on me hearing it in the first place. But I did. And it made me kiss him harder.

He slid a hand down my side and around to my lower back, the tremble of his nerves giving themselves away against my heated skin. A second later I was lifted onto the counter, Regan seemingly impatient with our ridiculous height difference. He wanted my mouth as much as I wanted his and needed to be closer.

Our mouths didn't separate as we ran fingers through each other's hair. Heavy breaths surged through our nostrils as our tongues took up all the available space in each other's mouths. I let out a shrill noise from the back of my throat. Excitement. Muffled by the fullness of his tongue, it rang through as desire. Need.

I did need. More.

God it felt good. Amazing. His hands felt in my hair exactly how I wanted them to feel. His rough, tight hands over the back of my neck and up through my hair.

No. I had to stop.

Now.

"Shit," I whispered as I pulled away from his mouth. Hard and breathless.

Regan's lips remained parted, at the ready as his eyes opened.

"Shit," I said again, sliding off the counter and walking to the far side of it. "Sorry."

Regan looked around. Back and forth on the floor, to each window, the ceiling and the floor, and back to me. I bit my lip to take away from what the intensity of his gaze did to my insides. He looked fantastically deranged in his post-kiss glory. His hair a mess, half out of the elastic holding it away from his face.

"Sorry? Sorry?" He was as breathless as I felt, though my own breathing was remarkably measured.

My voice, though, shook from my error. Premeditated, maybe. But lots of premeditated things are errors. "I...I'm sorry for...I didn't mean to just...I got carried away." My words spilled out like marbles on a tile floor.

"Georgia..." The seductive Celtic caramel of his voice preceded him as he walked toward me in a hurry. His hands were on my face this time, and damn it if it didn't look like he was going to kiss me.

"What?" I said it inside of an exhale. A sigh and a prayer rolled into one.

"What do you want?"

You.

"I...I don't...what do you mean?"

"I think you want to kiss me again."

I nodded. I'd completely lost any sense I had.

He reached for my hands. His were clammy but strong. I let them hold mine.

"But for some reason, you don't want to kiss me again right now, right? Not yet?"

It was like he was singing me a lullaby as he reached up and stroked my cheek with his thumb.

I nodded again, undone were my defenses against him getting inside my head. He'd found an underground tunnel, the bastard. Probably through my tongue.

"I want to kiss you again, too. I don't know when, either. But you're going to be the next girl I kiss. That...that I do know." He moved his thumb to my mouth, gliding the pad of it across my lips as if storing the address in his body's GPS system.

And, as if nothing happened at all, he turned and went back to the flours. To the chocolate chip cookies.

And me? I was racing full speed away from the Red Queen. Screaming at myself to wake up.

Regan

She tasted exactly like I thought she would. Sugar. That's not meant to be some cute sort of mental tie-in my brain made because we were standing in her bakery. Her lips were actually sweet. Dipped in nectar and pressing against mine.

The look in her eyes before she kissed me did not lead me to believe that wrapping her arms around my neck was going to be her next move. Her nostrils flared and eyes widened like there was a giant spider crawling on my shoulder and she was about to brush it away. Instead…the kiss.

I hadn't stopped thinking about what it might be like to kiss her since the day I almost had, several weeks ago. It was over so fast tonight that the only solution was to do it again. Not yet, though. It wouldn't be fair to her or Rae if I went ahead kissing the hell out of Georgia the way I badly craved without first truly addressing the card from Rae. Making sure that what I was doing was kissing Georgia. Not Rae's ghost.

I finished in the bakery as quickly as possible, lying to Georgia that I'd received a 9-1-1 text from Ember and needed to get over there. The only 9-1-1 text was from me to Ember. Georgia didn't question it, or seem weird about it, even though it was encroaching on five o'clock in the morning. She seemed just as desperate as I was to get into her corner and reassess what the hell it was that had just happened between us.

We mumbled agreement to meet again the next night. I assumed she spent a lot of time with her mom during the day, though I knew talking about it was still really hard for her, so I didn't push it. I had to record with The Six tomorrow, but wasn't about to be a girl with Ember in front of everyone. I could do that just fine in private.

"It's been a while, Kane," Ember mused as I let myself into her house. She was pulling a whistling kettle away from the stove. Two mugs were ready to go.

"I just saw you today." I hopped onto the barstool across from her.

"Yesterday." She yawned, which reminded me that for Ember it was a new day. For me, it was a continuation of the last few hours.

She looked up, a smartass grin bringing lightness to her face. "But, I mean since a 9-1-1 text. Or call, for that matter. You didn't even send me one when, you know, you got mail." Her eyebrow twitched like a period at the end of her sentence.

I sighed. "Sorry. I didn't know if I wanted to tell Bo...and I didn't want you to have to keep secrets from him, then you all showed up—"

"At Georgia's." She poured boiling water over loose tea leaves. "You're a grownup, Regan, but you didn't have to hide that. If you're hanging out with Georgia..." She shrugged like she couldn't commit to the unspoken second half of her sentence.

"It's not like that. Well, it wasn't. Wait...back up." I put up my hands then grabbed the steaming hot mug of tea. "How are you and Bo doing after...the letter?"

She smiled. The kind of smile she had while looking through little kid pictures of Rae before her funeral. A syrupy melancholy. "We're fine. You're adorable. How are you? I read the words, Regan. I remember you telling me you wished you'd said them to her."

She stood next to me and leaned onto the counter, our forearms touching and both of us looking at an imaginary spot on the counter. Ember had been excelling in her training in the art of talking about heavy things with guys. Eye contact is discouraged. Makes us feel naked. Which is only okay if naked is what we want to be at that moment.

"It was like ringing the doorbell to hell, reading that card, Em. I couldn't fucking believe I was staring at the words I'd forced myself not to say to her. I..." I put my chin in my hand and took a deep breath.

Ember took a hand and ran it up and down my back, not saying anything for a moment. When she spoke, finally, her tone was thoughtful. "I'd ask if we could talk about Georgia later, but I feel like this is all kind of muddled together..."

"Hell fucking yes, it's muddled!" I stood with the growl of a tantrum-throwing teenager. Taking my tea to prove to myself I was well past those days.

"Sorry..." Ember shrugged, facing me without leaving the counter.

I paced the short length of the living room. "I was kind of liking Georgia, you know? She's fun to be around and she's also aggravatingly complicated, but she's so...raw. So real you couldn't fictionalize her if you tried. She even tries, but it's not...she can't..." I stopped to take a breath, feeling the sticky sweet wisp of her kiss on my lips.

"Was?" Ember turned to face me, leaning against the counter.

"Huh?"

"You said you were kind of liking Georgia. What is it now?"

I pursed my lips, looking at Ember and realizing I had to say it out loud. To someone. Before I exploded.

"I really, really like her. I trust her. She's trusted me with some really heavy shit, too. And then she said she wanted to open her bakery, and I said I'd help her, and then we kissed."

Ember's eyes widened, a peacock-green billboard screaming, What the fuck did you just say? as her mouth formed a perfect "O."

"Say something." I huffed and sat down, setting my mug on the dark wood of the coffee table.

"Well...I'm trying to read your reaction to see if I should formulate my supportive response or my rescue response. How was it? The kiss, I mean."

"How was it?" I curled my lip, having not signed on for this level of girl talk.

"I mean, pervert, how did it feel? Emotionally."

I shrugged noncommittally as I formed the exact opposite sentiment with my words. "Awesome. Seriously. It felt so good to have my lips on someone else's...to have someone's hands in my hair and on my shoulders. Then she pulled away and it felt like a cold gust of Rae ripped across the back of my neck."

"Why'd she pull away?" Ember joined me on the couch.

"I don't know. She's got walls built by walls designed by walls. She wants to do it again, though. So do I...I think. I just...if I hadn't gotten that letter from Rae I might still be making out with Georgia in the bakery."

Ember laughed so loudly and suddenly that I jumped.

"What?" I asked, incredulously.

"Your honesty when you're tired is priceless. Anyway...did Rae's letter change your feelings about Georgia?"

I shook my head.

"Did they change your feelings about Rae?"

My eyes stung, but I shook my head, again.

"What'd they change?" She put her hand on my knee like she could read my goddamn mind.

"They changed," I managed through an uneven voice, "how I feel about my healing. I thought I was done with that part. I want to pursue things with Georgia, but I don't want to cheat her out of a real relationship if I can't even give her a real person. But...I feel like Rae's letter reminded me that I haven't come to terms with those things undone. You know? Like...things I can do absolutely nothing about. I can't tell her I love her and have her hear me and smile back and tell me she loves me, too..."

Ember squeezed my knee. "You're rambling. Slow down. First of all, you are a real person capable of a real relationship. Second of all, I don't think any of us will ever be done healing from Rae's death...she'll kind of flow through our lives like that gooey stuff in a lava lamp, filling in empty spaces, but never creating more emptiness. But I want those little holes, you know? For her to fill. And last of all, it definitely sounds like you need to find a way to tell Rae you love her."

"Loved...right? Loved?"

Ember shook her head. "No. You love her. I love her, Bo loves her, we all love her. She's just not here."

I nodded, swallowing the jagged edges of she's not here one by one.

"So...what will you do? Just for Rae, just between you and Rae, find your way to say goodbye to her that doesn't involve a funeral, doesn't involve hiding in Ireland for three months. Tell her you love her, Regan." She leaned into my shoulder, her head tilting down and her hair falling down my arm.

I wrapped my arm around her. "You're smart, you know that?"

“I had stuff I wasn’t able to say to her, too, you know...” Ember didn’t look at me, she kept looking forward.

“Like what?”

She sniffed, but made no move to wipe away the present tear. “Like that her brother and I finally got our heads out of our asses.” Ember chuckled a little at the tear-pinched end of her sentence.

I squeezed her into me as her shoulders shook. “So what’d you do?”

She sat up, finally wiping under her eyes. “Bo and I wrote her letters, then made a bonfire, and burned them, sending the spirit of the letter into the universe.”

I laughed. It was completely inappropriate and poor timing, but I laughed. Then Ember smacked me.

“Don’t be an asshole!” she shrieked playfully.

“I’m sorry. I just...was that your parents’ idea?”

She laughed and pressed her forehead on my shoulder. “Yes!”

I kissed the top of her forehead. “Did it work?”

She nodded. “We felt a lot better after it.”

I bit another smile away. “Is it okay with you if I...don’t do that?”

“I hate you,” she growled into my shoulder.

“I know.”

She sat up, cheeks rosy from laughter and tears. “Do something, though. I don’t care how looney it might seem to me or Bo or anyone else. Do something.”

“First,” I yawned as I stood, “I’m gonna go home and go to bed.”

Once I was at the door, Ember tugged on the back of my shirt.

“Regan?”

“Yeah?” I turned around to find her smiling softly, mostly with her eyes.

“I like what Georgia’s done to your face.”

I pulled my eyebrows together and Ember reached for my cheeks.

"The smiles. The reddish color that rivals your hair. If she does that to you, then she's okay by me. You don't need my opinion, and you didn't ask...but I want you to know that I see the life in your face again. And I'll kiss her for it someday."

I grabbed Ember into a tight hug. "I love you, Em."

"I love you, too. Now...go tell Rae the same thing, okay?"

"How?" I asked as I backed away.

She shrugged. "You laughed at my idea," she teased. "Seriously, though...you'll figure it out."

The truth was, I thought as I drove away, I knew exactly what I had to do.

CHAPTER *Sixteen*

HELLO, GOODBYE

Regan

SO, OVER THE next couple of weeks, I started. I started working on my final love letter to Rae. In between recording with The Six, which was only going to last another few weeks, and helping Georgia with the bakery, I worked on my goodbye.

It wasn't ready yet, and I hadn't really thought through what I was actually going to do with it when I was done, but the working on it was enough for now.

In the post-kiss atmosphere of Georgia's still unnamed bakery, I was thankful for her gritty ability to compartmentalize her life. There were no awkward pauses in conversation or bizarre back and forth dances trying to pass by each other as we moved around the kitchen. We seemed to only be seeing each other in the bakery these days, and that was a lack of sleep well worth it.

We were both exhausted from the hours we'd kept over the last two weeks since I started helping her, but according to Georgia, it was working. She'd had business cards made, with just her information on it, since the bakery had no name—a fact I mentioned to her whenever I could—and she would deliver her baked goods to local businesses and set up stands at various farmers' markets, too. Her phone had been buzzing like crazy with people telling her the things they liked best, placing large orders for private parties, and asking, of course, when she'd be open for business.

"I just need to get people in here on a regular basis, now." She spoke in the middle of a train of thought I wasn't riding. She caught on to my confusion. "Sorry...I was thinking it's one thing to have people know where you are, but you need to get people into the habit of coming to your place, to put it on the maps in their brains and make it part of their daily or weekly routine. Sure, they can place orders and pick them up, but I want people, like, here, too."

I gestured to the large windows that butted up against the booth. "At least you have the location working for you."

She shrugged and tilted her head side-to-side like she was half disagreeing. "The vista works, right? But...this is a back street in a largely residential neighborhood. There's a boutique on the north side of the street, but this part of the road looks like a long driveway. There's not a ton of foot traffic...almost none, really. And very little through traffic."

"Okay," I sighed, putting my hands on my hips, "time to get some traffic, then."

She looked up, biting her lip. "How?"

I wandered into the dining area and took a few laps around the space, willing an idea to come to me. I looked back at Georgia, who was watching me closely through the large cut-out in the wall. It was as open a kitchen as the space would allow without completely removing a weight-bearing wall. It was a fantastic space. Warm, open...

"Classes!" I shouted with a loud clap of my hand.

A clearly exhausted Georgia felt the volume all the way to her bones, it seemed. She jumped half a foot back. "What the fuck is wrong with you!"

"Sorry," I exaggerated a whisper, "classes."

She flipped me off, and whispered back, "Explain."

"You could offer baking classes here. For one, people love to say they're taking classes of something that sounds fancy. That's just how people are. Throw the gluten-free angle into it and you've got something. People want to learn how to bake G-F stuff whether they need to, or not. And, if they do need to, you'll be doing them a huge favor. You could charge per class or per session...like...I don't know, you could either have a course, so people could learn to make cookies, cupcakes, breads, whatever all in a week, or you could have cookie week..."

I trailed off as Georgia walked into the dining area to meet me toe-to-toe. My tattered six-year-old Converses against her ancient combat boots whose scuff marks were colored in with black permanent marker.

"What? Too much?"

"No," she blinked like her lashes were the fluttering wings of that rocking horse fly, "it's fucking brilliant!" A rare wide smile crinkled her eyes as she leaped from her spot on the floor and wrapped her legs around my waist.

Instantly it reminded me of the day I'd met her and she'd greeted CJ that way. It seemed like forever ago, but I know that there was no way back then that I was thinking I'd be in his position someday. The recipient of Georgia's full-body experience hug. I crossed my arms under the full curve of her hips and circled us around once before setting her down.

"Jesus, Regan, seriously!" She squeezed me one more time before running into the kitchen and returning with a calendar and a notebook. "That's brilliant. I had so many people this week saying, Oh I wish I could bake like this. I could teach them, and they might do it a few times to impress people or when they're feeling down, but we know they'll still buy from the bakery. People know how to cook but still order out, you know what I'm sayin'?"

For the first time since I'd known her, Georgia's Eastern Massachusetts screw-you accent slipped from her mouth.

"Yeah, I know whatchyou're sayin'," I echoed the accent back as I sat across from her.

She blushed deeply, looking up at me through noticeably tired eyes. "It's like that when I'm tired. Fuck off."

"How has everything been, just, in general?" I watched her hands produce a fascinatingly flowy cursive penmanship as she marked boxes on her calendar and made lists of ideas for classes.

"I can do an introductory class to start. Offer those on the next two Saturdays and Sundays and then schedule the grand opening for, like, three weeks from now?" She looked up hopefully, but frowned when she saw me studying her. "What?"

I gave a half smile. "I asked how things were going, you know, with life. I only see you in here these days...just checking in."

She sat back in the booth. "Things..." She looked around, just with her eyes, not turning her head. They seemed to glass over a bit.

"Hey..." I reached across the table and held out my hand. "Would it help if I went first?"

Georgia placed her always-warm hand in mine, and I took a deep breath as I wrapped my fingers around them. "I'm working on a final goodbye to Rae."

"What kind of goodbye?"

"An answer to her letter."

Georgia looked confused. "Did she...ask you something?"

"Haven't you read it?" I tilted my head to the side.

"No."

"But when..." I trailed off, trying to recall why I'd assumed she'd read it.

She pulled her hand from mine and ran it through her hair. She had thick roots growing in. The only reason I thought anything about it was because CJ said her hair used to be dark, and I'd spent an inordinate amount of time imagining her with dark hair.

"The night Bo and Ember were here, they sat with you and read it, remember? It was clearly a very...personal moment. I wasn't going to intrude."

I reached into my back pocket, where I'd been keeping the card since I first read it. "Read it."

"It's okay, Regan, I don't...need to." She shook her hands and head at the same time.

"I need you to, Georgia." I slid the card across the table, eyeing the already wrinkling and fading edges.

"Why do you need me to?" She didn't reach for the letter.

"You've been really open and honest with me, Georgia, and... you were there for me, really there when I read the thing. I figured you should know where I'm coming from." I tapped the envelope. "This is where I'm coming from."

Her look took on the pallor of guilt as she swaddled the letter after taking it from the envelope. She looked at me once before opening it. I nodded, reassuring her. She paled further as she read. Her eyes brightened at what I assumed were the cute and funny parts Rae had written. Then, it was like I was watching a flashback of myself when I came to the I love you portion of the event...Georgia's hand went to her mouth and she dropped the card, looking at me.

"I'm so, so sorry." She kept her hand hovering over her lips and she fled our booth, exiting the bakery door and taking deep breaths in the fresh air of the quiet Sunday morning.

Carefully, I slid the card back into its envelope, tucked it in my back pocket, savoring the limited time it would reside there, and followed Georgia outside.

"She loved you," Georgia started as the door closed behind me. "She loved you, and never really said it, and you loved her and never said it, then she died and no one said it and, holy fuck, Regan." She paced in circles.

"I—"

"And she died," Georgia repeated, and as if she were just learning of Rae's death for the first time, she started to cry.

So did I.

"She did." I wiped under my eyes.

"How are you standing here? How did you...what...shit and then we kissed." She ran a knuckle under her eye.

"I wanted to kiss you, Georgia. And, you wanted to kiss me... judging by the way you, you know, kissed me." I cracked a smile, not fully understanding her meltdown.

She leaned against the building just as it started to drizzle. "I knew you'd been in love, Regan. You told me. Rewiring your insides and all that, but...why would you want to risk it again?"

"Risk what, love?"

"Losing it," she whispered as more tears fell.

I shook my head, words jamming in my throat. Insecurity crashed into hope, fear rear-ended happiness. I walked over to Georgia and put my hands on her shoulders. "What if I don't lose it?"

I had to believe my words. Had to. There was no other way to take another breath. Ever.

"What if you do?" She stared through me, like she was etching an imaginary future into my brain.

I squeezed her shoulders, almost shouting over the fear that tried to drown the words as the rain fell harder around us. Crashing cymbals of water. "What if I do, Georgia? What if I do?"

The wind picked up, directing the rain to slam in sheets against us. Georgia didn't blink as she met my eyes, water covering every inch of her face.

"I have to go." She shimmied away from my hold and walked to her car, pulling away without another word.

Thunder crashed as I watched the car pull away. I retraced my steps back into the bakery, locking the door behind me, and turning off the light in the seating area. I couldn't shake the fear in Georgia's eyes as she talked about Rae...and love. Georgia was afraid to love. I was afraid that I'd never love again.

Had been afraid, until that blinding swirl of exclamation points and question marks masquerading as Georgia Hall barged into my life. Or did I barge into hers? How the hell did we get here? Kissing in her kitchen, promising more kisses, then doing nothing about it?

I didn't know what all her fears were, though she was clearly afraid of them, as odd as it sounds. But she wasn't a girl who could be pushed.

As I entered my apartment and pulled out my violin and composition notebook, I took a deep breath and reasoned that to love Georgia was to be patient. Let her come to me.

I was loving her.

As I drew my pencil across the lines of the notebook, sculpting the last goodbye to Rae, I didn't feel apologetic about that. Loving. Rae would want me to love again. Hell, love would want me to love again.

I was falling slowly.

And I didn't want there to be a bottom, because what greater feeling in the world is there than to actually be falling into love?

Georgia

My windshield wipers whipped too quickly back and forth across the glass as I sped down the highway. The thumping of the rubber took me out of my head, making me listen to something other than my excruciating heart.

I was running away.

Regan loved Rae, she loved him, then every worst thing in the world happened and he showed up at my doorstep. I invited him there, yes, I'm aware of that minute fucking detail, but there he was. War-torn? No. Faithful. A disciple of all things pure.

I'd been afraid that maybe if he was kissing me it was a rebound thing, but Rae had passed away almost a year ago—9 months, I think—and Regan didn't even like me when we first met. At least it hadn't seemed that way.

I slipped. I knew better. I shouldn't have ever rented him that apartment, but since there was nothing I could do about that by the time I realized what was happening, I should have kept him at a firm arm's length. Instead I'd had my arms around him exactly one too many times.

I couldn't tell him I didn't want his help anymore with the bakery. He seemed so happy when he was in the kitchen, and it was a constant reminder of why I loved being there in the first place. And, opening the bakery was something I was genuine in wanting. He was the only person who would let me go at my pace.

Then there was that fucking letter.

I shouldn't have read it. I wish he hadn't shown me. I knew all of it, but to see it outside of the folklore of Rae: former girlfriend was overwhelming. It wasn't her words or her character that so cheerfully bubbled through the ink that got to me. It was that she so certainly laid everything bare for him. I know they never said those words together, but reading her note and hearing stories from him, I knew they were a real couple. The kind that talked about things and then worked through them.

That was nothing I could ever live up to, even if I wanted to. I wanted to, but didn't want to want to.

I pulled into my mother's driveway right when my mind started somersaulting down a hill. The rain hadn't been this heavy in as long as I can remember, and I knocked louder than necessary just to be able to hear the sound.

My mom came to the door looking better than she had in days. Her recovery time between shock treatments was getting better, easier to manage. She was looking more like herself than I'd seen her in years, which was good since I was a total mess and needed her like I hadn't needed her in just as long.

"What's wrong?" she shrieked and pulled me in out of the rain.

The door shut behind me as I buried my face into her shoulder.

"I'm in big trouble, Mom."

In that moment I was thankful for gravity, because there was nothing else holding me to the Earth as every piece of strength I thought I had seeped from my eyes and onto my mother's freshly pressed blouse.

"That's quite a story." My mom brought me a fresh cup of hot chocolate as I finished telling her the Regan and Rae love story, and the Regan and Georgia tragedy in the making.

I looked into the swirling mini marshmallows, my eyes swollen with tears.

"What are you afraid of, Georgia?"

"Hurting him," I answered before I could craft something witty.

"I don't understand. From what you've told me, you two have an easy relationship. You're friends, you each have your own interests but are interested in each other's, respectively. What's the holdup?"

I took a deep breath; it tripped over lingering tears, but satisfied me just the same. "The women in our family don't really get happy endings, Mom. Grampa killed himself and with him, took Gram's chance at one, and you…"

"You don't think I'll get a happy ending?" Her eyes pinched at the edges, clearly hurt.

"I meant you and dad. He was a drunk and then you had…"

"Georgia, your father and I—"

"Had alcoholism and schizophrenia as supporting characters in your love story. How romantic. Regan doesn't seem to have any discernible mental illness, so I won't be robbed of a happy ending like Gram, but given my genetic inheritance—"

"You're not still hung up on that, are you?" My mother rolled her head back in exasperation.

"Caught up on my chances of getting schizophrenia? Yeah, I'm hung up on statistics."

"Georgia, you were more likely to get killed on the drive over here. Especially knowing how fast you drive."

"Thanks," I mumbled.

"So, let me get this straight. Regan is helping you open the bakery, and has been supporting you every step of the way for the last few weeks, and you're pushing him away because you're afraid you might, at some point, get a mental illness that's treatable?"

"Don't patronize me. He doesn't deserve a love that has to be medicated."

"He doesn't deserve to be cheated out of it, and it doesn't sound like he wants to be cheated out of it the way you talk about him."

I sat forward, my face growing hot. "Whose side are you on?"

"Yours, Georgia. Always."

I sat back in a huff, crossing my arms. "You weren't on my side when you took off and left me to be raised by an alcoholic father and his pack of misfits at Dunes."

My mother turned her face from me, gripping the edge of her chair as my words cut through her.

"Mom," I started, "I'm sorry..."

"No," she sniffed, "you have a right to be upset with me. I was doing what I thought was best for you at the time. Treatment wasn't like it is now, and I didn't know how long I'd be functional, or where the disease would go. Your father had never once been violent, but, if we can remember back two months, you've had bruises from me. Sure, your dad pissed away most of his money, but not before keeping food on the table and buying the building you live in now. There were no good answers there, honey. No right answers. I just tried to make you as strong as possible before I left."

"Because you knew I'd end up taking care of myself."

She didn't answer. She just sighed and looked down. I hadn't intended on showing up and blaming my mother for my life, so I stood and made my way for the door.

"Why are you leaving?" My mom followed me, staying a measured three steps behind me.

I turned as my hand touched the knob. "You know, Alice didn't even get one. A happy ending. She just...woke up, and everything was the boring old goddamned way it had been before."

I pulled the door open and stepped onto the top stair. The rain had stopped, finally, leaving everything gasping for breath after the onslaught.

"There was no ending," my mom called after me as I walked into the rain-soaked air.

"What?" I turned around.

"There was no real ending to Alice in Wonderland, Georgia. Go ahead. Read the books, watch the movie again if you don't believe me." She gave a challenging smile.

"What am I supposed to do with that?"

"Write one."

"How?" I grinned, feeling a riddle coming on. I'd learned from the best.

She smiled back the same knowing smile. "By writing it and living it, by living it and writing it. You have to do both, and in both orders at once. Make it. Mix it together. There's no timer, though, so you're out of luck there. Just use your nose."

"Things can get burned that way," I mused.

She shook her head and as she closed the door, she said, "Not if you breathe deeply."

Just like that the Hookah-Smoking Caterpillar swirled away into a cloud of smoke and butterflies and I was left with the most challenging and simplest riddle of my life.

Love.

Him.

Love him.

CHAPTER *Seventeen*

GO ASK ALICE

Regan

WITH ANY OTHER girl, it would have been maddening, the way Georgia went back to work with me Monday in the bakery like nothing had happened the day before. We hadn't texted or really seen much of each other, which was normal, but how we'd left things on Sunday was far from normal.

Well, far from normal with anyone else. With Georgia, the out of place, slightly off-kilter way of things was normal. True North on her compass seemed to be somewhere between "N" and a little left of there.

In truth, I'd been so focused on my project for Rae that I didn't let myself wallow in the "whys" and "what ifs" with Georgia. She was a straight shooter, and I trusted that she'd shoot when she was ready.

"Guess what?" she asked as she lined wicker baskets with cloth napkins.

I pulled two tins of muffins from the oven and put another two in. "What?"

"I set up a website for the bakery and posted information about the baking class, called all of the contacts I've made from the local businesses and the farmers' markets, and today alone I got ten people signed up." Her smile was contagious as she took the warm muffins and put them in the baskets, closing the cloth napkins around them to keep them warm.

"Really? Georgia, that's huge!" I crossed over to the large sink and started cleaning up the dishes.

"Uh-huh. I'm going to start the first class this weekend. Just a one-day introduction class. After that, I'll run another weekend, and the weekend after that I'll have the grand opening. Is that crazy?" She put her hands on her hips and took a few quick breaths.

"No." I shut off the water, dried my hands, and walked over to her. "It's not crazy at all. You've got this. What's the permit status?"

"I have my inspection Wednesday, and everything else will be good to go." She shrugged, leaving her shoulders by her ears as her face shifted to disappointment. "Shiiiiit," she sighed.

"What?"

"I…have this…fucking appointment…thing on Wednesday and it's like around the time the health inspector is going to be here." For a second it looked like she was going to cry. Like a child who was about to question the reality of Santa Claus, but didn't really want to know the answer.

I reached up and touched her shoulder. "Don't worry about it, G. I can be here for the inspection if that's okay with them."

She looked relieved and, in a flash, smacked me. "Don't call me G."

"What? I thought your friends could call you that. Did I miss something?"

She scrunched up her nose. "It just…sounds funny coming from you. And, I don't kiss my friends…or people who call me G. Those are one and the same, you see?"

I playfully growled and shook her a little. "The riddles! When do they end?"

"Look around you." She laughed and spun around the kitchen and into the seating area. "Never! This is the world according to Georgia, brought to you by the Mad Hatter." She twirled again, one smooth circle with her arms out and chin lifted to the ceiling.

"Can I call you Alice, then?"

Her chin dropped, lips formed a thin line, and she crooked a wicked eyebrow. "Not if you expect me to answer."

"Why not?"

The air around us shifted. Imperceptible to passers by, for certain, but I was afraid to look down, thinking the floor would suddenly be missing. Georgia's shoulders and breasts rose and fell quicker as color went from her cheeks to the scooped neckline of her grey t-shirt.

"Because," she started with nervous breath, "because...Alice was a lonely girl. With no prince."

I cleared my throat. "Yeah? What, then, are you?"

"Who."

"What?"

"Who, then, am I, you mean." Her voice was shaky.

I nodded. "Who are you?"

She took two steps toward me and grabbed the ends of my index fingertips. "I'm not a lonely girl anymore."

"And the prince?" My voice came out as a whisper.

"It's like Alice with the unicorn. Book, not movie. I see one, I think, but it's in the convincing, you know? Of myself. Can I believe it?"

We were both speaking in whispers now.

I didn't know what to say. I wanted to tell her she could, but things with her were better presented as questions. "Can you?"

"I'm afraid, you know."

I nodded. "I know. Listen...I have something I need you to help me with." I cleared my throat again, willing myself not to kiss her until this last part was done.

"Oh? What's that?"

I sped into the kitchen, grabbed two cupcakes and handed them to her. "Meet me on the pier in, like, five minutes."

"With these?"

I nodded. "We'll need them, I think. Kind of a re-do of a few weeks ago. Only I promise you that this time I won't curl into the fetal position and sob."

She stared at me with a comically quizzical look on her face. She wasn't used to being part of a plan, just the master of them.

"Just go." I nudged her arm. "I'll be there in a minute."

A few minutes later, I made it to the pier with my violin in one hand, and a paper bag in the other. I stopped at the edge of the pier for a moment, taking in the view. Not just the welcoming sun, peaceful in its fury, but the peaceful and fury bit of human being dangling her legs over the edge of the splintered wood. She'd rolled her black jeans up to her knees and her shoes were resting next to her. Just as she rolled her head back and took a few deep breaths of warm sunlight, she caught a glimpse of me out of the corner of her eye.

"Oh, hi!" She seemed startled, even though my invitation was why she was there in the first place. Georgia stood and un-cuffed her pants, staying barefoot, as she walked toward me with the two cupcakes in her hands. "Did you, uh, want these now, or..."

"Not yet. Set them over there. I have to play something first."

As she set the bright cupcakes on the tattered grey railing, I played a couple of notes.

"What are you playing?" The wind picked up slightly, and Georgia wrapped a bandana quickly around her hair, keeping it out of her face.

"The song you asked me to play a couple of weeks ago was called Nocturne by Chopin. I've been playing it whenever I think of Rae. And not because it sounds sad, I actually don't think it's sad at all...anyway," I took a breath, refocusing myself, "I composed a piece based on that one and mixed in some notes that I felt really expressed Rae, to me. And how we were with each other."

"Oh...wow..." Georgia looked uncomfortable as she studied her fingers.

"But," I sighed, "if there's anything I learned about love and loss at all, it's that I can't do anything alone. That's why I want you here. To help me say goodbye to her."

She opened her mouth like she was about to protest, but then her shoulders sank as she exhaled. "I'm here for you. Go ahead."

Georgia rubbed her hand up and down my back a couple of times and stepped back, giving me space to play.

I'd kept the beginning the same, tears spilling from the strings in the form of high-pitched vibrato, wailing for everything I'd lost. I shook up the middle of the song, though, and gave it some reprieve. Breath. Healing. Working on the notes over the past several weeks, I'd focused on all of the good times Rae and I had, and everything we felt for each other, said and unsaid.

As I transitioned to that section, I looked out into the ocean and heard Rae's laughter yet again. My eyes shifted to Georgia, who had tears in her eyes and down her cheeks as I swayed to the notes. She did a horrible job of keeping her tears hidden, and eventually they fell from my eyes too.

I smiled through them, though. Life is an endless ocean of tears, happy and sad, and it's our job to smile in their wake. Ending the song was easy, peaceful, resonating with a tranquility I'd spent almost nine months forcing into my bones. Letting go was all I needed. Not a forcing in of peace, but a letting go of hurt. Peace is always there at the center of our souls, and I had allowed anger, hurt, and hate to shove it in a long forgotten closet.

As I pulled the bow away from the strings, I closed my eyes and whispered, "Goodbye."

At that, Georgia's arms were around me. I rested my chin on the top of her head and took several breaths, feeling lighter than I had in months.

"Regan, that was beautiful." She stepped back and gestured to the bag. "What's that?"

My throat constricted. "It's the last part."

I had her hold my violin as I knelt down and removed three items from the bag. First was a glass bottle I'd picked up from an antique store around the block the day before. It came with a large cork, which was the selling point for me, really.

"What are you putting in there?" Georgia took off her coat and laid it on the ground, setting my violin on top of it as she knelt next to me.

I pulled out a crisp sheet of composition notebook with the words For You written on top. "This is the song I just played. See?" I handed it to Georgia, who took it in her hands as if it were a baby bird, never closing her fingers around the edges, just letting it float in her palms.

She nodded and I took it back from her, rolling it into a telescoping tube and sliding it into the bottle. I reached into my back pocket and pulled out Rae's card.

"What are you doing with that?" Georgia arched her eyebrow skeptically.

My voice shook, even though I was certain. "She wrote her love letter to me, and I wrote mine back. They belong together in here." I rolled the card up as tightly as I could so it would snuggle inside the rolled up song. Finally, I put the cork on it, pressing as hard as I could, until my thumbnail turned white.

"Regan," Georgia's voice rose in panic as I stood, "what are you doing?"

I held out my hand, helping her up with a sweaty palm. "Walk with me. Please."

Her short legs moved quickly to keep pace with me. "Don't you think you should…think about this?" She seemed to figure out my plan pretty quickly, though what else was one to do with a corked bottle and a whole ocean?

"I have. For eight months, three of which I spent trying to forget about her in Ireland. I don't want to forget about Rae, Georgia, but I need to say goodbye."

"You can't throw that fucking letter in the ocean. That's insane!" Her hand trembled as she tugged, begging me to slow down.

We reached the end of the pier and I stood with my eyes closed, filling my lungs with salty fresh air.

"Seriously, Regan, you can't throw her letter away." Georgia's voice was pleading.

I faced her to find her pale and nauseated looking.

"I'm not throwing it away. I'm just…sending our love into the universe. Maybe someone will find this. Maybe not. If they do, I want them to know what our love was. If no one ever sees it, then we'll know. Rae and me."

I brought the bottle to my lips, kissing the cold glass once. Georgia held my hand tighter, resting her head on my shoulder; her breathing was even as she seemed to wait.

"I love you, too," I whispered, my lips still against the bottle.

I reached my arm back, and, as hard as I could, I threw it into the ocean where it bobbed, rather undramatically for a few moments, before a series of large waves took it under and out of my view.

I stared for a minute at the spot I last saw the bottle, filled with the part of my soul that belonged to Rae, and the part of hers that had belonged to me.

"Are you okay?" Georgia's voice came from nowhere and reconnected me to our clasped hands.

I peeled my eyes away from the ocean. From my past. Georgia looked unsure, nervous, maybe, as she locked eyes with me and waited for my answer.

With a smile I pulled her into a hug. "I think I'm ready for those cupcakes now."

She didn't try to berate me with the ins and outs of my psyche that created my bottle-tossing idea. She simply nodded and led us back to the land-end of the pier, where our cupcakes waited.

We sat silently on the edge of the pier, fumbling with the paper wrappers and finally biting into the gorgeous therapy.

The salty air around us made them all the more sweet.

Georgia

As I waited for my mother in the waiting room on Wednesday, I thought back to my morning on the pier with Regan a few days before.

"You're doing it wrong," I teased.

"Eating a cupcake? How do you do that wrong?"

I rolled my eyes. "God! Stop! Eat the cake part first, like this. Save the frosting for last. That's the point of a cupcake, you know... it's a vehicle for the frosting."

I'd laughed until my sides hurt as he took the entire top of the cupcake in his mouth at once.

"Mmmm. No. You're wrong. It's always better to have the sweetest part first." He licked his lips, and my eyes followed every move.

"Why are you such an optimist?"

At my question, he just shrugged and said, "There's no good reason to be anything but."

He chose happiness the way people choose to put on clothes in the morning.

Thinking back to the way he played his violin for Rae on that pier, I knew I had to be fully honest with him about my mom, my life, just...everything. I didn't have to, I suppose, but I wanted to. My phone buzzed with an incoming text. I smiled at his name across the top.

Health inspector here. Everything's good so far. Hope you're doing okay.

Thank you so much! I texted back.

*Everything *is* okay...right?*

I instantly felt bad about being so vague about the "appointment" I had that was keeping me from an important step in the opening of my bakery, which was only two short weeks away.

Everything's great. We'll talk when I get back, K?

Just as I sent the text, the nurse came out to let me know my mother was ready to be released. It was going to be her last appointment for a couple of weeks. She was feeling stronger and more in control of herself than she had since I was a little girl. The hours immediately following the appointments were still tough. Effects of the anesthesia and varying degrees of memory loss were difficult to navigate.

Once my mom and I were in the car and on the road, I turned the radio down.

"Mom?"

She slowly rolled her head in my direction, seeming to be more tired today than usual. "Yeah?" she asked with a yawn.

"Is it okay if I bring you back to my place for a little while? I need to meet with the health inspector, if he's still there. You can rest in my bedroom, if you'd like."

"Sounds good, Alice..." My mom trailed off with droopy eyelids, her head rocking back to the support of the window.

That wasn't the first time she'd called me *Alice* during her treatment, and it usually came when she was fighting sleep. I welcomed the slip of the tongue, reassured that even though her short-term memory was spotty in the days surrounding her treatment, her brain still clung to the most precious moments of my childhood.

I'd planned to tell Regan everything. To tell him that the mortar holding my walls together was pure fear, certainty that I'd follow the same path my grandfather and mother had. Only, now they weren't fears. I couldn't do anything about the genetics, and I had to let that go. But watching how my mother handled her life, her diagnosis, and her treatment taught me that fear was more debilitating than almost anything else could be. I needed to tell him about what my mom and I had just been through over the last few weeks. He deserved that. Frankly, I deserved that, to be honest with another human being about something without them dragging it out of me.

When we arrived at the apartment, I helped my mother up the stairs and she insisted on sitting on the couch in front of the television, claiming she needed some brainless entertainment for a while.

Her joke, not mine.

"Be right back, Mom." I kissed her on the forehead and she dismissed me with a wave of her hand.

"You worry too much. Pretty sure *The Young and the Restless* and I will do just fine while you're downstairs."

I shut the door behind me and raced down the stairs and into the bakery, where I found the health inspector talking with Regan, handing him papers from his clipboard.

"Here she is now." Regan gestured to me and the inspector turned with a smile.

"You caught me just in time, ma'am. This place is in such great condition, I was finished sooner than expected." The averaged-height, overweight man with more hair on his arms than on his head looked pleased as he swiftly took the papers from Regan and handed them to me. "Two weeks is your intended opening date?"

"It is. Two weeks from Saturday."

"Best of luck to you. Make sure you phone my office when you decide on a name for the place so we can fill out the certificates accordingly."

Behind his shoulder, I watched Regan lift his fists to the air in supportive victory.

"It's all set? I passed?" My eyes widened and I looked between the papers in my hand and the inspector's face.

"All set. Good luck again, Miss." He gave me a firm nod and left through the main door.

I turned around, my mouth hanging open in my excitement. "Holy shit!" I screamed, raising my arms in the air as Regan had seconds before.

"You did it!" Regan lifted me into a tight hug. Fully lifted me off the floor and spun me around. "Come upstairs with me. I have champagne."

He set me down and grabbed my hand, racing up the stairs.

"Slow down, legs," I teased, "some of us aren't twenty feet tall."

"Some of us aren't two feet tall, either," he shot back, reaching his apartment and opening the door.

"Gee," I mused, "love what you've done with the place." Bare walls and a single couch seemed to be accents to a music stand and his violin.

Regan pinched my cheek and stuck out his tongue. "I'm not here much, jerk."

He dashed into the kitchen and pulled a bottle of champagne from the fridge.

"Hey," I started, putting my hands in my back pockets, "there's something I want to talk to you about." My heart beat in triplet rhythm as I prepared for total emotional exposure.

"Hang on." He reached into a cabinet and pulled out two plastic cups. "This is all I have...sorry."

"It's okay." I cleared my throat, afraid I'd lose my nerve.

Regan popped the champagne and it made me jump, feeling like I was shoved through a keyhole, riding on an umbrella with a dodo bird, circling in a pool of insecurity. Before I opened my mouth again, he looked over my shoulder.

"Oh, hi, Mrs. Hall," he said nonchalantly. "I didn't know you were here, sorry. Want some champagne? The bakery passed the health inspection!"

Dread nearly crippled me as I turned and found my mother standing in the doorway. In our excitement, Regan and I had left the door open. She must have heard us. She was pale and looked like a foreigner, the way her eyes darted around the apartment, settling on Regan's face for a few seconds at a time before moving on.

"Is everything okay?" Regan asked when my mother didn't respond to his first salutation.

"I'm sorry," she shook her head, "have we met?"

Regan slowly set down the bottle of champagne, taking noticeably quicker breaths as he stared at me.

"Mom," I prompted without looking at Regan, "this is Regan, remember? You met him a month, or so, ago in my apartment. CJ's cousin."

I said as many prayers as one can say while waiting for their facade to shatter.

"CJ, the drummer boy your dad used to let play at *Dunes*?"

I swallowed hard, nodding at the repeat conversation we were having about how I knew Regan. About five minutes too late, recognition snapped my mother's eyes into focus.

"Oh, shit. Regan, yes, of course. I'm sorry, honey, it's the goddamned shock therapy messing with that pesky short term memory." My mom giggled. A light and airy sound that was instantly soaked in the darkness of Regan's face.

"The what?" Regan came around the counter and stood next to me in the living room. I knew he couldn't believe what he'd just heard. I wouldn't have believed it myself.

"Sorry, I shouldn't say *shock therapy*. That's kind of tacky, isn't it? The ECT."

The *Please be quiet and go away for five minutes* vibes I was sending my mother with my bugged-out eyes were not being received by her, but they were loud and clear to Regan.

"I didn't realize, Mrs. Ha—"

"Please, call me Amanda." She smiled, though it was starting to fade as it became clear Regan's lack of understanding was more like a lack of knowledge at all. "Oh…I'm going to…excuse me."

My mom left as gracefully as possible, closing the door behind her.

I looked at Regan who was, as I'd expected, watching me. "Let me explain."

His eyebrows lifted as he held out his hands. "Shock therapy, did she say? Like to her brain?"

I nodded. "Yes, for the past four weeks she's been—"

"Four *weeks*?" His nostrils flared and he dropped his hands to his hips.

"I can explain, Regan."

He snorted. "Sure. Just like you could explain her existence at all, right? How you were *going* to tell me she was alive."

"I *was* going to tell you. I just needed—"

"Needed what?" he snapped. "Time? Did you need more time to watch me come apart and expose every inch of my soul to you before you deemed me worthy of knowing what makes up yours?" He brushed past me, grabbing the bottle of champagne and pouring it down the drain.

I caught up to him and put my hand on his wrist. "Regan, you don't understand. Don't cut me off—just listen. I'm not made like you. I don't trust like you do. I've never had a reason to."

He pulled his hand away. "I thought I was reason enough for you, Georgia. For weeks you were the only one who knew about the most heartbreaking letter I'd ever received. Jesus, I cried with you. Hard tears, Georgia, not the sniffles of some dumbstruck asshole trying to play on your emotions to get in your pants." His face turned red as he continued. "Then…then I asked you to hold my hand as I said goodbye to her. As I threw that *fucking* letter into the *fucking* ocean! Explain to me, please, how that gave you reasons to keep something like this from me? Damn it, I could have helped you. Been there for you somehow."

"I was scared, Regan!"

"Scared? You were scared? Georgia, we're all fucking scared. This is *life!* It's scary. People divorce, disappoint us, die, walk away. I thought we had something here." He pointed between us.

I held out my hands. "We do. Don't you see? You're the only person who has made me become more of myself. You pushed me to open the bakery—"

"Don't even get me started on the bakery, Georgia. That's when I thought we were getting somewhere. I thought that was you letting me in. The last bit of the real you that no one else had seen yet. I felt special to be in there with you, to be part of the process. Was the last month with me in the bakery so awful for you that you knew you just couldn't open up to me all the way? Even after that kiss? The one *you* initiated, I might add?" He clenched his jaw.

I refused to look away from him. "Forty-two days."

"What? Enough with the goddamn riddles, already." His face screwed up incredulously as he tried to sew my words together, walking past me again and heading for the door.

I sucked in breath and demanded confidence from myself. "You've been in my bakery with me for forty-two days. And, each day for those forty-two days you've broken down more barriers than I even knew I had. Please, *please* listen to me. I'm sorry."

He shook his head, stopping my train of thought. "I'm tired, Georgia. I'm tired of the games, of the riddles, and the half-truths not quite bold enough to be called lies. Rae taught me a lot of things during her short time in my life, and the most important was, you know what? Sometimes there really is such a thing as *too late.*" Regan opened his door, staring at me with eyes so empty there wasn't even a hole for me to jump into in a final appeal.

"Regan," I pleaded, my eyes filling with tears.

He stared at the space around the door, not able, it seemed, to look at me.

I wanted to grab him and tell him that I loved him. That I really, truly did. He'd view it as the Hail Mary I didn't intend for it to be, though, so I had to leave. I pursed my lips to keep my mouth closed as the tears started to fall. When I walked past him at the door, I took a deep breath, taking in the molasses smell of rosin that always seemed to linger on his skin.

As the door clicked behind me, without so much as a goodbye, I forced myself to dry my tears. If this love stuff was real, and I believed it was, and if we both felt it, which I believed we did, then I had to trust that he'd come around.

I believed in him. Now, I needed him to believe in me.

CHAPTER *Eighteen*

WE'RE ALL MAD HERE

Regan

"So..." Bo cracked his knuckles and leaned back in his chair, sipping his beer.

"So." I took a swig from the anger bottle.

Ember rolled her eyes. "God, you two could take a century having a conversation. Regan, it's been a few days. Are you ever going to return Georgia's texts...or go home?"

I sat forward, placing my forearms on my knees. "She hasn't been texting me for the last few days. And, I've been home, smartass. I've only stayed here one night."

She threw her head back, growling and sighing to the ceiling. "You know...I'm the last person in this little group here that should be qualifying Georgia's character, since I was such a raging bitch to her when we first met, but you know she wasn't being malicious, right? At least not from the story. It's only your version I've heard, anyway, and that's the impression that I get."

"Mighty Mighty Bosstones. Nice reference, Em. What was that...1997?" Bo cracked a smile, setting his fourth bottle of beer in the sand. I laughed, picking up my fifth.

"Dear God, drink some water, lightweights." She couldn't help but chuckle along with us.

I cleared my throat. "You're right. She wasn't malicious, I get that."

"So why are you here? You're not the theatrical ty-...oh, wait... there was that *hiding in Ireland bit.*" Ember shrugged and polished off her wine.

The air was cold coming off of the bay, and I pulled the hood on my sweatshirt over my head, scoffing at my flair for the dramatic.

"I'm just licking my wounds. Animals do that, you know—run off to a cave somewhere and come out when they're all better."

Bo sighed, like he already regretted what he was about to say. "You know you're not going to feel better until you talk to her."

Ember's eyebrows shot up in surprise. "Says the guy who spent two months stalking his ex-girlfriend at the club where she sang."

"Worked out for you two, didn't it?" I air-toasted them and finished the rest of my beer.

"Barely." Bo shook his head. His voice was low and serious. "Sure we both did some healing and growing in the three months we were apart, but I promise you I would have rather done that healing and growing with her by my side, no matter how uncomfortable it would have been at first."

Ember rose from her seat and placed herself in Bo's lap, nuzzling into his neck as he wrapped his arms around her. "And, let's address the elephant on the beach here. Haven't you said that you learned from Rae to live every second? Not like it's your last, or anything, but just *live*. Don't you say there's no point in wasting seconds not living when living is what we've been charged to do?"

I winced as Ember spewed my well-rehearsed mantra back at me, and my stomach turned as I realized I'd used similar words to hurt Georgia a few days ago in my apartment. I turned them around and threw them back at her from my own anger.

"When does the bakery open?" Bo asked.

"I'll make you cupcakes, calm down," Ember teased. He stuck his tongue out at her.

"No, I mean, Regan, you were a huge part of giving her the courage to push forward there, right?"

I nodded and shrugged. My noncommittal stance as the knife in my stomach twisted left and right.

Bo continued, "Don't you think you should be there to support her on that day?"

"The girl can hold a grudge, Bo. I mean, she has to, she doesn't have many friends."

Ember scrunched her nose. "She's friends with CJ, for Christ's sake, how big of a grudge can she hold? Just because she doesn't have a ton of friends doesn't mean she holds a grudge. Look at you, you're private but not a grudge holder."

"I really do like her, guys."

Ember sighed. "No, you love her. At least that's what's brewing in there. You're not a *like* kind of guy. You don't put your emotions on the line for *like*."

"Argh," I pinched the bridge of my nose, "what if I really, *really* fucked up? She has trust issues and, *shit*, I kicked her out of my apartment."

Ember sat forward. "Well, it's safe to say you fucked up, Regan, but so did she, kind of. She was scared, you were insecure, it's just...nonsense."

"What'd you say?" My eyes shot to her.

"Uh...nonsense?"

"Ha!" I clapped my hands and stood up. "You're brilliant. I gotta go."

"Oh, no you don't," Bo nearly yelled. "You just swallowed five beers. Tomorrow. You can ride in on your white horse tomorrow."

He was right, said my head, as it seemed to move separately from my body. I sat down in a loud thump and looked at the love birds perched on their Adirondack chair together.

"Rabbit." I smiled.

"What?" they said in unison.

"Bo said *white horse*...it's a rabbit."

"Christ, you're weird." Ember stood and gathered the bottles from around the chairs. "It's my hypothesis that you and Georgia will do just fine together."

The next day I left as soon as my eyes opened for the first time which was, regrettably, five in the morning. I knew that would be my only chance that day to talk with Georgia, since she was doing her day-long introductory class today at the bakery.

She'd already be in the kitchen, whisking and whipping away, so I wasn't worried about waking her up, though if I had to, I'd do exactly that to get her to listen to me.

I slammed my hand against the steering wheel in frustration at what a jackass I'd been to her. Just because two people don't trust on the same timeline doesn't mean one is more or less trustworthy than the other. I'd quantified Georgia's trust and told her, in not so many words, that her total wasn't good enough, high enough, for me.

What a dick.

As predicted, when I pulled into our driveway, I saw the light shining in the bakery kitchen. I knew the door would be locked, and I didn't want to scare the hell out of her right before I apologized by bursting in through the interior door, so I knocked on the glass door outside.

And knocked.

And pounded a fist.

My pulse became slightly frantic, as she seemed to ignore me, until I caught the bright pink outline of her earbuds and noticed her phone tucked into her shirt pocket. A few seconds later, she looked in the direction of the door and jumped when she saw me.

I waved, pointing to the door, asking to be let in. She seemed to take a deep breath, but exhaled with a smile as she held up one finger. I watched her lean forward as she pulled a baking sheet from the oven and set it on the stainless steel table behind her.

She jogged over to the door a second later, and I smiled at the short shorts and combat boot combination that first caught my attention a couple of months before. Her smile widened as she unlocked and finally pushed the door open.

"Hi," she said, holding the door open.

"Hi." I tried to take a step in, but her hand stopped me.

"Wait a sec. Don't move." She pulled her hand away from the door and nearly skipped across the seating area to the far wall, flicking two light switches.

The pre-dawn darkness was still heavy enough for me to notice pink and blue lights turn on at the front of the building. I leaned my head to the side, to try to see what she'd done, but she yelled as she ran back to the door.

"I said don't move!" She laughed nervously as she met me outside and took my hand, bringing me to the front of the building. "Well…now you can move." She shifted on her feet, nodding upward toward the sign.

It took me a while to tear my eyes away from studying the way hers lit up. She seemed hesitant to look at me as her eyes remained fixed on the neon sign above us. Finally, I looked.

Sweet Forty-Two.

The letters were in no particular pattern, some blues were two in a row, some pinks three, and most of them were in a different font.

"You've got a name! But...wait..." My excitement at this tiny detail that had been annoying the piss out of me for the last couple of months waned. "Forty-two?"

She nodded, pouring everything she had silently from her eyes into mine.

Forty-two days. You've been in my bakery with me for forty-two days.

"This is...from our conversation the other day?" I swallowed hard, looking between the sign and her face.

She smiled. "It is."

"But...we kind of...ended on a shitty note there."

"It wasn't about that day, Regan. It was about the forty-two before that. You didn't just help me in the bakery and break down my stubborn walls." She took a deep breath and reached for my other hand. "You broke down the walls and lead a search party for the pieces of me you knew you could love, and you dragged those out of the fucking rubble I'd let pile up around my soul."

"Georgia," I whispered, moving my hands up to her face, letting the warm fullness of her cheeks warm my hands.

"It was," she cleared her throat as I watched her eyes water, "the sweetest forty-two days of my entire life, Regan."

I pulled her head to my chest and kissed the top of her head. "What if I didn't fucking come back? Or, what if I did and we didn't talk anymore?"

She shrugged beneath my arms. "It wouldn't have changed those days and what they did for me. Plus," she pulled away and wiped under her eyes, "you asked me if I could believe in a prince. I believe in you. Will you believe in me?"

"What?" I shook my head in confusion.

"Will you believe in me? Will you be patient with me and hold me and trust...me. I realize that's a huge thing to ask, given everything that's happened—"

I cut her off. "I believed in you from the second I laid eyes on you, Georgia. There was never anything unbelievable about you. Well," I laughed, "it was *all* a bit unbelievable, but you know what I mean. You're real. Raw and jagged. Confusing and curious and... nonsense. And, I believe every single bit of it."

"Do we get to kiss now?" She sniffed, an unsure smile tugging at the corners of her mouth.

"Don't you even want to hear my apology?"

Her brow furrowed. "For what?"

"Being an ass. Kicking you out of my apartment. Telling you it was too late. Pick one, I've got more..."

Georgia lifted up on her tiptoes. "That, I believe, is called being human. You don't have to apologize for that."

As our lips got closer, our smiles faded and our breathing got heavier. Clouds of anticipatory breath swirled around us, highlighted by the freshly rising sun. Our lips finally touched, both of us taking deep breaths, submerging ourselves in the feeling.

Georgia's cold nose brushed against mine and we smiled and we kissed until the sun had fully risen and the world started a new day with new love.

The best kind.

"Wait a second," I asked as I pulled away. "How'd you get a lighted sign made in three days?"

"There's a sign shop in La Jolla. I'd been there a few times talking designs and names with the guy. When this name hit me, I knew I'd be out of luck, that there was no way they'd be able to make the sign before the grand opening in two weeks. But, I figure the outside should match the inside, so the guy took me to the storage room where they keep pieces of old signs, letters they never used, prototypes, all of that. There were enough there for what I needed. He came yesterday and wired everything in and...here." She held up her hand, once more showcasing the bright sign.

"But if the outside should match the inside...shouldn't it be something Alice-y?"

She bit her bottom lip, smiling wider by the second. "That's where we're in luck. When Alice was on trial...book not movie... for the rose painting incident, the King was in a tizzy about Alice being there at all. Near the end of the trial, he blurts out, 'Rule forty-two. All persons more than a mile high to leave the court.' So," she shrugged, "I suppose they can all come here."

"Nonsense," I whispered to myself, smiling at Ember's words, and the tone of my life over the last few months.

Georgia winked and kissed me again. "Exactly."

Georgia

The grand opening of Sweet Forty-Two was more than I could have ever expected. Since I expected nothing, and ended up with a bakery that saw probably a thousand people in the first two days. Truly, though, it was magnificent. Regan told members of The Six, and they told all of their friends. Willow Shaw even plugged the opening during a radio show she hosts once a week.

While my friends at E's were sad to see me go, they showed up in full force and traded one vice for another as they gorged on cookies and cupcakes. The classes I'd hosted for the two weeks prior to the opening were a hit, and I was already taking requests for more. Thankfully, Regan was finished recording with The Six, and had some time to kill before they started their regional tour, so he was just as busy as I was in the kitchen and helping me advertise.

It's been two months since I made my first dollar from something I created, and, pardon the cliché, but it keeps getting sweeter. As I looked through the kitchen into the cafe area—which is what we call it now since that's hip—my stomach twisted a bit at the thought of having to share my boyfriend with The Six once summer rolled around.

Boyfriend.

Such a simple, ordinary word for a relationship that is anything but.

Regan wiped down the tables after locking the door and turning the sign to Closed. He tucked his always-wild hair behind his ears as he cleaned the tables and benches, humming a song I didn't recognize underneath his breath.

"See something you like?" he teased when he caught me staring, my lips slightly parted. Regan put the rag over his shoulder and glided toward me, pressing his hand on the small of my back when he reached me and giving me a warm kiss on the lips.

Maybe it was the unnatural long length of his legs, but he always looked like he was gliding whenever he moved by foot. A lot of tall people are awkward in their body, but Regan is awkward in nothing. He wasn't thrown off balance when I asked if we could wait a while before spending the night together. It was part of my trust thing, and, really, there's nothing more vulnerable than sleeping next to another person. Leaving yourself defenseless in their arms.

Tonight, though, that was going to change. I laughed under my breath about the card that slid under my doorway first thing in the morning. It looked as though he'd had help from Ember, or some other female, because it was quite crafty. It was on thick card stock and had all the suits of a deck of cards stamped along the border. I was invited, the letter said, to an unbirthday celebration in Regan's apartment after closing time at the bakery that would last until the next morning. Seemed he didn't want to come right out and ask me to spend the night in his bed. I appreciated the tact.

"What do you have planned for tonight, exactly?" I asked, kissing him on the nose once before lowering myself back to my heels.

"Oh, you know, cabbages, kings, bits of Cheshire running about." Regan twirled his hand through the air with a crazed look in his eyes.

I smacked his chest. "I'm serious."

He picked me up and set me on the large worktable behind me. "Will you just trust me?" He grinned.

"Oh, I do. I really do. I was just saying—"

He laughed, pinching my chin between his thumb and forefinger. "I know you do. And, I know it's not easy. Thank you..." He trailed off, his eyes locking on my lips before moving back to mine. The look he got right before he kissed me was enough to seize every muscle in my body.

"What?" he asked, studying my face.

"That look in your eyes...it's so intense."

He kissed me, letting his tongue trail the length of my lips once before pulling away. "Bad intense?"

"No," I said in my exhale.

"Come upstairs with me." Regan held my hand as I slid off the table and walked next to him up the stairs. My pulse thumped in my neck.

He opened the door, letting me in first. The usually bare interior of his apartment was alive. White twinkle lights were strung around the perimeter of the room and framed the picture window at the far end. The couch had been pushed aside, and in the center of the living room sat a small bistro table and two chairs, with a bottle of wine and two glasses sitting in wait.

As if crafted for a script, the timer on the oven dinged just as Regan closed the door. I whipped around to face him.

"How...what? You were with me all day today."

He ran his thumb across my cheek and kissed me on the forehead before walking into the kitchen. "Ember."

"Oh..." I trailed off, watching him remove what looked like chicken parmesan from the oven, and pulling two plates from the cabinet.

"Fantasy is fun, Georgia. It's how we met...and fell in love. Being at the Mad Hatter's tea party day in and day out in the bakery is a joy, and watching you handle customers in character with that theme is fantastic. But," he brought the two plates over to the table where I'd been standing, "normal is underrated. Sit."

I looked around, tears forming at the way normal had taken my breath away when I opened the door. White lights, a simple black table, one guy, one girl. I sat and took his hand from across the table. He smiled and squeezed my hand.

"I love you," I blurted out, letting a few tears roll down my cheeks.

"What'd you just say?" His cheeks reddened, obvious even in the barely lit room.

"The most normal thing I could think of. I love you, Regan."

Regan sniffed and didn't try to hide the tears in his eyes, either. "I love you, too, Georgia."

And there, under the soft glow of perfectly normal twinkle lights, two perfectly imperfect people did the most normal thing in the universe.

Loved.

Made in United States
North Haven, CT
13 November 2023